TRUE
LOVE

TRUE LOVE

by Herbert Gold

ARBOR HOUSE
New York

To all optimists and pessimists
in love:

SWM 45 interested in philosophy literature movies running exercise 6' 170 lb goodlooking educated financially secure an admirer of the Stoics and the life of the mind, wants a very special woman to love and make happy. This woman is extremely attractive athletic not overweight between 25 and 35 lives in San Francisco and is more interested in finding the answer to the riddle of existence than in acquiring material goods, more interested in happiness than in fun, in love than in lust, in substance than in show. Write Guardian Box #14-CC.

My Ideal Mate

I want a relationship complete on all levels: spiritual, mental, physical, involving a deep committment to serving each other and the world. I want a man spiritual, metaphysical who accepts his divinity and responsibility for creating his life, a man gentle, affectionate, sensitive,—a prosperous professional who loves his work but not consumed tall, slender, attractive non-smoker, semi-veg who likes classical music, movies, sailing, sun and desires marriage and children too. I am tall beauti-

ful brunette, professional
woman into spiritual growth
singing art and playful romantic intimacy. Ideal
mates send photo and
story to Guardian Box
#14-Y.

And also to Boxes 14-CC and 14-Y of the Bay *Guardian*; may
they
find each other, or if not,
may they find an answer to the riddles of existence and spiritual
growth.

"It might be what I want also,
dear, which doesn't mean I can have it.
But since it's what you think you need,
it might just serve you right to find it."

—*Bethany*

TRUE
LOVE

# 1

She was wise about her hair, Bethany was; how the corn-silk bangs over the forehead made both the most and the least of her long straight nose. It was the kind of nose Watkins associated with intelligence and occasionally, in times of adversity and sulks of soul, with his own lack of intelligence for associating it with intelligence. "Kudos, kudos!" she cried after he made a comment which struck her as strong, sensitive, very Watkins: "*Très* kudos, Wat!"

She was echoing a critique she must have heard in her time as a drama student at UCLA, when she was planning to become a star of stage, screen or television; but of course she was too clever to keep nagging at such ambitions past the point of no more fun. She had married an Olympic track contender and dentist instead. It was the right thing to do. She was now a star of real-life family drama and over-thirty tennis, living happily forever afterward in Davis, California, one of the top ten small towns for comfort, culture, primary education and health in the whole United States.

She and Dr. Andrews were deeply involved in solar energy, the logic and renewable power of it, not mere ideology—not the flakiness aspect. Investors in tax rebates, they constructed state and federal write-offs and prize-winning condominium projects right in their home town. Atriums, sun-saving brick, heat pumps, greenhouses, hot water. Their three children were also partners in the projects (Bethany and her husband trustees until the kids turned eighteen for dividends, twenty-five and thirty for principal).

And so after Bethany took a wonderful hour or two with

Watkins, her lover and personal lawyer, she sometimes whispered with a smile, "Very good, *très* very good," before she fell soundly asleep for exactly twenty minutes and then awoke alert, refreshed, grateful and brisk in her dressing. Bethany caught up with lost time before it rounded the bend. She was that way at afternoons of passion and she was that way when she served at doubles, too—straight to the net unless she smelled a soft high lob coming.

Due to the intelligence demonstrated by her long straight nose under the gleamy, glossy, corn-silk bangs, she gradually learned not to say, during these afternoons in Watkins's town house on the edge of campus: "Kudos."

"You're smart," Watkins told her.

She looked suspicious and showed her teeth. Was this a soft high lob coming? "I'm smart enough to be smart," she conceded, "but not smart enough to hide it. So I'm really just ordinary conniving. That's why I've taken up tennis. I'm becoming a tennis vestal virgin in my white dress. Which is not a saint or a truly sacrificing individual, Watkins."

"You're not hiding it."

"No, probably not," she said. "I'm learning to give up pleasure, though, for convenience. That's *extra* smart, don't you think?"

"No," he said. "*What? Give up pleasure?*"

The smile passed and the suncreases and sunlines showed what she would look like at forty, which was pretty soon now, despite emollients to the contrary, although her smile and her skinny limbs and her tennis dresses kept her looking quite a lot like a girl or a girlish student of Theater Arts at UCLA. "The best I can prefer to do with my life, Watkins," she said. "Here I am in the flatlands of California. Near Sacramento. A real estate dentist's wife. Playing games. Smart. Gone solar. And not too smart—oh, I'll miss you when I'm gone, Watkins."

And although she was laughing (he thought), there was a real longing and tenderness and grief and need in the way she now took his hand and moved her behind and adjusted his hand so that his fingers—

Bethany, dearest. Sometimes it was the teasing and clever estimations of the sun-crinkled eyes, but sometimes it was her ass. The curl of well-exercised muscle, and how a line, a fold, smiled up from below the fall of cloth from her tennis shorts; those two exercised fistfuls of buttocks, oh! She wiggled and wriggled and he treasured her mind.

Watkins's postdivorce town house was adjacent to the campus, but he was too old for collegetown funky—instead, redwood beams on the outside and a combination of glass and Middle Eastern white plastered nooks and cozy alcoves and thermopane skylights and lazy leg-stretch pits on the inside, with plenty of indirect lighting and long planks for books which took up the redwood theme. He had a king-size bathtub. He didn't believe in California hot tubs, but on the other hand he did believe in a nice large space that could be flooded with hot water for two in case of thermal company. Bethany liked to come from her tennis to splash around with him, scrub backs, slide soap hither and yon, get really clean. Once she brought a set of her younger son's plastic boats; the kid had decided he was too old for that kind of play, but his mommy and Watkins were not.

Watkins always made sure the place was especially tidy on Bethany's afternoons. Tidiness was essential to the whole blessed routine, when they would sip a cup of tea or a glass of wine, take their bath together, becoming young and carefree and easy, and then run to the bed. And then she returned cheerfully to her husband and children. And he tended to his briefs and his books, or to dinner with a friend or colleague, and felt he deserved this much pleasure and peace after two pathetic marriages.

"Tragic," Bethany had once commented.

"No, merely pathetic," he answered. "I should have liked my first wife and I should have persuaded my second wife to like me."

"You're so good with words, my dear. But I don't mean tragic. I mean funny."

And he soaped and scrubbed and tickled her nicely, and they had more need for jokes than for words. So she was right. Since Bethany made him enthusiastic, Watkins couldn't see himself any longer as tragic or pathetic. She treated him as funny.

Nevertheless, it was not just funny. Love is funny only for those not in love. When he entered her, everything nearby was white and yellow from the sun—the corn-silk hair of her head, her groin, the tiny corn silk of her arms—it was summer and he felt that he was entering a summer field, it was parting softly for him, blowing in the midday wind; and his body was soft and hard as a lazy boy's as he disappeared within her, so much in so little, she was a magician. She was so beautiful. Bethany, you're so sweet and beautiful. Bethany, you are what I live for.

Her eyes were closed, her lips parted. She was happy with him, too. "You're nice, Wat," she said.

She smelled fizzy and sharp after they made love. It was an odd kind of sweat, too perfumed for sunny afternoon lust. He guessed at some secret cologne in there someplace. Her breath had more beast in it, and it was hot on him, hot when her tongue took him, hot when she just laughed and blew down on him, but when they kissed, there was still that sharp fizzy taste.

"Women don't smell like this right and left," he said. "You've got something special."

"In your mind," she said, laughing at him.

"That's the place, always was. Also you've got something ordinary in you. That's what's peculiar. I'm afraid you've got everything."

She propped herself up on one elbow. "And you've got a problem," she said. "It's Bethany Andrews, faithful mother of three."

The preceding remarks had been registered on Tuesday. Watkins studied the oral deposition until Thursday, when he knew, not being stupid, she intended to continue a line of discourse which he felt—pains in his stomach, down below, where jealousy is located; pains in the sinus, frontal lobe, where anxiety can be found—she had been considering for a while now. On this afternoon of the irregular nine-month summer of the Sacramento Valley, on this spring afternoon, a day of fresh winds and the usual brilliant late sunlight, she arrived with a smile, some bath oil for a special pleasure, a briefcase and the remark: "I never asked you to sign a power-of-girl-friend, but darling, I'm afraid you'll have to agree."

"To what?" Watkins asked.

"To the neatest possible conclusion. Darling, after today it's over. It's really getting complicated. I'm not going to leave my husband. I'm not going to break up my family. I told you— convenience covers pleasure. I certainly won't say it's boring with you, it's really not, always highly interesting and precious, but we've also fallen into a routine—"

"Ah," said Watkins, and this was a short sharp gasp.

"For one thing, you count on me. You're lonely. I can't stand the pain of thinking of your long lonely, oh, you think I'm kidding—"

He tried to tug her skirt down.

"I'm not kidding, Wat."

"How would I be less lonely if I didn't see you than if I do? Come on, come on, let's have a shower this time for a change— opposed to mere routines, aren't we?"

She pulled his hands away. "You're making turmoil!" she said sharply. "Don't."

He folded his arms.

She took a moment to regulate her breathing. She had these little lifesaving devices, a yogic and thermostatic linkage. It wasn't lifesaving, really, it was just a matter of good housekeeping. It would be best, she had decided, to head for sensible, for gentle.

She touched his hand ever so lightly.

Softly, gently, sensibly, she said: "Listen, spider, I know your sort. You pretend to have superficial feelings for me—" And she could head a little toward comradely teasing, too. Or maybe just rush forward with all she had on her mind, fullout telling the truth. "—you pretend, Wat, you talk a good game, you do that nice little ironic superior smile at the corner of your mouth

13

when you're getting dressed sometimes, or more likely you're watching me getting dressed and you recline there propped so nicely on your pillow—you're laughing at me because I'm in a hurry, can't keep the kiddies waiting at their soccer practice—you *pretend*, Wat, to have superficial feelings for me, but all you want is my body and soul and true love. You lie to me in the dark, you make promises, you tell me you're just a moth in the night, you whisper stories till the kids come home, but I happen to know, Wat, and it's a commotion to a happily married woman—you're secretly a one-woman man. You live from Monday to Thursday. I smell singed chicken feathers where that torch you carry gets at your eyebrows. Goddamnit, Wat, I hear, I *know*. You just mope away your life, especially on weekends, when I'm doing all those wonderful sports with my loved ones and my wonderful athletic happy-go-lucky husband. I have time-sharing on the ski place, I have the family membership at the club. Watkins, what you need is a regular seven-day woman, and I mean weekends and national holidays, too."

"Can we talk about this later?"

"Wonderful idea, darling."

So they ran to the hydro area, used her bath salts and bath oils, scrubbed, dried, fled sweet-smelling to the bed, cuddled and crept into each other—that curious sharp fizzy taste again—turmoil, sleep. When he awakened with a start, perhaps after a half hour's doze, she was dressed, wearing glasses, this was serious; she had made tea, had opened her briefcase at his desk, "Come on, we've got some paperwork to get through," she said.

Bethany, his married true love, was not capable of abandoning him to lurch about drinking too much beer, chasing female persons who were too young or inappropriate in other ways, such as married. Yet, in this small university town, the market for a twice-divorced lawyer of forty-four was restricted. The disgrace, the immaturity, the griefiness of his hunger for true love got in the way of his academic expertise in torts and property, plus a part-time practice as a small-town legal adviser, just keeping a foot in the real world, in case anyone thought torts and property in the university law school were not real. Bethany's husband, for example, the outstanding endodontist of the area, kept busy with his practice, his work in gum disease and write-offs, his sailing and skiing, his condo project, his cheery wife, his happy family. *He* was not immature or contemplative. She wanted the same for Wat. But how? How to achieve such a goal?

"Yes, and also why?" Watkins, wrapped in his bathrobe, asked. He was relaxed after sex and a nap. His voice was a little hoarse, as if he had shouted with joy or delivered a lecture with a cold. Grumpy was the most he could manage at the moment; morose, deeply masculine and pleasured after a sweet half-hour snooze in her arms, the last ten minutes without her arms. Tear ducts were inaccessible for the moment.

"To explain. Notice, Wat, the material I have here neatly spread out on your desk."

Watkins got a whiff of something serious. He had better acknowledge the seriousness of which he had just previously taken a whiff. A whiff of the awful is not the same as coming to terms with it, not by a long shot, but in the jungle it's a start. This was Davis and not a jungle and he was an adjunct professor of law with an endowed chair and he was in jungle trouble. The heat came up in his body as if the thermostat had gone haywire. Trouble is always inappropriate, Watkins firmly chose to believe, but here again it came; he recognized the evidence in that heat of terror which is so much like gratified desire; the fresh plaster of his town house, the redwood and the thermopane skylights and the various nooks and the nonhot tub only put the general fear at half a remove. It was no haywire thermostat; it was the meaning of his present life. This was Hostile Outside Force, a blazing sunstorm of cataclysm. (Ah, Watkins, he thought, too much thinking of yourself, which is one more bachelor error—please take control of your life, as Pete Positano would advise.)

"Look at me." Watkins opened his robe. "I'm covered with sweat. I'm nervous."

"And you're not even horny. And you just had a bath and all —a shower today. Poor boy. Now listen, sit down, I invite you, your lover has figured everything out so it'll be nice for you, Wat. Look."

He looked.

He looked and he said, "You're humming. I don't know what that means."

"I'm working on your behalf, darling," she said. "I'm trying to give you two Sabbaths in a row."

"Try to tell me what you mean. It's inappropriate that you're doing something awful—"

"Just because I'm saying good-bye to you?"

"—you're doing something awful and all you do is hand me cute puzzles."

Concern for his welfare drew her lips down at the corners. That late-thirties collegiate look of hers, weather-worn skin from tennis, skiing and swimming with her family, that laugh-wrinkled sun-washed blue of eye, that dear deep fret which good manners forbade that she inflict on either her lover or her husband, had enraptured him for years. It wasn't just their afternoons, their very rare evenings of laughing and cuddling. He was in love. Or at the least he was addicted. Now, whatever passion is, or cozy friendship, or whatever love might turn out to be in heaven or limbo, he thought he felt it for Bethany Andrews, contented wife and mother of three.

"You don't know about two Sabbaths in a row, darling?" she asked. "A great rabbi, one of your people, said the Savior will come when there are two Sabbaths in a row. And you, with your optimism, every Sunday we're together you think you're half-way there."

"My people don't call him the Savior. We say Messiah. West of Chicago, we don't even say that very much. And what this means is you're kissing me off."

She studied him through the serious horn-rimmed glasses she used for paperwork and said, "Down to business. I'm just kissing you good-bye. I can't handle it anymore. I like you a lot. I love my husband devotedly." He winced. "At least I love something about him more. He's different. He's my husband. We have our kids. You're different, too, Wat, *très* different, but really I don't have to explain all this. I can live my life with him. You—"

"I'm a loser? You can't live our life together?"

"Oh, dear. You're not a loser, you're just foolish. I love rolling around and getting down with you, darling, but that's not love and don't you start lecturing me. I'm not lecturing you, either. It's all decided and I want you to look through this portfolio."

She pulled him to his desk. She tucked the chair near. She opened the portfolio and showed him the top sheet, a newspaper clipping neatly Scotch-taped to a full sheet of paper:

> BAY AREA PROF, midforties, div., straight, no physical defects, high IQ, distinguished chair at major univ., healthy, unhappy, mild-mannered except no astrology, tarot, or est . . .

It continued in like manner. It was a classified biography of him, as incomplete as any official account. She had filled it with negatives—"a nice touch, I think"—and inciting quirks, such as "mild-mannered except." "Distinguished chair" would not hold up in court as a synonym for "adjunct professor." "I wanted to give the impression you're a beast at times," she remarked. "Does that meet with your approval?"

He shrugged and mumbled. When stunned he played for time by playing dead. It was a jungle instinct he had carefully preserved from Paleolithic times.

"Well, I had to make some literary decisions here, Wat. I realize how hard it is for you to choose your words about Theodore Roosevelt or Judge Learned Hand or whatever fuzzy stuff you happen to be teaching about this year. Premises, premises, as you like to say."

"I never did."

"Or maybe I like to think about you. Anyway. Anyway, without even touching on your immortal unique soul, I received seventeen replies, darling. So the prose drew pretty nicely. Your bio makes a nice advert. Of course, a little less than half are crazies or dummies or the, oh, unattractives, but that leaves seven or eight possibles. And I've arranged them in order of interest, one through eight—"

"What? How?" These were not words but sounds. She pretended they were questions.

"Of course, I said you would consider all of California, north and south, plus Nevada, Tahoe if necessary, you can afford to travel on weekends. I think it's more important you find the right woman than she be *très* convenient, like me, just in the neighborhood, like me, dear, and available, dear, like me. Numbers one through four are really promising, I think. Want to look at their letters? Peruse in detail?"

Wat had said What? so often he felt he was quacking like a duck. Bethany must have been a little nervous, too. Chatter wasn't her normal style. She was a woman of action.

As long as she presented herself as brittle and brisk, which was how she now chose to present herself to her lover, and of course the only safe way for a loyal wife and mother to present herself—or this loyal wife and mother, anyway—she could live up to his expectations and understanding. It was essential that he be wrong and unjust about her. That was sufficient for her game. If creepy loss and grief leaked out of her, what good would she be to anyone? And she had so many responsibilities. Even to Watkins she felt responsibilities, although he might not suspect how good she was at them.

So it would be indulgent to show character just now. What Watkins and perhaps even Bethany herself might call character was the enemy. It was the wrong procedure; therefore, no character. Let Watkins be unjust to her. A neat package was appropriate for these trying circumstances; neat packages make do without loss and grief.

Perhaps he needed a moment for the new file on his desk to become a part of his routine. The papers were hers, not his, but soon they would be all his and none of her concern.

Please, let Watkins be unjust. It was not merely more comfortable; it was essential. Intelligent management was what this emergency required. So far, it was working out. While Bethany gave Watkins a moment to take in the folder and paper, she could take the time she needed, too. All the good players did that.

Watkins was staring at the folder and papers on his desk. Bethany showed her teeth in a smile which (she was pretty certain of this) had no loss or grief in it. The smile was meant to be 100 percent California whiteness and dental care. That's what she was giving out just now. That's what the situation demanded. How else to get through it? "All you get," she said aloud.

"What?"

She would amplify this portion of a sentence with the stillness of command. She would keep loss, grief and most of Bethany out of it. "Look at the letters, Wat," she said.

He looked at the letters.

Number One. A woman lawyer for MGM Studios in Los Angeles; the movies, not the real estate. Photograph showed thick lashes, slightly overcoiffed hair, sturdy small body. Letter showed money, impatience, a degree of intelligent discomfort about the whole goddamned situation, an interest in adventure. Divorced. Children but no babies. A sensible first choice.

Number Two. An assistant professor at UC-Davis. She explained that she was a Semite, a liberated Arab, a Christian from Iran, not a Persian—complicated in that part of the world—and if he was Jewish that was okay. Sociologist. No photograph. But a nice mildness in the few facts she divulged. Wary but hungry. "I'd put her number four, maybe," he said.

"Shush," said Bethany. "This is my project."

Number Three. An advertising woman in San Francisco. Never married. Ex-surfer gone smart. Likes Doris Lessing and Sylvia Plath. The main attraction was the photograph: a winningly sexual look of singles-bar championship. She explained that she had retired from the foolishness of casual encounters at the end of noisy evenings, and was now ready for other sorts of foolishness, but if he was a reformed gay, he needn't apply. "It's an easy trip down Eighty and across the bridge," said Bethany, "and that's one reason I put her Number Three. For neighborhood fucking. To ease the transition from me. Of course, she might not be telling the whole truth about herself."

"Who's Number Four?" he asked, plus: "Who does?"

"Number Four!" said Bethany. "She may not be the prettiest, but when you're tired of just messing around, by that time—"

"I'm tuckered already, Beth."

Number Four. A widow. One small child. Likes to cook, likes to talk, likes to make no demands, likes not to dwell on the past, likes to change her life, likes to take a chance when all else fails. "Las Vegas time, Wat," said Bethany with great good cheer. "You might need a little vacation."

"I'll go for Number Four first," he said.

Bethany left the manila folder (GUM DISEASE TODAY) on his desk. She informed him he had the option of putting the applicants in a different order. Being a free man, he might accept that option. She was only making suggestions. She was only trying to be helpful. She was ready to make her getaway fast. She wanted no clinging, no argument, God forbid no tears from either one of them. She was saying, "What the rabbi said about two Sabbaths in a row interested me. I think he meant for us to hope, but never to get what we might possibly dream of, darling."

He said nothing.

"I'll do anything I have to, Wat. I don't care how bad it is for you because I'm doing my best and it doesn't matter—"

She was too smart to say the rest of it. She was too serious. She was too good a player to hand him any weakness, need, grief and loss which happened to be lying around in Bethany. He was now the opponent. In this game, she absolutely had to win. For Bethany, today, the win was the right—the ability—to say good-bye.

She lifted her wiry little shoulders in a shrug, she lifted her eyebrows, she gave him her most white smile, her shoes made no sound at all, the door opened, the door shut.

And so Bethany left him. She left him with dreams, but no hopes. He would have to make do with what she left him.

He sat at his desk for an hour, not looking at the manila folder which used to hold information about gum disease today, just holding it in his hands. These white plaster walls, this print of Pieter Breughel's *Hunters in the Snow,* this space from which Bethany had excused herself forever. It wasn't an hour; it seemed like an hour; maybe it was. Pieter Breughel the Elder or Pieter Breughel the Younger—he couldn't answer that, either.

Rapid damp had closed around him. It was night and it was dark. That's the trouble with going solar. He was staggering without moving.

Then he picked up the telephone to make an arrangement to meet when convenient for two strangers. A few steps away, on the grassy campus, bicycles were creaking and chirping, those chains, pedals and gears; lovers were creaking and chirping. Eternal springtime lay only a few steps away. That was out there and he was in here. Obediently he rang Number One on Bethany's list.

 *2*

Davis used to be a town to which young people came to study agriculture and old farmers from the Sacramento Valley came to retire. The smell of rice huskings, horse, burn-off and fertilizer blew over the campus and the settlement. Then money came to the university, and it became a prosperous suburb of Sacramento; and solemn-eyed science students, law students, even arts students, multiversitarians, wandered the long, straight, flat streets of the town and the winding grassy paths and bikeways along Putah Creek on campus. The counterculture grew solar developments along with the write-off culture's malls and condominiums. In the mood of a daily visiting circus, double-decker buses from London, a project of student government, swayed through town from "living arrangements" around pools toward classroom high rises.

After midnight a new shift came on duty. The town alkies and oddballs were joined by university burnouts, speed lobotomies and earnest all-night students and lovers at Sambo's, brawlers down near the tracks, food-stamp scholars, the rock wounded and counterculture disabled, faculty temporarily out of marriages, ag industrialists not wanting to miss the eighties as they had missed other decades, and motorcycle clubbers who had retired to do a little drinking at the Antique Bizarre. They scorned the new fern bars.

Bicycling was the dominant religion. More ten-speeds per soul than any other town in America. Green "Historic Bicycle Lane" strips lined the geometric grid of streets. Since there were few heroes from Davis, a slim past and overall a scientific temperament, the geometric grid was labeled A, B, C, D and E streets in one direction, intersected by First, Second, Third and Fourth in the other. Logic filled spiritual needs. It made things easier for students and teachers who were just passing through. Most people here were wayfarers, and some even managed to get lost at the corner of Second and D. Watkins feared he was taking his inspiration from the wayfarer folks.

Sometimes, in the dog days of summer, the California desert blew into town. Thistles rolled down the feeder roads from the desert-rock mountains not far on the Interstate. There were strong smells of rice and tomatoes, sun heightened, diesel mixed. Trucks bumped red smashlings onto the roads. Some of the older wooden houses had gardens where driveways used to be, spike-headed flowers and herbs cultivated by widows. The Plymouth down the street was parked at the curb, up on blocks, by agreement with a kindly, compassionate, civic-minded police force. When the lady got over her stroke, got young again, she would drive her Plymouth out to the delta, where she liked to steal new plants for her garden.

Watkins liked the ancient wife's driveway garden better than the white gravel of the town-house condominium and tended ferns where he lived (upkeep was part of the deal). Still, her plantings made him pensive, which is the next thing to sad. Never, never, never, no matter how lonely he ever became, would he take up the consolation of gardening, no matter how successful history showed it to be.

At present, instead, he ran. He tamed onrushing age with his Adidas and shorts and sweaty tee shirts that said Lawyer—a gift from Bethany, of course. Running tamed age as Bethany tamed loneliness. It was easy to make things work when a fellow was smart, determined, lucky and not overly susceptible to shin splints.

The clapboard farmhouses marooned in town, the redwood suburban tract developments, and the condos for investment abided peacefully together, as did the young faculty, the commuters to Sacramento, the retired, the dropouts, the students in their boarding houses with reggae music reaching from the windows and Goodwill couches melting on the porches and cars and bikes and motorcycles stacked in the driveways. The yards were full of transportation. Once, during an insomniac no-woman midnight run through one of these streets on the edge of the campus, Watkins heard the sounds of Bob Dylan's "Sad-Eyed Lady of the Lowlands"—it took him back a decade or two —and he tracked the nasal keening to a window with a broken screen on it, which must have served both to admit and to keep out flies, and behind the screen a couple was embracing, a girl with a back like a snake's as it moved, a boy with long straight hair, just like the old days—Watkins was on campus and about their age when he first heard about the girl with amphetamine eyes. The boy's thumb was hooked under the elastic of the girl's bikini underwear, pushing, and as it slipped down they began to sway and move against each other in a kind of dance, the girl wearing nothing but hobbled by her half-slipped bikini, the boy wearing a tee shirt and nothing else; and entranced, Watkins felt not like a Peeping Tom but like a supplicant, a worshipper; it wasn't nostalgia he felt, but the grip of the happiness of others; not jealousy, but a dizzy constriction around his forehead, a lurch in the belly. Perhaps this was celebration and envy all confounded. His eye hurt; he was proud to be alive. Those lucky wonderful children! He celebrated them in his own dizziness because he too used to enact a sadness he had not yet earned.

Suddenly there was a sound which startled him. He heard himself laughing and muttering like an old man under his breath and moved on. He muttered that he was a midnight thief and a stinking voyeur. He ran.

He avoided that street for weeks. He felt shame. He felt envy. The girl with the snakelike back and the boy. The music he remembered. He wished too much to see them again.

When he forgot and strolled one night down that street, just happened to be going that way on a visit to the 7-11, needed bread, apples and cheese, the quarter was over and there were new tenants in the house, two young men with mustaches and short hair and the wedding-cake look of stylish homosexuals. But the light of their painted false Tiffany lamp was soft and marvelously cozy. Watkins wondered if the boy and girl were still together or if that was only last quarter's love. He preferred to turn those graceful children out of his memory. Why should he feel their love judged him, when he was an adjunct professor and practitioner of law, settled in a respectable path, while they were surely worried and harassed about grades and applications and an uncertain future? They had to deal with all the years to come—more of those years than he had! Why should he envy their uncertainty and troubles?

Because he still wanted a moment like that with his thumb pressing against a snakelike back.

The next morning Watkins stood up in a School of Law Senate meeting to debate the allocations of funds for the ABC program, A Better Chance for minority law students, blacks, browns, women (a majority of the minority), military retreads, plus lesser groups, such as the Organization of Middle-Aged Handicapped Single Fathers. . . . His colleagues sighed, shifted, creaked in their seats and paid attention. The approach was now calm; there wasn't enough money for rage. Social conscience was running amuck *correctly.* Listening to his own persuasive voice, he wasn't quite sure what to make of his commitment. He referred to the Bakke decision. He made distinctions. He referred to Justice, Rectitude and the lessons of History. He sat down and noted, amid the flush of recent performance, the usual mix of approving nods, glum frowns, indifferent fiddling with pens, paper clips, small mechanical instruments. A young Chinese woman was plucking at a pocket calculator, dividing the lessons of history by justice times rectitude. He wasn't sure he had made the proper distinctions.

Not reconciled to his personal life, it was correct that he had difficulty valuing his public and professional life. Yet he made every possible effort to do the right things. He believed in conscience; he hated interviews with the IRS. He was above average in many ways, as Bethany was kind enough to admit when she had a mind to praise him. Heart, IQ, hairline, physical stamina, even principles—sometimes well above average. Native doggy decency. His IRS audits were consistently clear wins.

It couldn't be, could it, that below average would be more correct for the survival of a Watkins just now?

Then, before lunch, a stroll to his office in the John Muir Redwood Professional Mall. On a bicycle path, just before the city street took over, he met Pete Positano, professor of family relations in the med school, wearing one of his tie-dyed tee shirts. Watkins preferred these to the ones with messages— LEGALIZE COMPASSION. Pete was like a veteran of the Spanish-American War and the charge up San Juan Hill—the last of the sixties psychedelic heroes. "Hi, Plutocrat," said Pete. "Hi, Human Potential Fascist," said Watkins.

For Pete, the Law was part of the problem and Watkins was a sellout to the military-industrial-academic Establishment. For Watkins, Pete was someone he knew several wives ago, when everybody was a kid. Skinny, ravaged and unyielding, Pete was speaking a language that seemed more ancient than Church Latin. Only among tenured associate professors could a person still find those tie-dyed tee shirts and expanded minds.

"Good-bye, Mr. Uptight."

"Nice to see you, Dr. Positano."

They curtseyed and continued on their way. They were two middle-aged professors who shared the campus diseases of face-tiousness, affable mutual dislike and boyishness. Was that tightness Watkins felt on his face the little ironic smile that Bethany mentioned? Was she right about the corners of his mouth?

He turned to look at Pete and wave a friendly farewell, and did so, but Pete was rounding the path with a bit of hustle and Watkins's wave just stirred the air sweetly, unacknowledged through no fault of anybody.

What a nice town. Watkins could walk from the faculty senate to his office, and in the inner court of the building find Mrs. Gillems lurking for a bit of conversation, as usual. Her husband, a tomato farmer, a pioneer of factory tomatoes, square ones, suitable for easy shipment, but inedible, had left her this building without a mortgage. She owned the building plus industrial tomato patents. She always had something to declare, something to astonish or inform or enrich Watkins's life. Today she asked:

"I tell you what happened to my sister, Mr. Winsor?"

"I didn't know you had a sister. The name's Watkins."

"Yes I do. Did I tell you?"

"No."

"Well, she moved to Canada. Her husband got transferred overseas to Canada."

Mrs. Gillems was following him up the outdoor stairway to continue her information blitz. She handed him a stack of junk mail that had been put in the wrong box. Their shoes clanged on the redwood slabs attached to cast-iron supports. "I hope her kids get to go to an American school," she said. He was riffling through the envelopes. "Anything important in there you can see yet?"

"I let my subscription to *Running* run out. They'll give me a sweatband if I resubscribe for three years."

Marriage, he thought, is comfortable like this, the conjugal Muzak running in the background. I wouldn't kill her. I would hold off the police for hours, getting a good grip on things, making sure the cameras had it all for the evening news. . . . And then I'd slowly drink myself to death in front of it.

"My sister's brother-in-law, the young one, has really straightened out. He started at Stanford and now he's at some other school."

"Why'd he leave Stanford?"

"He's doing very well. He wants to be a doctor."

"Why'd he leave Stanford?"

"The other school is a really good school."

"Why'd he leave Stanford!"

She shot a curiosity-kills-the-cat look at him. Why did he have to keep asking questions, just because she was talking? "He's only twenty-four," she said, "but you should see how bald. He looks like a grown person."

"Some people move to Canada," Watkins remarked hopefully. "People do all sorts of things."

He bowed nicely, just as he had nodded to Pete Positano, an incline of the head, an open-and-shut of the fists, closed the door of his office and sat there awhile, sorting out the things he might or might not do later. The sun was bright through the slats at the window. He would not call Bethany. The sun was warm on his shoulders. He dialed Bethany's number but hung up before it had a chance to ring. He wondered if Bethany might resubscribe to *Running* with the offer of a sweatband. He heard the clang of Mrs. Gillems's steps receding down the outdoor staircase. She must have waited to see if he would dart out of his office.

Now he had a good reason to come out of his office. It would be more difficult to telephone Bethany. The silence, the files, the telephone, the sun on his shoulders were a menace. Better call this a day of rest and have another stroll in the park instead of a run. Perhaps he would walk and drink coffee today. He would think about turning off his pains. They were unearned. He had no rights in the matter. He would not telephone Bethany on this day of accustomed mildness.

In the center of the little city park stood a bandstand for Fourth of July concerts and dedications of new bicycle lanes. The mayor had declared Solar Month here, and Wind Week, and Anti-Nuclear Year. Individual days he left to the minor diseases and incurable afflictions. This afternoon the playground was occupied, as usual during the hours after nursery school or day care, by young mothers with circles under their eyes who had not planned to spend their late twenties plotting freedom while wiping the asses of kiddies. One woman of, oh, a little older, was holding the fat legs up and doing the necessary job with pursed mouth while her son stared uncordially at an upside-down world. The kid was okay, but here is the assumption made by Watkins: Desperate mother. Maybe she wasn't. Since those were redwood chips below, maybe it wouldn't hurt too much if she dropped the nice baby on his head. Watkins had had a few experiences with wives.

He strolled in a circle around the mothers near the sandboxes as if he were looking for something. Ladies, he was thinking, it all comes to this, does it? The rock concert, the walk by the bay, the weekend in Truckee, this is what it came to—behinds for the wiping?

What if, Watkins thought, what if she's not even angry with her husband? What if she still loves the father of that fat little dirty behind? What if, when day is done, she and her husband stroll this park with the kid mounted and sleeping on baby wheels and they just look forward to holding each other through the night, now and forever, redeeming the universe for all its heedless cruelty? When speckled and shimmering yellow of streetlamps lit the park, and a man like Watkins avoided it, no matter how balmy the evening, for the melancholy it brought him, this couple with their sleeping child would feel tenderness, not grief or longing. He achieved melancholy; they earned tenderness. A better way they had found to deal with the yellowish aura of streetlamps at dusk on a warm evening.

Oh, he wished this for himself and Bethany. Oh, he wished someone.

The older mother had a husband who was probably an honest man, an associate professor, or perhaps a dentist. He wore a fifty-seven-dollar Banana Republic safari shirt with his honest Levi's jeans, upon which he had performed no tailoring. Instead, he tailored his buttocks by running, not jogging.

Or perhaps like Pete Positano he was eternally young, older, Watkins's age; in touch with the Theories of Seth as taught in workshops all over Northern California, not just in the Bay Area; trailed an aura of silver and gold plus spicy smells, because in an earlier life he had been an Aztec craftsperson, which explained why he was so good with inlays and crowns; and also, on his father's side, Russian philosophers and sadists who, by the time his karma reached Davis, were caring, truly kind, fond of hiking and foreign films, baroque music, special meditation weekends, poetry of Richard Brautigan—nonsmokers only, please—true love, reply to my box . . . Watkins stopped himself. He had no right to punish this couple, the husband invisible, because he wished to stand in his place beside a somewhat worn, sweet-faced young woman with smudges of fatigue beneath her eyes. Watkins was the one with the box number, not these two. Watkins was the one whose Bethany had made an intelligent set of decisions for him.

In his quest for love Watkins was avoiding megalomania with a fury. Megalomania was an evil to be destroyed by total concentration. Watkins would kill for peace. All he asked was a secure and reasonable calm in which to live out his life. His requirement was merely comfort and caresses in the starlit hours of wakefulness. Humid mildness would do; he could give up luxurious afternoons with Bethany, especially since she had given them up with him. It wasn't what he had in mind anyway.

And so he headed for the Third Eye Bookshop on D Street to buy his Wall Street *Journal* and a few legal-sized yellow pads. These were items he did not absolutely need just now. Perhaps his face showed the stress of thought. There was a very young gypsy fortune-teller hanging out there, probably a sophomore from the East Coast, wearing layers of reddish fabrics, earth tones, crinkled stuff, exploded silver jewelry, earrings, a peaked little fox face. For unknown reasons he found himself in the Women's Studies section, which happened to be near the gypsy who had been measuring him up and down since he entered the shop. "You've heard of Out of Body Experiences?" the gypsy asked.

"Sure, that mystic stuff," he said. They should have put it with women's studies and isolated legal pads with cards, favors and stationery. "Mystic is on the other side of the store, I think just across the coffee machine."

"Sir, what I wish to offer you is an Out of Pants Experience."

Oh, dear. He measured his options carefully. She was zany, collegiate, a student trying to be a townie dropout, and trouble. Waves of avuncular swept over him, washing temptation away. "I'm sure it's a good deal," he said.

"Best deal you'll get all day," she said, reaching.

"Ouch,"—and he jumped nervously back into the Harlequin display. She began to giggle. He bent to pick up fallen romances and so did she. *"Her husband, a giant!—Her lover, a hero!—Her father, a beast!"* *"He pressed her throbbing bosom to his throbbing breast."* The gypsy bumped his head with her head. "Ouch," he said. She picked up tiny handfuls of tiny novels and whispered,

31

"Would you like a truly gothic experience, mister? I'm so bored, so bored!"

"Here, give me those."

He replaced the stack of books and stood back to admire his good citizenship. There was a castle on a heath; there were ruffled shirts; on one jacket there were identical twin beauties growing from a single neck, plus a long-lost portrait of Lord Byron in all his doom. The gypsy sophomore was whispering, "Or would you like me to use my foot or my hair instead of my hand and mouth?"

Watkins swiftly apologized for being so occupied with chores, shopping, running behind schedule, family obligations—that reminds me, shampoo!—good luck to you, miss. The gypsy seemed secure within her jittery being, but on the other hand, she might be a little crazy despite her apparent normal need to wile away an afternoon with a sentimental brief corrupt encounter. Watkins needed no such distractions in Davis. He was a respectable citizen and a seeker of true love. He was an established adjunct professor and visible town lawyer, although seeking true love. At selected times in his life he found resources of prudence deep within his soul and this was one of those times. Trusting he might meet her again in a different life, perhaps on a heath in Scotland, perhaps only in a galaxy far, far away, he tucked his legal pads under his arm (no Wall Street *Journal*) and stepped into the main street glare.

Indian Jewelry B'Teek.

Tower Records.

Frogurt Frozen Yogurt All Natural Type Ingredients.

Depilatory, Waxing, Electrolysis & Travel Kits.

A tangle of bicycle racks—students living upstairs.

Watkins might have preferred to be an Olympic acrobat and live entirely in the air, but that was not possible for him. He suspected even the vaulters and spinners who seemed to dwell only in the empyrean and in applause occasionally came down to earth, sought pickups on the street, accepted or rejected them and went home lonely after the competition. Even in their moments of triumph. This time in Watkins's life happened not to be a time of triumph.

Our bridge to earth is so frail, he thought, because we are frail. The planet and civilization have much to offer—the firmness of that concrete bandstand in the park, for example, or the grip of the older young mother's hand on the fat legs of her upside-down dirty-assed son. As he walked, using the overhang of buildings to give him shade—the glare brought a sweat he liked less than his runner's sweat—he took inventory of his bridge to the town. The planet and the universe would need a separate account.

The J. C. Penney's. The Ward catalogue store. The real estate doctors' mall with boutiques, vitamins, tee shirts, stationery, "Wall Hangings" (macrame), juice bar with kegs for sit-down juicing, Moulded Running Shoes Forsooth for stand-up running, Space Available for Leasing Coldwell-Banker. A redwood sign with an arrow made of bark painted green pointed upstairs to Kosmic Documentary Films & All-Purpose Media Services (Temporarily Closed for Corporate Restructuring). Bicycles were tangled everywhere; they sailed like air-powered vessels down the slight slope of the parking lot, past the automobiles which looked like an exhibition of Anti-Detroit (Mercedes, Porsche, BMW, VW, Toyota, Datsun, Honda and a few museum Chevies with bodies eaten out by eastern winter salt, smuggled across the Donner Pass by immigrants). The Quiche-Me-Quick had just replaced the Fro-Fro Yogurt, but the Foto-mat was holding steady, guaranteeing Your Fotos by Four If in by Ten or Free Film.

Kenny's Down Under, a Fern Bar for Us, had replaced Alfie Australia, the former straight fern bar, utilizing the leftover ferns, which are androgynous. Watkins took his beer ration at the Antique Bizarre because he liked the burly world of railway workers, even though the railway workers had been gone for a generation. The tracks rusted nearby. There were bicycle racks here too, a trap and a menace for the drunk. Coffee boiled down to the consistency of old shoelaces was free at the Antique Bizarre. They didn't want sleepy drunk drivers to leave the place, or wobbly bicyclists, or even mumbling pedestrians like Watkins, finding his way alone to the house on G Street from which wives and a secret love had departed forever.

On the whole, Watkins decided, despite what I and others might think, this is really not so bad. One should be happy in a California university town with its ten-speeds and its London double-deckers and no woman for a middle-aged lawyer. One could be really happy here; every broken heart asked to be broken into cheerful parts. A professor of English had informed him that the perfect medieval town, as described in *The Medieval City* by Fustel de Coulanges, contained thirty thousand people and so did Davis. "Then why are those archers shooting at us from behind the crenellated walls?" Watkins asked, and Lester Groton had answered, "I see what you mean. No cathedral. A certain amount of unavoidable noise pollution. You have a point there, Wat."

On a cross street, trucks heading out toward Woodland, stood the punker and harassed-mother resorts, Wendy's, Jack-in-the-Box, McDonald's, Gino's Tex-Mex. The smell of fast food and parking lot drifted across a stand of undeveloped trees to meet in a conflict of oxidation. A few country hoods cruised their cycles down and back, looking for speed, looking for girls, looking for each other, finding six-packs. A few lovers sat in postcoital gloom or precoital bliss at Sambo's (bless them all, thought Watkins). Someone called to him: "Hey, Broccoli-brain! You lose something?"

How did he know?

At forty-two years, which seemed to Watkins the middle of a life in California, he had lost his second wife. That was how it seemed to him: he had mislaid her by the side of a road. She ran away with a graduate student who offered her a life of marijuana growing and integrity in the hilly regions of outer Marin. She herself had been a graduate student a few years before when they met and fell desperately in love across the generation gap. And then broccoli-brain had lost her to a zucchini-brain.

And thus it occurred to Watkins that it might henceforward

be unseemly for him to run around with students, even graduate students. Their cute behinds and alert eyes pleased him, but they no longer conformed to his sense of the fitting. After all, as a lawyer and a professor of law, he was old enough to be a Responsible Negro Leader, if only he were black and had developed a bit of belly. Racquetball and running kept him lean and fit, and contributed to keeping him sane. He went through an exceptionally desolate period when his concentration was shattered. He stumbled on. Some brute patience saved him—he simply usefully gave up. Bethany Andrews helped, a dentist's wife, a leader of society in Davis, Woodland, Winters and Dixon, a passionate laborer at filling the day, a froster of hair until he told her not to, a women's tennis star, a subscriber to useful magazines, *Harper's, Prevention, Money* and *Architectural Forum,* and a reader of them while she waited for a court—a women's star in the over-thirty tournaments—and a loyal mother of three. Bethany saved his life was how he put it to her; thank you.

"Now Wat," she said, "I can spare a couple of afternoons a week is all. And maybe you sleep a little better in general. But the only people that their life I'm willing to save is my kids', my own and maybe my husband's. For me you're just a good friend and mingle."

"Mingle?"

"You know what I mean. I don't like to use dirty words unless it's absolutely necessary or I'm tossed on the waves of passion, you know, really mad at someone or, oh, you know, Wat—"

"*Mingle?*"

"Wat! Please! Don't quibble!" He said nothing and watched Bethany also busily saying nothing. While she was engaged in the act of silence, sweet fizzy smells, her athletic moves, her arms and legs wrapped tightly about his heftier but no longer plump griefs. Actually, of course, they weren't wrapped about the griefs. They were wrapped about his chest and shoulders or his hips and legs. The griefs were contained therein. They were not her primary concern, but since she was quick, intelligent, they were her secondary concern. Like certain insects, she made

35

precise articulations. She didn't want his griefs to impede their swift afternoons together in the fresh-baked condominium town house he had bought for convenience's sake, solar heated and solar cooked, shared tennis courts, racquetball and squash, pool, sauna and complete Neptune exercise facilities. Early on he was grateful to Bethany for her unmeddlesome acceptance of him. Later he realized—being inexperienced, this was something he had to learn—it came with the territory of being happily married.

Bethany saved his pride. She preserved his pleasure. She tickled him. In dark moods, or in moods of elation when he first met her—when he was getting stonewalled by the wife now with her young lover in outer Marin—he believed she had saved his life; but of course nobody really did that for anybody, not for long, only as a temporary stopgap.

A respectable professor of law, with a small buccaneer practice, he was now interested in seeing if he could save his own life. A savings and loan had endowed his adjunct chair in such a way that he had time for meditation on the philosophy of justice, criminal and business, plus (not stated in the terms of the bequest) justice for the boy contained in Watkins personally.

Sometimes it seemed that life pursued a punished man with new punishments. Just when he was thoroughly shaken by his wife's defection—and who was he anymore?—one of the leaders of Human Rights on campus visited his office, crossed his legs, showed a thread-filled rip in his jeans at the crotch, was wearing no underwear beneath the threads, and announced: "I've always argued gays don't feel any attraction to nongay individuals because we're so beautiful all by ourselves. That's my nonnegotiable position. Well, I was wrong."

Silence. There was silence except for the gentle sounds of the campus firemen across the way, throwing their Frisbees and expressing camaraderie. It was the wrong time in Watkins's life for this sort of invitation. He knew it, and knew the lad had no rude intentions. He was only uttering the honest truth about his feelings, as people ("viable individuals") must. Nevertheless, in his own honest truth, Watkins felt alarmed. He thought: A soft answer turneth away wrath. "Fuck off, Buster," he said softly.

That was wrong. That was piggish of him. That was uncontrolled.

So Bethany was very important in preventing these explosions, in putting him together again after the postcards from his second wife and the dunning letters from his second wife's lawyer and the occasional dutiful notes from the grown children by his first wife. Since he had learned to love the one he was with and he was with Bethany, he would not ask too much of her but she couldn't stop him from loving her, could she?

He wrote a little note to the chairgay of the Human Rights Society to apologize for his outburst, admitting he had come under psychosociological interpersonal pressure about something totally unconnected with the modern world and developments in the struggle for freedom of previously enchained or closeted minorities. He had been aggravated and he was sorry. He received a gracious reply, suggesting another meeting, this time in a bar in Sacramento.

A little poor health or impotence would have helped at this point. Perhaps a touch of ulcerative colitis, or a spectacular burnout on the launch pad or fizzle, with crowds cheering, at the moment of penetration; something of the sort. Bona fide disaster, delivered by pain and signed by doctors and women, might have made him feel more real to himself. Instead, disembodied, he floated in teeny-tiny adventures like a stroll in Davis, and maybe there was a deeper ill health or impotence in his nature, beyond his stubborn alertness and eagerness—not feeling after having put too much of a burden on Bethany, his last love after so much marriage. His metabolic optimism persisted. He sniffed the air of D Street where it crossed Second, and thought about following Bethany's instructions.

On the whole, he might have enjoyed a touch of impotence, which after all was no stranger to him. With his first wife he had sampled it aplenty, especially when she made rules about positions for sex—no one on top, no one on the bottom, just perfect side-by-side equality in a posture which suited neither of them. And as to ill health, he had tried that, too—headaches, turista, flu every third year or so, nasal drips in ragweed season, an appendix which almost (but didn't) burst. So his offers of pain were made with a full and knowing heart, of good mind and conscience, like a will.

Instead, his penis obeyed him, his stomach obeyed him—were they following the proper codicils of his living testament? How did they know what was good for him?

Well, don't look a healthy middle age in the snout and complain, he decided. It's not seemly, with so many friends fading, even dying. This is America, isn't it? And isn't it California? *Northern* California? On to the future, forty-four-year-old lad.

Bad news from too many women causes some men to decide enough is enough. At Watkins's age, it was a solution he had noticed. Some men grow mature, and that seems to work for them; maturity provides intelligent procedures. They were companions to wives who no longer loved them or whom they no longer loved; they attained friendships with these women, and a working friendship is no small gift. They gazed at women on the street or in restaurants. They went to conventions, on business trips, and experienced one glorious adventure per decade, plus a couple of inglorious ones. They returned, relieved, to their good working friendship. Their wives did the same, perhaps at the club, perhaps on odd sultry afternoons; the wife of one of Watkins's colleagues had a taste for Bay Area dope dealers, rock-and-roll musicians and car parkers aged nineteen (more car parkers than rock stars were available to her). She took a path which involved careful scheduling and showers at odd hours.

They matured in alcohol, ambition, property, money, despair and the love of their children.

They matured by growing older.

Watkins had a peculiar metabolism and an askew brain and a gaping soul. After the final bad news from a wife (it became real to him only gradually because he was filled with stupid, boyish hope), he decided in his own way that enough was enough. Early middle age would be the limit of maturity for him. He had a painful obsession, thank God, like the lonely dried-up gentlemen who sit in big-city cafeterias on national holidays, eating the turkey special and cutting out the bad news from the Thanksgiving edition of the newspaper. He dreamed of Miss Right 'n' Lovely, a fast-fantasy serving of woman. He knew she was out of sight in the past. He knew her chatter would drive him back to the blue plate special. He whirled like an athlete in the street when she drove by or walked past, heels clicking, or laughed along with some healthy racquetball player.

His love for his last wife was finally dead to him, like a severed snake, the head cold but the tail still twisting at night in his dreams. When he found Bethany, even the tail got buried. That was good fun.

Ah, this is dumb. He often spoke these words to himself: Oh, Wat, you are really stupid.

So he kept his madness in check, as far as the world could see. He did his jobs without disgrace. He did not rise as far as his professors in law school, nearly twenty-five years ago, had convinced him he would; but he had risen high enough for most members of the California bar—well, for some—and he had surely spent more time suffering through marriages and love than most of those who rose higher.

Watkins was mature now, but not exactly. At last he was grown up, but somewhat juvenile. What he meant to declare about himself: worldly wise, but an idiot. He had thought he was finally content with Bethany. A friendly arrangement had become a source of deep and regular awe. He could both tickle and worship a woman, and how cleverly they had buried any occasion for dissension. He had found peace! It turned out not necessarily to be the case that the experience of contentment meant a person had the actual cozy thing in his possession.

Enough.

 3

He rang up Number One on Bethany's list. "Uh, the person in Davis, I'm the one who received your letter—" Obedience to Bethany was not the optimal state of mind, he noted; start again. "This is Watkins. It's a peculiar moment for both of us, I imagine."

"Definitely weird," she said.

"But we're both normal embarrassed people. If this is too squirmy for you—"

"No," she said. She sounded cautious by telephone, unlike her high-spirited but sensible letter. "Yes," she said. "All right, a visit would be convenient this weekend. Please come to my house and I'll make dinner. I'd rather not go out—I'll explain."

"May I bring something?"

"Your good self," she said somberly, not convinced his self was good.

Wine, he thought. *Flowers.* Her welcome was uttered like an undertaker inviting the family to bring along the star of the show. *And your good self. And dread.* He was comforted by the distance between Davis and Beverly Hills; perhaps she was also reassured. If it's a traveling thing, it's not really real, it's just a foot in the water. Anybody was less likely to complicate things too soon, less likely to report back to anybody else. He was unused to these doings and so was she. She was scared, like him, and he tried to pass the time on the flight to L.A. International by imagining her distress. Since he didn't know her very well, he could only imagine his own. But he would try to go easy on her, hoping for magic—maybe she would go easy on him, too. *Think adventure,* he thought.

In his mind, as a gesture of adventurous independence, he resolved not necessarily to take them in the future in the order Bethany had given them to him.

Adela Jenkins lived in a high rise on Wilshire Boulevard. She told him to find a cab, not rent a car, and he did as told. He sped to her high rise on Wilshire with wine, with flowers, with a hotel reservation in his pocket, just in case, but thinking adventure. In the cab he also worried about details: Where do I put my bag? Nonchalantly at her door? As if I'm just staying a moment, surely not for the night? Nonchalantly?

These adventurous thoughts filled the idle half hour, forty minutes, of taxi. He was calm, but his heart and stomach were enfevered. They throbbed, but of course he was like ice, a pillar of strength and resolution and—dare he praise himself?—a certain daring. No, probably not; no heroes appropriate to this war.

No turning back, however, either.

The building had a doorman and a full closed-circuit welcoming machinery. Television, pipes, electricity. Button to press, replies to make upon demand, as described in a manual. He was walked to the elevator after he was introduced by a device which falsified both of their voices: Watkins . . . Come on up.

He throbbed at her door and she seemed to hear. She opened. Either those were her eyes or she wore glowing contact lenses. They stood and introduced each other to each other and he put down his bag and was quite sure, no choice about it now, he would not be using his hotel reservation. "Why I wanted to cook," she was saying, "has to do with my daughter's phases. She is going through a passage right now. In fact"—slant at left corner of mouth traced lineaments of humor—"she lives in one. You'll notice."

He was made comfortable. Dubonnet. Chipped ice. A woman lawyer who worked for MGM in-house, the-films-not-the-real-estate. She was a colleague in the law. She had an agreeable large mouth with a swift way of shifting into a stubborn firm setness, gleamy intelligent eyes with the hysteria under management, highly professional grooming of the hair. It was short, curled, fluffed and reddish in certain lights. If there are grades of henna, this was the best.

His fellow attorney's house was green with plants, ferns, cyclamens, airy with puffed pillows, stamped for contemporaneity with prints by Chagall, Picasso and a large Lichtenstein cartoon with dots like cannonballs. There were no photographs of men. He didn't expect any.

He was no more uncomfortable than God meant him to be.

"Sherry!" she called. "Sherry, you march right out of there now, please—then you can go back."

Sherry emerged, blinking, as from a cave. Sherry was her daughter. She was eleven or twelve, cute, blond, button-nosed and wearing a child-tailored World War II combat camouflage uniform with ammo clip and belt from which hung child-sized grenades. "Sherry, this is Mr. Watkins."

The child saluted smartly.

"Hi," said Watkins.

"May I return to duty, Ma?" the child asked.

Ma nodded. Watkins took a step or two with her, until Ma signed him to retreat. But he saw the tent pitched in her bedroom, surrounded by armament. "Sherry likes to play war," Ma said. "She's an island fighter. It's only a game, of course."

"Naturally."

"This is a crucial juncture in her negotiation with the Viet Cong," she said. "That's why I wanted to remain on the scene, monitoring developments, and have dinner in. You don't mind?"

"I so seldom get a home-cooked meal," said Watkins.

"Sherry's a delight, but my son has problems. I'll say no more, except he's older—you wouldn't think I'd have a son his age, would you?" Her eyes, Los Angeles beaver eyes, fluttered and lowered themselves with the kind of flirtatious winsomeness a mature woman achieves when she pays herself a compliment. "Pharmacuticles," she said.

"Pardon?"

"So I got to be an expert in pharmacuticles, too," she said, looking at her nails. "That's why I do pro bono work in drug abuse, like that famous master of ceremonies whose daughter did it. I'm like him. I didn't push my son around; he got to be a disbarred lawyer all by himself. Naturally, I shared my input into his decision-making process. As far as his addiction is concerned, I showed him the way. I'd say he's halfway cured already. He's in a halfway house. I'll say no more. Later we can share the problem of maybe getting his license to practice back. Or he can always do legal research for some understanding attorney. Some of our finest saints started life as sinners, I ought to know. And he knows that, too—a fine boy, like me."

Watkins listened attentively. Sometimes life took him elsewhere. This was one of those occasions.

"I happened to find myself with him, a teenage mother, just like he found himself a teenage legal prodigy. Then for me came marriage; for him, pharmacuticles. It's a halfway house all the way. A mother's anguish—a single parent's pride—a Parents without Partners life—an affirming crisis which separates the men from the boys. I'll say no more. You're not a vegetarian, are you—you eat carnivore?"

Watkins nodded. There was a jungle beast in him which demanded convenient high-density protein. He wished to mention, in addition, how he too was nervous in this situation with Adela Jenkins and had a whole life's story to impart. But perhaps the island fighter's mother understood. He would say no more.

She offered a glimpse of the carefree inventiveness and hope of adventure which breathed through her winner of a letter. It had won Bethany. It was first for her. Adela's eyes glistened; her lipgloss glistened. "I'll tell you one thing," she confided, "we're not having field rations out here."

He sniffed. "Beef Bourguignon?"

"You guessed it. If there's a smell of scorch, that's Sherry's grub on her alcohol burner."

"I brought a white," Watkins said apologetically, "but it's chilled." He zipped open his bag. The bottle lay snugly against shaving things, two shirts, socks. Swiftly, shyly, he zipped shut.

44

It seemed overly suggestive to let the zipper sound, to show his socks. "An unpretentious fine French chilled white," he said.

"It's not your fault. How could you have known? I might have been a fish person. We'll save it for some enchanted seafood evening." She turned the bottle over in her hands, reading their fortune in the green glass. "Chenin Blanc nineteen seventy-four." She cradled it in her arms. "Can't say I know that year."

He shrugged modestly.

"Or breakfast," she remarked, "when we're having cold salmon. Who says, in such situations, a couple must be bound hand and foot to German Riesling for the seafood omelets?"

They were both shy. They were both embarrassed. Some speak copiously to cover the silence; Adela may have been one of those, despite her rule about saying no more. "I used to have a Close Personal Friend," she said, "you know what that means in Ellay? But then I responded to your ad because it was such a very interesting appeal, Watkins. I mean I had this Close Personal Friend I was just totally sick of. He had no finesse, he lacked panache. On Sunday mornings when I said sailing, he said lie in bed and read the stupid trades. I said Tijuana, let's just be crazy kids, he said got to get up early take a breakfast meet. I said I haven't seen Venice, Italy, yet, he said it's sinking, let's wait till they float it again. Watkins, I'm so loyal, but I'm not in a coma. For spurts of zing, he was totally out of it. How could I have been so innocent not to notice till I read your vita and it hit me over the head what's really out there, an attorney like myself but a live one?"

He didn't have the answer on the tip of his tongue. Internal static and chaos often put Watkins, who had been obliged by fate to study living alone, in a brooding and paralyzed jungle play-dead mood. In which he sometimes talked a lot—jabbered.

One of these tangled moods was coming on him now. He vowed to fight his inclination. Unfair to the hostess, it would only challenge her. Surely she didn't need any more challenges, what with Sherry, plus her son, plus a close personal friend with a missing panache, plus the plain turmoil of existence in a world in which an attractive woman, dressed for success both mentally and personal decor-wise, could only find true love through the classified section. Since facts are facts, Adela Jenkins had no intention of letting her life continue in the downer mode. Thank God for advertising, and for all the finesse and panache just begging for a decent meal and a little attention out there.

"Are you always so silent?" Adela asked.

"You've given me a lot to think about."

"I like depth in a man. I was afraid you'd be one of those always telling me about his broker, his alimony, his Tamaran at Marina del Mar he only has time to sail one weekend a month, they asked him to Washington for a workup and he turned down the appointment in the White House, undersecretary of trilateral this or that—I prefer depth in a man. If the truth be told, it's sweeter—depth plus a devil-may-care streak."

"That's me," Watkins said gloomily.

Adela compressed her lipgloss together, shook her curls, pointed a finger with a winning cuticle job on it and just plain beamed out of her beaver eyes at him. They both knew what she was being so silent about. Let's face the fact that he was overwhelmed by all her knowledge, experience, control and general smooth; he was only a small-town academic attorney with an overnight bag near the outer door; this was not easy for anybody.

Having faced the fact, they could go on.

The kid with the combat equipment, slowing down any possible attack from either quarter, served as chaperone with her intercondominium ballistic missiles. Sherry eased matters somewhat. She was a godsend, a Medal of Honor candidate. The battle for atolls dwarfed the hunger for sharing. Eventually Adela and Watkins must speak about why they had, to put the matter straight, advertised for company. Definitely a must topic, and so far Adela had only sketched out the perimeters. Watkins's input was total zilch; his output, zip. Such terrific high-to-higher achievers as they were, or as one of them stated herself to be, they owed each other a few explanations. They could strive to be whimsical, frank, honest, a touch *triste*. Depth was not beyond their grasp. If push came to shove, they could put it in their own words.

Maybe he would tell her about Bethany. Despite her vow of silence, she might talk about her son and her close personal friend. It was essential.

On the other hand, maybe they had both already said enough, given their mutual tact and innate sympathy, and they could just move right along to the future, which is what counts when a person only has a limited patience with past errors and wrongs. Disco nights and lunchaholic all-day meets don't count anymore. True, herpes might count, and so might a non-fun-loving attitude. The important thing was to seize the moment on the wing, because every option expires unless it's renewed. That's the nature of life, red in tooth and claw when a person idealistically reaches out his or her lonely arms toward the bottom line. Face it, we're all beasts out here. Yes, we're also capable of gentleness, kindness, devotion, the purest kind of altruism and nonoffice giving, full of dreams and needs, whipping up a light supper without even being asked. We're just kids at heart. So naturally we have to twist a little knife now and then in the dark, just to forestall misunderstanding.

Watkins felt a little vertigo. Maybe the situation, or maybe Adela's generosity in taking so much of the initiative, made him a bit dizzy. He was learning. This was Wilshire and he had a lot to learn. Adela was the hostess and he would follow her lead.

Adela felt the same way. She would follow her own lead.

"That's neat," she said, returning to the main business of the evening and concluding the previous matter of the non-Riesling chilled white wine suitable for a seafood breakfast omelet or cold poached salmon. She stored it away. Deftly she inserted the daisies into a narrow-necked faded blue vase of some sort of crackly antique make, carried north or west from an ethnic society to remind everyone of truer values. There were fine ethnic crackle lines in the glaze. She didn't find it necessary to inform Watkins of the provenance of the vase, but he guessed Baja.

47

Watkins inclined his head modestly. Self-control was return-ing with the little wine-and-flower ceremonies. "You're wel-come," he murmured.

"And now a light supper, Mr. Watkins!"

"Wat," he said. "Watkins is my first name. Called Wat by my friends."

While scorch aromas of field rations wafted from the tent-stuffed bedroom, they ate the following: chilled vichyssoise, which she did not pronounce without the final consonant—she also did not say "bo-teek" when she meant *boutique*; a salad with a light herbal dressing—they both commented on the French habit of serving salad after the meat course; a meat course, the aforementioned beef Bourguignon with baby carrots in a sweet-ish wine gravy, which she called "au jus" and he did not dis-agree; fruit and cheese. "I don't believe in heavy meals at night," she said, while he thought: And she blushes. That's nice.

"My son," she said. "You have such a real face I want to lay it all out. I mean you have such a gentle, understanding, really human face I want to tell you about my boy. You have a genuine face, so about my son—this is hard for me."

"Go on," said Wat. Possessed of an entire physiognomy, with features, eyes, ears, nose, mouth, and skin joining everything in between, could he offer less? "Please. I'm all ears, nose and throat. No, sorry, I really mean it."

"You do?"

"I do."

"All right. You asked me, and a real person like you deserves to suffer no secrets. My son. This is hard for me, Watkins. My son, like his father, he has this tendency to ejaculatory impo-tence despite erection. We're very honest with each other, Wat. Normally, your average insensitive person, ejaculation is the forceful propulsion of seminal fluid along the prostatic urethra, due to spasmodic contractions of the bulbocavernous muscle and simultaneous closure of the bladder neck. Stop me if I left something out, Watkins."

"I think you covered it."

"Well, my son is different. Having a real bitch for a father

48

made him different. I'll say no more."

Watkins appreciated that. He appreciated discretion in a new friend.

"You like some extra au jus with your carnivore?"

"Delicious," said Watkins, slapping his napkin. "Really tasty, with a nice tang."

She dipped out some red-eyed sauce. "Say no more," she said.

She served espresso in little cups. Alertness seemed to be in the cards before the night's repose.

But first, having said no more, they talked. Her marriage, his marriages. The tasks of in-house counsel in a major conglomerate such as MGM, movies plus real estate plus hotel investments; the MGM Grand in Las Vegas, plus liaison with specialized firms in several overseas areas. Her work, his work. The destiny of humankind in L.A.

They talked around the subject. She went to look at Sherry. Sherry was sleeping in full field pack, sprawled precariously, little legs askew. With a trilling laugh Adela asked, "Why do we have to explain everything? Let's save something for later."

He nodded. She wafted a half turn around the room as his eyes followed her, and while she was remarking, "The cleaning woman will clean up in the morning," she wafted herself into his arms, onto his lap—actually, kind of between his thighs— where she took a firm grip ("Easy!" he cried), and she asked, "Right hand or left?"

A cuteness, he supposed.

Perhaps because he was so terrified and distant, he noticed no difficulties. What should have produced premature performance produced adequate performance. From a distance. From a distance he heard her voice asking amid the tumbled clothes, amid the beef Bourguignon remnants: "Am I beautiful?"

"Yes," he said.

"Was I good?"

"I think so."

"Am I wonderful?" This was an interrogatory. "Am I wonderful?" she repeated.

"To the best of my knowledge," he stated.

49

Tumbled there on a nubby orange carpet, of some kind of material which would wipe away stains (WipeAway Fabric of Sunburst Orange, he thought), she gazed up at him. Suddenly she was happily in love with someone, a person who was beautiful, good, wonderful—herself. This might be the only true love! She sighed and touched him. "You're nice," she said. "I'm glad you wrote to me."

"Me too," he said.

"Do you like to be touched *there*? Like this?"

"Will it wake up Sherry?"

"I doubt it, darling. She's a light sleeper, so I put a mild analgesic in her field rations—enough to tranquilize a veteran afflicted with night fears, my sweet."

He stared at the ceiling.

"You didn't think of that sooner, did you? Men! But she's ten miles out in dodoland, dearest."

To prove her point, she temporarily removed her hand and turned the music up. It was Jean-Pierre Rampal playing Japanese folk melodies on his romantic French flute, softer before and not too loud now. Returning, she touched him lightly with a wetted index finger. It was an oddly ingratiating gesture, like a pointer to a blackboard in an accident damage suit demonstration. She was presenting evidence for consideration of all present, including him. "Right here," she said. She was persuasive in her analysis. It was right there. To her lips, to his right-there. To his right-there, to her lips.

He remembered the leaves of faintest autumn falling, letting in the sky, on the campus of the University of California at Berkeley, where he had found a girl to do what they were now doing on the WipeAway Fabric of nubby Sunburst Orange. They were both good students, so they deserved each other. This was a generation ago. She had tired finally of using her fingers, and before the first winter rains, her tongue had fallen to this work; she discovered a greed in herself which astonished them both; and thus he married his first wife, alas. Now she was the one he liked the least of his wives—her greed did not mean the true love he thought it meant at nineteen, it meant only greed plus a small amount of intelligent calculation—finally all those choked gasping cries had painful implications when property-settlement time came along . . . "Are you thinking of your baby," the in-house counsel from MGM Pictures and Real Estate asked, "or are you, perchance, woolgathering?"

"Woolgathering," he admitted. At his age he sought to be honest; had no choice; sometimes didn't care to lie.

"Well, pay attention. I want you to do this now."

With firm hands on his ears she directed him where to go. The campus, Indian summer, autumn, then first storms, glorious in their brisk sharp chills, disappeared. Well, it wasn't a long happiness. Now he was committed to humid, oily, hot work, kept busy, urged to keep busier. After a while, the hands gripping his ears let go, trusting him, and with her climax came some nice friendly pats on the head. He rested where he was. "Nice," she said, "that's nice. I like how you just stay still there now."

He was trying to recall Bethany and succeeding all too well; her clean fizzy smells, her eager chipper laughter, her caring.

"I'd like to get to know you," she said, growling a little. She must have spent some time in MGM screening rooms.

"Me too," he said.

"You're good. You're very good. You Northern Californians are surprisingly good," she said.

He was the peripheral canal, bringing irrigation to the parched southland.

"And now I want to ask you something," she whispered, the growling of passion subsiding into the curiosity of a thoughtful temperament, "and then I'll say no more. Are you happy, too? Did you? . . ."

The roar of her engine must have drowned out his own little revving-up on the proving ground. "Just hold me," he said, "that's enough."

She clutched him to her creamy sallow skin. He felt yoga classes, nonfad diets, cosmetics from Rodeo Drive and not too much sun. She was also grateful, and that was nice of her. He was aware of Adrian—Adelle—no, Adela—as she held him, but through her eyes he seemed to see himself receding, receding,

51

into the middle distance. Into the far distance. Gone.

Now what. A long night ahead. It didn't make sense to pick up his bag, retreat, try to check in late at a hotel. It also didn't make sense not to, but there seemed no fair way to find the right thing to do. Also a practical matter: to pee. To pee or not to pee was not a question; it answered itself. He couldn't quite recall, in a state of partial somnolence, where the bathroom was, although he presumed he must have used it already, perhaps before dinner—oh yes, past the hanging plants, past the door leading to the tent and Sherry's field exercise, then hang a sharp right into the black tiles of comfort station.

As a practical matter, while he thought about it, his crotch was sticky and he felt a small unalert wiggle against his thigh, as if the wiggler sought a place to hide. The wiggler was retreating fast; the sensation of itch persisted. A travel memory came to him. Tahiti. A giant land crab clutched a coconut and broke it with one straight convulsion of its claws, and the milk flowed. He was no armored clattering tropical crab. He was in the grip of things.

Watkins climbed up. Adela's lips were parted, her teeth gleamed, she looked childish and vulnerable, there was a little childish vulnerable snore when he disturbed her on nubby fabric. She caught her breath, moaned and continued her sleep. He was heading barefoot down the long verdant trail, past bubbling aquarium, ferns, pots, greens suspended from wires, a Far East of plants, toward the black-tiled bathroom. What he felt must be more than the sadness after sex. At his age postcoital melancholy should be put into perspective. A grown man reckons with it, then cancels it out. Relief lay ahead when peeing, but not yet.

He crept past darkened trees, flowers and souvenirs. No, this was the honest midnight grief of the bus stop and the no-bus-coming blues.

He stood before the commode. The itch stopped him a moment. A reflex of withdrawal. Relief came in a stream of warm and wet.

Suddenly a blast of sound shot forth from nubby fabric central. "Don't leave the seat up! My husband always left the goddamn seat up, and you know what that feels like when a person sits down? Goddammit, what makes you think you're better than I am, just because you stand up?"

He said nothing. He finished. He shook. He thought to return, where he would inquire into the welfare and dreams of his lady, reassure her of his consideration. At the moment he felt naked, and was; and as he turned, he found himself in Vietnam, with Sherry facing him, the size of an enemy, her electronic rifle aiming to cut him in half, the combat child crying, "Ack-ack-ack! Ack-ack-ack!"

Well, what did you expect? This is the dramatic part of the state, he thought as he packed up to leave in the swift silence after battle. An eerie silence fell over the troops. The mother was back at the command post, watching in the dark. She had radar eyes and control of human waves of infantry ready to sacrifice themselves. Better not to speak.

On the street outside, wondering how to find a cab on Wilshire Boulevard at midnight, or how to commandeer a civilian vehicle, Watkins realized that in his chagrin, haste, terror and doomed carelessness, he *had* left the toilet seat up.

He trudged, carrying his overnight case, toward a distant marquee. It seemed to promise a lodging for the night.

4

Carrying his overnight bag at 2:00 A.M. on Wilshire in L.A., Watkins had turned to see if there was life in the high rise where Sherry and her mother had made him feel at home. Lights dotted the steel-and-glass tube. Here and there folks lay awake, or left their lamps burning the way he sometimes, in Davis, left the radio on for company in his absence, so he wouldn't be alone when he returned.

He found a bivouac in a building where they were selling executive condominiums. The guard, whose shirt was covered with little snippets of black curls, wanted to know what he had in mind, mon, and where he had stashed his wheels. No, at this moment before dawn he was not shopping for time-sharing suites, but perhaps a deal could be made for a few hours. The negotiation was brief. The watchman had to interrupt his self-inflicted haircut. He offered to show sample accommodations in several sizes, but Watkins chose a stripped-down one-and-a-half bedroom plus wet bar. This was only a temporary. The watchman accepted a twenty as compensation for the momentum he had lost in doing his sideburns. He threw in his own time-shared towel in case Watkins wanted to freshen up a little in the morning. If you snap the towel, the hair comes right out.

Probably Bethany didn't want a complete report on his visit to Los Angeles and the Wilshire high-rise bunker. Even though Adela Jenkins stood Number One on the list, an attorney with a fulfilling job in middle-level management, a sharpshooting daughter, a son in a wonderful halfway house, Watkins's profound conviction was that Bethany was not in the slightest, not even faintly or incipiently jealous. So the only reason to tell her

55

would be for the comradeship of it, and he didn't feel he could face her nonjealousy. There was a gentle concentration of bile in his belly. He knew it would spread, it would take on acid and mucous, it was desire made rancid. He had never been jealous of her husband. The athletic young periodontist used to seize her on Saturday night and maybe one or two days during the week, but her joy was with Watkins. No more. Bile, food in bad repair, longing enmeshed in desire to hurt.

He spent the week sighing and recovering. He proceeded despite himself, a man startled from sleep, hurried into life against his will, his head filled with mists, his soul caught between dreaming and waking. He seemed to have chosen this slap in the face of a comfortable middle age. Unlike Vic Lonkin, he was not doing the great things people had expected of him. He was agitated. He chose to let Bethany choose for him.

The days passed.

No herpes, no painful urination. He recovered his spirits, and recovered spirits inquired: Where the sense of adventure, old boy?

On to the next on his list. He wondered if anyone noticed how he shifted his obligations around in favor of white spaces on the appointment book which remained unaccounted for. His secretary may have thought this the prudent slowing down of a man in the middle of his life, a sort of silent jogging. Or may not have thought about it at all.

On to the next on his list.

Of course he could write anonymous letters to Bethany's husband, he could offer venomous proof, birthmarks, words she cried, her tanned arms flying up to claw at his back—what proof is that? A letter to the dentist-sportsman-investor would express his hatred of Bethany. But it would not express his love. He wanted her, not to punish her for abandoning him. If he couldn't have her, he could hope on a certain February, with the winter flowers blooming, the hedges throwing their scents into the winter sunlight, she might remember him. That wasn't much for a lover. It was even less for the lover of a woman who was not a sentimental brooder but a wife, mother and tennis player, intelligently entertained by the distractions that came her way. She had stopped thinking about her soul when things got busy. She was several moves ahead of him there, wasn't she?

It was a heartbreaking autumnal Saturday afternoon, the leaves blowing, dry and warm—the weather here sometimes played for a day at being an eastern autumn. A bunch of town kids slid by on roller skates; a sweet-faced Chinese couple from the university was walking their dog past his house, making sure it did its dropping near his house and not near theirs; a jogger with Walkman music plugged into his ears was making his turn around the campus before going home to something. Surely they all had something to go home to. Watkins was alone with a weekend underplanned. He peeked into the box to see what Bethany had rejected on his behalf. He decided to study some of the advertisements in the *Guardian* she had clipped for his instruction. There was company here, seeking comfort or magic, or if they had given up on the big things, looking for distraction, a passing of the time, a near reminder and approximation of their hopes.

My Former Lover
(and now my best friend) will be 40 soon, and I'd like to find him a new playmate for his birthday. He's a charming, sexy business executive, slightly eccentric, very funny, sweet & sensitive, and if that's not enough, he's rich, too. If you are a beautiful woman with a trim but voluptuous figure, in your 20's, smart, classy, sensuous, adventurous; if you prefer excitement to commitment, and want a taste of the good life, please write to me about yourself, and include a recent photo or complete physical description. Vanessa, 1850 Union St. Box 107, S.F. 94123.

Would You Believe

W/M, 35, 5'10", 175#, attractive excorporate president (I sold my company last year), semi-retired (I work 3 half days a week), highly entrepreneurial—I am a devout capitalist. Enjoys running, lifting weights, exploring California inns and wineries, intelegent conversation, touching and sharing feelings in front of a warm fire on a foggy night. I am seeking a woman who is exceptionally intelligent and attractive, who is slender, non-smoking, vivacious and not particularly interested in drugs or children. You are probably extremly successful, slightly overeducated and hopefully very sensual and openly affectionate. With luck you enjoy film, gourmet dinning and are free for extensive international travel. Your age, race and religion are interesting but not important. Please write (photo appreciated) Guardian Box #7-DD.

Lady Wanted To Hold In My Arms

to listen to classical music, also bluegrass, some country and rock. Looking for a serious, sharing relationship, and with much to give, I'm a Berkeley professional, W/M, late 30s (youthful looking), tall, attractive, trim, unencumbered life/-lifestyle, affectionate, communicative, playful, energetic, emotionally secure, have good sense of humour and diverse interests, including outdoors, running, photography, travel, literature, chess, music. You: non-smoker, very attractive, slim, tall (preferably), below 35ish, any race, mutual qualities/interests. Please respond (photo appreciated). Guardian Box #8-TT.

Come And Join Me

In the peaceful central California coast, where the air is crystal clear and the wide open spaces stretch as far as the eye can see. I am a forensic psychiatrist, formerly of Berkeley, and just emerging from a broken relationship. I am very intelligent, well educated, creative, witty, sensitive, have many skills and interests and am seeking a beautiful, intuitive, talented woman who is artistically oriented and has a strong sense of ethics. I am 42, 5'7", 135 lb and in excellent physical condition. Please write P.O. Box 991, Atascadero, Calif. 93422.

Herper Seeks Herpette
Good-humored, attractive professional W/M, 33, 175 lbs., 6 ft., with herpes seeks woman in same icky circumstances. I like: P.G. Wodehouse, Faulkner, V.S. Naipaul, Be-bop and Phobe Snow, the comic pages, fuzzy-minded liberals, elderly sport cars, very dry martinis, large dumb dogs, and the great outdoors in carefully controlled amounts. I abhor: self-help books, disco and new wave, astrology, hot tubs, heavy dope, Reganomics, consciousness raising vegetarianism and cowboy hats. If some of the proceeding makes sense, and if you are trying to come to terms with your pet virus, let's meet somewhere for lunch and get acquainted. Guardian Box #7-NN.

Are You There Lady
Tall athletic build very handsome aware alive non macho psychologist musician PT father easy going honest passionate real seeks lady counterpart 20 to 33 5'6" + in touch with her inner feelings who wants a good friend and lover. PO Box 657 Redwood City 94064.

Beginning professional woman 27 attractive stays slim dancing likes cooking culture clothes travel families rock music seeks strong supportive adventurous warm somewhat liberated literate generous man who likes sex but takes time to know a woman first makes 30,000+ looking for serious committed relationship maybe have kids someday. Jackie PO 362 Larkspur 94939

Spirits Of Air And Earth

Gemini, W/M, published writer, engineer, workshop leader, nationally-known photo-artist, meditator, gardener, baker, living very simply. A powerful, airy person with earthy interests. Sensitive, youthful, compassionate, complex, single. Trim, energetic, 5'-6½", attractive mid-forties. Seeks joyful, spiritual, powerful earthy woman with airy interests. E.B. or S.F. Guardian Box #46-J.

White male, 37, attractive, vegetarian enjoys reading and writing poetry, reggae and third world music seeks understanding, professional female 25–35 for sharing music and reviewing each other's poetry. Guardian Box #5-H.

Image Maker

Let me draw your face and see into your heart. A picture can be worth a thousand words. Slender, tall, sensuous, affectionate W/F. Poetess, cosmic thinker, dreamer, animal lover, well educated professional. Phi Beta Kappa, feminist, music and film fanatic. Comfortable dancing under the stars or to "Down Home Girl." This artist has new canvas to fill for special "subject." You are a creative, intelligent, psychically and psychologically aware close to nature, health conscious, tall, slim, handsome, caring man, an ex "Desperado," 33 to 43, who understands and likes himself, can appreciate a very attractive, complex woman, thrives on intensity and knows how to handle it. Letter, photo appreciated. Guardian Box #2-FFF.

Technical Affinity

Warm, impetuous, feminist woman with a passion for electronics, would like to meet a sensitive politically conscious man with technological work interests open to long term relationship of honest communication, sharing of creative technical projects and free flowing playfulness. Guardian Box # 10-C.

I'm Tired Of Turkey

I want a man who is gentle, romantic, responsible, employed, sexy, sensual, loyal, loving, friended, willing and able to lean, and be leaned on, and ready for commitment in his life. He should not be too well educated, but should have a lot on the ball, and, well, there is a lot more. Chemistry too. I am a 28 y.o. Phillipine-American, pretty, bright and ready; I am a construction worker, a firecracker. I love "drugs, sex, and rocknroll." I wear bright clothes, keep my word, and I am tired of turkey. Guardian Box #4-CC.

I'm: Tall WM 26, handsome, bright gentle. You're: WF, intelligent, attractive, (the taller the better): We like: bicycling, hiking, snuggling, rainy days, beaches, ice cream, frisbees, honesty. We dislike: smoking, drugs, the "Moral Majority", shallow people, and one night stands. Guardian Box #4-K.

You: comely, boyish-figured W/O-F 20's, bright, feminine, spunky, concerned, romantic, adventurous, Me: W/M, 39, attractive, robust; thinking, gentlemanly, fisty; humanitarian, sentimental, philosophical. Interests: hiking, dining, history, nude beaches, movies, parapsychology, old cars, tantric yoga, travel, writing, growth, etc. Box 249, 1476 Calif. S.F. 94109.

Remarkable Jewish female requires man with exceptional sense of rhythm, humor and style. Prefer enticing male of profound intelligence with combined looks of O.J. Simpson, Lawrence Olivier and Elliot Gould. I love lobster, Cole Porter, finger-painting, Motown, jazz piano, the seashore and existential literature. I hate beets and Alan Hamil. I have long dark curls, am 28 and beyond belief. Guardian Box #8-S.

Professional W/M, 32, 6'-1" who is looking to meet a special woman who I know
exists but is hard to find. She is probably
25–35, career-minded, non-smoking, and
could share interests in sports, music,
and theater. She's definitely quite attractive, slim, affectionate, fun to be with,
happy about herself, and has a good
sense of humor. I'm warm, sensitive, and
loving and truly interested in meeting
someone with the same qualities. This
special woman may be someone who
likes to read these ads but would never
think of answering one. Hopefully, I've
interested you into answering this one.
Guardian Box #9-E.

Character Not A Caricature
Are you an "A"-type woman? Competitive, professionally accomplished and a
risk-taker? First born, well educated who
values style, her individuality and sees a
man as a peer, who's physically fit, athletic and trim in her 20's or early 30's?
Someone who despite appearances
seeks out hot sun, Monterey Char-
donays, Tom Wolfe, Satie and early
mornings at the Sur, who can cry, hold
children and talk about feelings, and
above all be witty about who you're not.
Write: Esq. PO Box 10459, Oakland
94610.

Between us the play will please. You are
a heroine of beauties truly blent—lovely
and literary, accomplished, and athletic.
A prince among professors, I am 32, tall
and trim, luminous and lusty, solvent and
searching. I long to have some chat with
you, to thrive and ideally to wive. A photo
would be appreciated and returned.
Guardian Box #2-000.

Bethany, of course, sought only the best for him, good nature,
beauty, intelligence and enough womanly power to keep him off
her case. Respect for her judgment helped him postpone reading

the rejected letters, those put low on her list. She had stopped ranking them after Number Eight, but she left the other replies neatly clipped together. Some showed thoughtful penmanship, being written with nibs, not ballpoints, their *i*'s neatly circled; most, of course, were businesslike and typed, no matter how much compositional turbulence had gone into the mere words.

Well, perhaps Bethany wasn't perfect. Adela from Wilshire Boulevard could be considered an error. Maybe he would find a diamond here among the unnumbered and unranked, a genius at true love, a woman of intense spirit unlike Bethany's carefree but cautious one. Surely she meant for him to make up his own mind. The inside of his head, where part of the mind is located, felt like an old clock radio, rusty, bunched connections and solderings, and noise, but it worked unnecessarily. The switch went on and off, waking him up at odd hours. He could kick it or wait for it to die, or take it to a garage sale.

He settled down to read the file near Pieter Breughel the Elder's or the Younger's *Hunters in the Snow*, shoulders bent under the cold and his staff, faithful dogs following, homely chimneys smoking nearby and, in the distance, skaters on a frozen pond. A lonely crow overhead, huddled in its feathers on a naked wind-stripped branch.

Dear Box Number 109-A:

I am writing to you with great distress in my emotions. My doctor tells me that, were I to aspire to "motherhood" and all which that ensues, I must make the decision soon. For reasons too complicated to tell, I have been sellebate since the age of 18, and before that I was a "virgin," innocent of men and men's ways. As you can see, judging from how I just write down the word "virgin" to a man I hardly know or am acquainted with, no one can call me a "prude."

Yet many "lovers" have been mine for the "asking." There was hardly a big-budget movie I was not invited to see up until the age of about thirty, always, I frankly add, by a man who seldom was content with a bite to eat, a serious film and a sharing of an evening. They always wanted more than companionship. To date,

I have not found the man who deserves "more." Yet now there is a crisis. You, Sir, sound like a man who might deserve <u>more</u>. (I underline the word because I am filled with emotion.)

There are many films in the contemporary cinema which can fascinate serious-minded connoisseurs. I am willing to view one I have already seen, should that be your desire, confident that a second viewing plus heartfelt discussion might reveal depths and complications which . . .

Into the file. Watkins imagined drooping hemlines, unresolved religious stirrings, description of film as the contemporary art form *pour excellence*. He imagined a good position as an "executive" assistant to a fast-food mogul. He didn't have to imagine very much, since she told him what he needed to know. Videotape cassettes might be the definitive contemporary art form *par excellence*. Into the file.

. . . I trust you be interested in a woman with a head balder than Grace Jones's baldy, and you know who Grace Jones is. She is black and she is beautiful, tall, sassy, and mean and so am I. If you are into water sports or S & M (for Smiling & Moaning, babe), I'm your squeeze.

Now you might wonder, if I'm so bad, and I am, cross my heart, why I need to inquire about some stranger. I'm glad you asked that wonder. Because all the men around this town is a damn faggot is why. So if you be a damn faggot just looking for a hag, save your postage. But if you be a real man who appreciate frilly underwear on himself and jockey shorts on a tall, handsome, Jonesy gal, get on that box and <u>call</u>, man . . .

Watkins liked to refresh himself sometimes with what he was missing. The Grace Jones lady seemed to have a sense of humor, he would grant her that. She be making a stab at writing dialect just to get under his skin, man. She rang a bell—he esteemed the singing of Nina Simone. But she took disco, punk and the obligations of brinkiness too seriously for him. Watkins wanted to wear the jockey shorts around here. He wanted no preprogrammed Smiling & Moaning because the world gave enough of it in the natural avalanche of events. The Grace Jones lady went into the back of the file, even if she therefore decided he was some sort of damn faggot, like all her friends.

Thank you for your advertisement. Normally I never reply to such queries, but you sound so nice I shall take a chance. I can be described as a Roughneck Western Girl because I am a Girl of the Golden West, prefer to rock-climb and hike, and wear flannel shirts because of their proven dampness-absorbent qualities. Companionship is my major goal in life if you are similarly inclined. I love people, dogs, cats, birds, and cooking by an open campfire. Since a love affair which left a deep wound at the age of twenty, I am now celibate and forevermore must so remain. If you can find it in your heart to join my way of life, I can promise many pleasures, including a gradual program of fitness training, both aerobic and the development of major muscle system, if you're not too old. A kind of Mutual Federation, Sir, not that Total Union which leads to deep wounds . . .

The lady sounded healthy and sound, yet she caused him distress. Bethany's judgment was correct. Back into the file.

. . . My late husband, the anesthesiologist, left me reasonably well provided for, thanks to a life insurance policy inaugurated shortly before his tragic demise, plus his normal income as a distinguished doctor and the investments and the Keogh Plan authorized under the Internal Revenue laws of the United States of America, and the house happened to be in my name all along, heated swimming pool, tennis court needing only a little work, gazebo for private conversations plus meditation singly or in small groups when the children were little. . . . My kitchen happens to be a full restaurant kitchen due to gourmet training at Cordon Bleu West, plus I do Mandarin and Harbin, the first complete set of woks in El Cerrito. My late husband, before his unfortunate demise, always said his pride and joy was, firstly, an inner city program of precancer testing for our downtrodden fellow racial citizens, and, secondly, my culinary skills in the gourmet style . . .

Watkins made an exploratory telephone call to the wok-wielding widow. Her late husband, during his unfortunate demise, seemed to have expired of some inexplicable fatal poisoning, mainly due to an erroneous mushroom. She invited Watkins to dinner.

Watkins suggested, instead, lunch at an inn by the bay which he had always wanted to try. (In fact, lunch at the inn had hardly entered his mind, but he had seen an advertisement.) She informed him that the food in that plastic place was bland and phony, and instead, she would be glad to serve him a light but tangy noontime repast in the gazebo beneath which her husband's ashes were buried. In good weather, they could see downtown El Cerrito.

"Too much trouble for you," Watkins pleaded. Instead, just a glass of wine perhaps. He would bring a bottle.

But she loved cooking for her friends. Could she count him already, on the basis of this friendly debate before their meeting, as a new friend and lifelong acquaintance?

Hypnotized, he nodded.

"Hunh?" she asked.

Dehypnotized, he said unfortunately he was on a strict diet. He ate nothing but protein wafers from a sealed box at lunch —a box he carried with him at all times.

"Then do come for breakfast," she suggested. In her full restaurant kitchen she kept a Tiger's Milk blender for energy emergencies. In her cupboards, a low-cal mix. In her mind's eye already, a protein shake that would inspire him to great flights.

Beginning his flight already, he implied *eating was out*.

Her sadness began. Men's appetites even let her down by phone.

May the anesthesiologist rest in peace beneath the garden gazebo supported by insurance, Keogh Plan, investments and a no-mortgage little estatelet; may the lady avoid autopsy in future loves. Farewell. Watkins and she were not destined to break toxins together.

5

He telephoned Number Two on Bethany's list, the Iranian professor of sociology. That was easier to manage; required no airplane or freeway travel; and if she was nice, he would visit her on his bicycle. They could bicycle together, feeling right at home in Davis, California 95616, bicycle-use center of the U.S.A. He liked the idea of a sophisticated refugee from the war-torn Middle East, and imagined hearing about winding seaside roads heading down to the sea and crystal beaches, perhaps never again to be enjoyed with youthful abandon. He was sure they both knew about nostalgia, unlike Adela Jenkins. *Tristesse* had not been Adela's strong suit.

"When?" said Aviva. "I live just off campus."

"I live just on the edge of campus," said Watkins.

"I live on the west side of campus."

"I live on the east side."

"I have a bicycle."

"Why don't you bicycle over?"

"And we'll have a bicycle ride together. Then we'll have coffee. Dinner."

"My practice," said Aviva, "in my country, is first the dinner and then the coffee."

It was agreed, although she had adopted a new country with new practices. Watkins wheeled out his ten-speed. He pumped up the tires. He was preparing to meet a young scholar from a former Switzerland of the Middle East. He decided to take another shower. This was for the sake of international *savoir faire et vivre* after fretting over skinny racing tires. He mounted his bicycle and wobbled off toward the campus, which he would

67

cross in the company of the fleets of youthful cyclists who, like birds, migrated in flocks, silent, with silvery spokes, not wobbling even at takeoff.

Although they were mostly pensive and considering their next class, plus the entire future, these airborne creatures sometimes murmured soft cries, "Hi . . . hi . . . hi." An amused young woman pedaled alongside with straight bangs cut low across her forehead, dark flat eyes, some sort of white floppy suit which succeeded, thanks to wind, in acting like a clinging garment—it must have been soft-woven Indian cloth. Watkins was sure she was lovely and naked under her clothes. It was a thought that used to come to him often as a boy. He tried to banish reactionary concupiscence from his heart as she took up speed ("Hi." "Hi."). He tried a deeper thought: Would she be as lovely in a slithery polyester pantsuit? But before he could come to the answer, which might have been no, he heard a metallic pinging clatter and a vocal aria in the path behind him. Ouch, she was singing. She had hit a rock in the path, her bike skidding, she was down.

The concerned lawyer dismounted his Suzuki ten-speed to tend to the wounded. Personal Injury was not his field, but he disbelieved in specialization. She was gently consternated rather than severely hurt, it seemed, for she was saying, "Shit. Shit. Shit."

"Are you okay?"

"Shit and *dog* shit," she said, submitting an amended brief. In store for her the future had held contusions and irksomeness.

Fortunately the soil was mostly on her wheel. He helped her to her feet, discussing all the while the recent economies in state support of the university, which meant that Grounds & Maintenance was cut, the pooping dogs that ran free were not scooped after, standards were being let down all over. "What's your area?" she asked.

"Coffee," he said.

"Pardon?"

"Oh. The law school—I'm an attorney. I also practice in town. Coffee?"

"Okay, why not, we'll go to the Coop," she said.

They walked, wheeling their bicycles. She wheeled hers on the green, asking grass to do the ecologically sound thing, gradually cleaning her spokes and tires. Chlorophyll helps. A bit of unhelpful grass stain on her white Indian-cloth pants. A little flush, a hectic little flush on the cheeks, which were normally brown or tan or Spanishoid. "Are you related to the folk singer," he asked.

"I look like her," she said, "people say more like Joanie's sister, but no. My name is you tell me your name first."

"Wat. Watkins."

"Make up your mind. Alicia," she said, "but since I got accepted in grad school I've accepted, contrary to California habit, a last name, too." This was an impressive speech for a California student. It was full of subordinate clauses and social criticism. UC-Davis was an institution for high achievers. "Alicia Marboro. No," she added quickly, "don't say it."

He laughed. How many declared themselves to be the Marlboro man? "You can draw the tattoo on my hand over a cup of French roast," he said.

"That's a variation. That's nice. It's not much of a joke."

"Best I could do on the spot," he said, "terrified as I was by your near-serious accident."

"I was just going to the library, but there's mud on my knees —well, it hasn't rained—dust anyway—I'd like to wash. Yucch. Why don't you come to my cottage and—"

Never mind the Coop, she would make coffee. Poor Alicia decided to have a bath first. She needed to be scrubbed a bit; there are parts even a contemporary woman can't reach by herself. Watkins helped. He climbed into the bath, an old-fashioned ceramic vessel on little metal feet; claws, rather. Meeting a woman was an odd thing to do on his way to meet a woman. Wasn't a certain Iranian person waiting for him? In the bath, splashing a bit, Alicia and Watkins performed acts of cleanliness together.

Then Alicia and Watkins had a heart-to-heart conversation about Alicia. She had been an industrious young woman in high

69

school in Santa Barbara, working as a baby-sitter and finding some housecleaning in the neighborhood. She spent the proceeds on necessities, mostly soft drugs like marijuana, ludes, cocaine, LSD and occasionally—only on weekends—a little PCP. Well, a bit of heroin during the summer doldrums. Finally her parents threw up their tired arms—her father a wounded veteran from Korea—and advised the police to pick her up. In Juvie Hall she found Jesus. Then she graduated to a "Christian Commune," but there she fell in love with another Christian delinquent and they left the commune because each, at eighteen years of age, was stronger than Jesus. A few months later she refound the love of learning, and now this former recreational drug user, former evangelical, was a present graduate student in French because she couldn't see the point of just doing something for the business advantages. Her parents still thought she was nuts. She was interested in her soul—Gide, Montherlant, Saint-Exupéry and Lévi-Strauss, the structural anthropologist, not the jeans. Barthes. Derrida. Some really neat games those boys play.

Watkins tried to pretend the names meant something to him. He could pronounce Cordoza, Friendly, Holmes, Lon Fuller, Learned Hand and Felix Frankfurter with the same assurance.

"You believe in the missionary position, sir?" she asked.

"Pardon? Depends. It's not an article of faith."

"Man on top?"

"I know. There are many circumstances, such as whims . . . lower back pain . . . Should there be rules, Alicia?"

"I mean *the first time*," she said.

Truly, he did not know what was expected of him, nor what he expected of himself. He thought saying nothing might be the right thing to say. She watched his silence with close attention. He began to take courage as she took on confidingness.

"Well, the first time, I say go ahead, whatever's right—whatever he has on his mind. The first time and there'll generally be others, won't there? Won't I get my chance in due course?"

Since silence had already served him so eloquently, he practiced it a while longer.

70

"You're nice," she said. "No rules. I like that." Her mouth made the prayer silently, *no rules,* and she shook her head with the wonderment of just finding an intelligent gentleman like that, all due to dog shit on her bicycle spokes.

Getting to know you is intense work, so then they took another bath. She used to be flighty, nervous, irresponsible, capricious, *existentielle* (her word), but now her affairs tended to endure—at least Watkins was, for her, a two-bath lover. Dainty finally, a foundation of daintiness firmly established in her makeup, she confessed that, for her, due to childhood trauma, including the embarrassment of a one-armed father, not that she thought it merely inconsiderate of him to leave an arm in Korea, but still, but still . . . Total union was out. With her, total soul interface presented problems. This, of course, precluded nothing they could whomp up together on the existential plane.

Watkins could accept that. Anyway, he had to live with it. A gentleman mustn't force total union on a lady with whom he has taken two baths in rapid succession; dry puckered skin was a beginning.

Then they had a conversation without words. Watkins had not locked his bicycle, leaning it against her little white picket fence, but he didn't care. If it was stolen, it was stolen.

She ambled naked, long legged and tanned, with a slight reddening where she had scraped her thigh on that fateful spill, to peek out the window. "Bike's there," she said. *"Voilà ton vélo."*

"I'm not worried."

"Now I really have to go to the library," she said. "Thanks for the interlude."

"Interlude?" he asked.

She looked at him with flat, level, gray—they were gray in the fading afternoon—smiling intelligent eyes and said, "Don't think more of this than it is. Not that I plan to lose you. I never lose a lover, Watkins."

She had learned efficient behavior in her world of psychopathic equilibrium. That was Watkins's unspoken judgment. Rapidly he found himself dressed and Alicia dressed and the two of them remounting their bicycles in the last light of

71

day. Only patchy grass grew near her front stoop. Probably all those old lovers, trampling the sod. "You didn't give me your phone number."

"No," she said, "I didn't," and pedaled off to the Romance Literature section of the library.

He owed an apology to Aviva. He would have to make it up to her. He had a certain duty, even if he had never met her, even if some people, certain former addicts and Christians, didn't recognize their duty. Personally, he, Watkins, a member of the California bar, was a man of higher standards. At that level a man can be allowed a few mistakes, a little slippage in the post-existential structuralist ruins.

He dialed Aviva's number at the first operative corner telephone booth. For some reason he didn't have to refer to the piece of paper. He must have memorized it while he bathed twice in the off-campus cottage of the bicycle lady. His mind was sharp and refreshed. He imagined Aviva impatient, hurt, cultivating a sense of injustice in her apartment which he could not visualize. He could not visualize Aviva, either, although she had sent a Polaroid of a dark Persian beauty in purples and violets. She answered and he asked: "There's been an accident. Will you forgive me?"

"What accident?"

"It's too hard to explain, but it was not in my control, it truly wasn't my fault although perhaps some quotient of human error might have been involved—"

To be or not to be is *not* the question, he was thinking. Not to be is our certain fate. But while we exist—during that brief moment—to *be*! To be here and festive for a while! And then okay, we must get ready not to be for the rest of eternity.

"What?" she was asking. "Are we disconnected?"

"Excuse—mind wanders because . . . I'm sorry, a little shock," he said. He was also thinking: You may come in a lady's mouth, yet she's not yours forever. That's California. That's modern times. "Will you forgive me?" he repeated.

In her silence he came to a focus on the matter at hand. He

stopped thinking about Bethany (he always thought of her), about the bicycle lady, and now thought about Aviva. He could almost hear her Middle Eastern breath as she considered the matter. That was only static on the wire, poor telephone maintenance in Area Code 916, but he knew he was still breathing and he thought of breath. Since he hadn't met Aviva yet, he loved her—he had hopes. Since he felt apologetic and culpable, he didn't like her very much.

"Yes," she said.

The deponent was replying to what? Oh yes, thanks very much, she was forgiving him for having failed to meet her. The tone was generous. She was even forgiving him for what she didn't know. She must be an Iranian Christian, not a Moslem; dark armpits, salty and friendly.

"Will you see me again?" he asked.

"I haven't seen you the first time," she said.

"I mean—"

She had probably studied in a religious girls' school in Teheran which taught Aristotelian rather than existential logic. Her throaty Middle Eastern laughter helped his confusion precipitate into nonconfusion, nonculpability. Out of gratitude for her good nature he was ready to say I do, I do, I do; and out of weariness he was ready to add, But I feel kind of tired and headachey tonight, dear. They set a date to try again. Aviva sounded patient and nice. Next Thursday, to be confirmed.

He hoped she was not a free-lance guilt artist like his first wife.

Or a sunset-loving esthetical skinny like his second, who thought karma was something she could earn by not eating.

Or a perfect woman in every way that counted, like Bethany —but then didn't want to leave someone else and her perfect family for him.

The flat evening sky was like the eyes of some forgotten woman. The high California gray blue shallow sky. The edge of wind coming up and blowing smells of industrial fertilizer from the surrounding farms across the town and campus. A warm dry

73

flat wind scraping this earth on which, before white man's time, so many flowers used to grow that a person could not step without crushing them.

In God's country, Watkins thought, the natives shouldn't be this hard to please. He was conforming to the traditions of Eden.

6

Upstairs in the greeny redwood mall where Watkins kept his office, the clever old lady, Yorda Coblentz—a faculty widow—who served as his secretary sang out, "Hi ho, Mr. Solo Practitioner, a client has been calling." He noticed the continuing present tense and cocked his bushy solo-practitioner eyebrow at her. He liked making Yorda happy—the tired skin could still blush through its mourning and leatheriness—with friendly, almost flirtatious gesture. Her husband had been Chair of the Music Ed faculty; she seemed more like a colleague's wife than a half-time employee. She wiggled like a younger woman, which in her heart she was.

"Elaine Jones. She said to tell you Elaine Positano. *Imperitivato,* as they say in a little-known Swiss mountain language."

"Call her back in English, Yorda."

"Pronto, Mr. S. P."

Elaine asked did he remember her and he said sure and she said well it's difficult even more difficult sometimes the second time and he said he understood from dire experience himself and Elaine said she needed help and he said most of us do and Elaine said when could she come in, and he said he had a lecture to prepare and she said When then? and he said okay, right now, since this lecture was one he gave at the same time every winter quarter and he could use last year's notes and Elaine said she was grateful, she knew he would come through for her, and he said, Don't, not yet, and Elaine said she would be there directly.

When she hung up, Watkins tried to organize some recollections of her. Elaine Jones, Elaine Positano. Elaine what? Something previous. She didn't say, "I'll be right there," she said, "I'll be there directly." A few years ago she was married to Pete Positano in the med school. Now she was married to someone off-faculty, a builder, a contractor, a manufacturer of solar panels, something in that line, but not a periodontist. Bigger money, bigger fun. Well, it would all come clear in due time.

Due time, in Davis, nice small California town, was twenty minutes later. The nice thing about small towns, Watkins reflexively thought, is the getting there and parking, plus that marvelous sense of American community. (I'm *glad* I didn't take the offers from the Washington or New York or San Francisco firms, I'm *glad* I took the academic not even the judicial road, I'm *glad* I live in bicycle-riding Davis, where people sell solar panels and heat collectors to each other, I'm *glad* the former Mrs. Positano feels free to call on me when another marriage shorts out . . .)

Just before Elaine arrived there was a call from the dean saying, "Bakke again," which he often said intead of hello, since minority admission and the problem of publicity about it—*issue* was the preferred word—were what made the University of California at Davis Schools of Medicine and Law famous. There was this black kid who was not doing too well, managed to squeeze through as a freshman, now a sophomore, normally an easier year, and since Watkins was such a nice, friendly, easygoing fellow—he was *not,* of course, that was mere oil of dean—maybe he would talk to the kid and see if he might just sort of voluntarily withdraw and become a disc jockey or a minority entrepreneur of some creditable type because he wasn't dumb, he just wasn't cut out to apply himself to a whole bunch of taxing details, such as the law. . . . Would Watkins like to take on a little task of counseling here?

"No thanks, Frank," Watkins said.

"Just thought I'd ask. You used to be so helpful."

"This is the eighties, Frank. God helps those who help themselves."

"You know, Watkins, sometimes you know what? Sometimes I long for the Sixties. I never thought I'd say that, Wat."

When Frank hung up, Watkins strolled toward the outer office to welcome Elaine Jones, remembering how even during the Sixties he knew he had liked that decade and would learn to like it better as time went on. "Of course, of course, of course I remember you well and warmly," he said to the overthin, overnicotined, overmarried woman who was trying to look both troubled and sociable for an old friend.

"I was happier when I knew you," she said. "I was happy to get dumped by Pete. I'm not happy to be dumping Will Jones."

"Come in and we'll explore the paradox." Watkins did his office cordial routine. He was a professional and could do it with his heart broken or bored. Uncordially, internally, he added: Up to a point. Up to a point, my dear.

During these difficult times of the Eighties he was, truth to tell, reluctant to deal with any tears but his own. He appreciated his own regrets, griefs and losses to excess. These were selfish times, and this was to be regretted.

"Please speak up, clear and to the point, Mrs. Jones, Elaine— not that I don't remember our days of nonprofessional acquaintance and lots of banter. Years ago now."

"I understand," she said. "Hi, Wat." She composed herself. Her fingers on one hand snaked around the fingers of the other, all twisty in her lap. The wedding ring was removed.

Mrs. Jones, Elaine Something-Positano-Jones, explained that she had lost her passion for solar panels. She realized she had a completion problem; that is, about finishing things, including men. When she was married to Pete Positano, she had started the definitive research work on sodomy in suburbia—"buggery," she explained parenthetically, "but not merely as a form of contraception"—because she wanted to please Pete. At first he encouraged her. His mother thought she was competing with him, not pleasing him, and perhaps that's how it turned out. The subtitle, she said, was *Above and Behind the Call of Duty*, and some of the chapters included, at least one of them did, the title "I'll Be Turning Around to Look for You."

"You do comedy, too," Watkins said.

"I guess I was serious about pleasing Pete, that's how I am.

You remember those days, Wat. The stylish thing would have been something sensational like wife-swapping or group sex, but that would have been wrong. All the spouses were taking up easy projects. I looked for something fresh. I looked to hold Pete's attention."

"Okay. What's the problem?"

Pete's attention was not holdable. So she gave up the book, to which he wanted to add his name as cocollaborator—a redundancy—but he was given to and liable for redundancies, which always irritated her, like hiccuping in bed . . . "Where was I?"

Watkins was about to try to jog her memory when she sailed forth again under her own steam. She dropped the book when Pete found a skinnier, more boyish pair of girl's buttocks to fulfill his research needs, to reeducate and form and move. So Elaine started a real estate course and met this advanced builder. And then came Aloysius ("Solar Deal") Jones and she put buggery behind her in favor of an energy-saving future, plus tax write-offs and a condominium at Tahoe and terrific fun trips to see congressmen in Washington, D.C. Al was both hip and high powered, natural but blow-dried, a doper but also a man who worked within the system. Elaine liked that. That was for her.

She learned to ski; it's not so difficult.

She tried to have a baby, and almost did. You can't get everything was one of the lessons she learned.

"Maybe trying like that," she remarked, nose reddening, eyes reddening, "is what kills it."

"You mean your feeling for your husband couldn't survive a failure, as you saw it, to conceive a child—?"

"I tried. I tried so hard. He said people couldn't make photovoltaic batteries commerical, either, not in this country, so not to worry. But I tried so goddamn hard."

"And you blame yourself?"

"He was so sweet. He helped. He let me do everything. Oh, Watkins, I fucked him silly!"

Watkins patted her hand.

"But one thing he neglected to inform me," she said. "He

didn't tell me. A few months before we got married he had a vasectomy."

Watkins deliberated, continuing the domestic-relations mode into which he had switched for her, but not speaking the words aloud: It probably means all your efforts were in vain.

"So he made me feel like a failure, and all the time he—"

"That has the look of deceit to me," Watkins said. "I admit, if you're seeking grounds, I think you could stop right there. In olden times, that has the look of annulment. Would you like some coffee or a banana?"

She was snuffling and ducking her head miserably, cutely (a little), and uttering, "Both. Al said photovoltaic solar storage batteries worked in the Negev, but not in this climate, not yet. But they will—" She stuck a dab of Kleenex to her nose.

He got two cups, moved to the maker, started the maker, watched the lights go into Making Mode, opened the little fridge, no banana; looked on top of the little fridge, only one banana. "I'll divide it with you while we wait a second for this pretty fair coffee, Elaine," he said.

"Never mind. Just coffee."

Watkins silently peeled, looked at her, gestured the naked banana toward her with a final offer, took a bite of the end which he normally cut off. He had read that one of the symptoms of potassium deficiency was existential dread. Perhaps banana-lack was Alicia Marboro's problem. Since he had long suffered from existential dread, and the university health plan did not carry it on their list of approved diseases or conditions, not even ranking it with the allergies, he ate a banana regularly every work day. He skipped Saturdays and Sundays, when he ate eggs at a little brunch place on D Street. So perhaps what he felt was not existential dread, being banana-potent, but potassium-proof loneliness and isolation.

It occurred to him that weekends were the worst times of all and therefore they really should be the banana times. While he contemplated internal domestic crisis, Elaine Jones contemplated him. "You're gone," she said. "Wow. You're not here at all."

"I'm not charging you for this conference," he said. "Please continue."

"Are you treating me like a child? In this situation I find myself, I suppose I'm not an old friend from the good days but a client, am I? I want to be charged. Your minimum, if you're nice."

Pat pat, hug hug, he thought, beaming with lack of knowledge of how to respond.

"Why not just tell me the facts in a businesslike domestic-relations manner, followed by a definition of the problem concerning Al? Al Jones? As you see it and how to resolve the problem as you understand it, Elaine."

All that without wheezing or panting for breath.

She sketched out the quick design of her marriage. A lot of standing in mud on construction sites. Four-wheel drive vehicles. Guys in plastic hats with lumber company names on them. Energy-saving sun statistics. Panels and mirrors. Faggot architects making kissy sounds at her and only meaning hello by it. "That wasn't how it was supposed to be this time," she remarked.

"How was it supposed to be?" Silence. "Elaine?"

She began to cry as she described roaring fires in fireplaces, bottles of champagne, skiings and holdings of hands over vistas of sparkling snow, pink cheeks from perpetual lovemaking . . . "It's never like that," Watkins said.

He remembered very early days with his first wife, before they were married. Monterey. Beer and abalone on the beach. He remembered early days with his second wife, even after they were married. Paris, Venice. More abalone on the beach, plus white wine. He remembered romantic moments with his daughter when she was the world's sweetest five- or six-to-eleven year old, and they sat at cafes over ice cream and confided in each other. He thought how hard it was to make Elaine seem foolish when he was, give or take a few hormones and fixations, the same kind of persistent yearner. All they both wanted was the merging of souls before fireplaces that didn't smoke too much, over ice cream that didn't spill in laps, with a partner that never caught on, in a time that never ends, in a world that never was.

"True understanding," Elaine was saying. "To care and cherish forever, like I have felt ready to do, even if I made a few terrible errors out of pure hoping and dreaming, just loneliness and missing my loved person, like that one time with the busboy at Tahoe."

"These things happen," said Watkins.

"He was in Sacramento talking to the goddamn lobbyist again. I was snowed in. The busboy was cute. I didn't want to, but what choice did I have?"

"How'd he find out?" Watkins asked.

"Suspected, but it was only an assumption. Some jerkoff in the restaurant wrote him a letter. There was no reason for this —no avalanche or life-threatening which would cause me to risk all I hold dear, so I convinced him it didn't happen. Watkins, I was sincere. When everything was perfect, which it was, why would I risk throwing it away, even for a moment, with a pimple-faced busboy?"

"You wouldn't."

"He believed me, but the damage was done. I offered to retrace our steps—roaring fire, champagne, ski, you know, the whole trip—the pink cheeks . . ."

"You can't go back," Watkins said. "You've always got to go forward, not that I don't try, too, Elaine."

"But I can! I did! Because that's how it was for us and that's why I was willing to try again!"

Watkins was willing to learn. In his own case, he found difficulties in keeping a marriage going, either with the wife he didn't like or with the wife he liked. They tended to dim out on him. There was an ache of anger with his first wife, and an ache of loss with his second, and an ache of time passing when he thought of his daughter, but these were pains he did not seek to dwell on. After all, life is still to be lived, and the rest is history.

81

Even getting to be, say, a state Supreme Court justice only confirmed the future if you had one and did very little for the past.

Yet there was something lacking in this analysis. Watkins looked seriously into Elaine's eyes until she wondered what he was up to, stopped crying, dabbed, and then he could ask, "How long was it perfect, Elaine?"

"For two whole weekends, plus the Thanksgiving holiday, Watkins."

They sat there, sipping coffee from Cost Plus mugs. Watkins felt the need of another banana. In his head, not his stomach. His stomach felt tight against his belt from the previous banana, but his head felt light, dizzy and unanchored in this final fifth of the twentieth century, badly requiring Chiquita, craving Dole. He began to tell Elaine Jones how intelligent she always seemed to him. Actually, as Elaine Positano she used to seem cute and sexy, and therefore bright; *intelligent* wasn't the word, but it was the word he used. He thought, he hoped it might please her. "Perhaps we ask too much of love and marriage," he stated. ("No!" she said.) Naturally his business was not counseling but representation; however, the two things are so intertwined you wouldn't believe it, Elaine. *("NO!")*

He suggested considering a serious try at reconciliation, including therapy, or a different kind of therapy to supplement what already hadn't worked out. Maybe even trying to reverse the vesicular litigation, if that's what it's called.

Silence. She gazed on him with blue eyes that had known both deceit and disappointment in the high Sierras. "I've considered it," she said. So that's what the silence meant. "I've considered it for months now. Since Thanksgiving. When we had representatives of lending institutions over for baked ham instead of family for turkey. Okay, so family was far away. But Golden West Savings and Loan? But raisins in sugar sauce, all mooshy, Watkins?"

"No ski weekend afterwards?"

"Washington afterwards to see a congressperson about tax helps. Al is a big man in solar, Watkins. I stayed home and

82

brooded. Shelters, write-offs, depreciation allowances, and I thought it was going to be fur rugs in the ski house. I do love my very own bearskin and a fireplace. So he got me a ski condo on time-sharing. That wasn't how I thought it'd be—some stewardess's hair in the sink when it came our turn to share was how it was." She stopped to breathe. "I didn't even go to the Ramada Inn and pick up some busboy. I deny it. So now I want severance pay—you know, for when the going gets severe."

Watkins considered the matter. He put a space of silence between them. He appeared to be thinking. "You really tried," he said at last, "but the problem is, I want to disqualify myself, being a friend of your previous husband, Pete." She went blank. "Pete Positano," he explained. "You may think this awfully finicky of me, Elaine, but I don't do divorces for friends. I don't like to do them at all anymore, since my own last one. I think you need a younger, tougher representation. You're a plucky person—"

"Plucky but unlucky," she said. "Cut the crap."

"It's not a personal judgment."

"You're turning me down. Not only by men but even by *lawyers* I'm rejected."

"Come on, now, there's a problem." He organized his thoughts to explain himself minimally. Fully was not the ticket here. He resuggested reconciliation. ("No! Try to listen to me!") He suggested that okay, in that case, he still had to disqualify himself.

"But you always did divorces."

"I used to. Now I only do them for myself."

"Do me, too, Wat."

"Because of Pete, who used to be your husband—"

"I remember now. He won't mind."

"—there's almost a conflict of interest."

"You mean too much interest? You don't make much sense, Watkins."

"Whatever. I think you're half right about that, which goes to show, I'd like to send you to another attorney, perhaps a woman —I'm doing mostly academic work now."

"Watkins, you're stouthearted enough for me. Plucky, is that your word? The more you deny me, the more I want you."

Is this the way of the world? Watkins wondered. Although he wasn't playing games, except very earnestly and in general, and that's fate, he toyed with the pipe on his desk. It was now a paperweight. He had given up smoking it ten years and a marriage ago. "I'm not free enough of feeling, my dear. I might have some crippling sympathy for your husband, whatever sort of wretch he might be. I can't."

Elaine Jones stood up. He noticed with sudden regret her tight hips in corduroy jeans on which the designer label stood stiffly up. "Then you sure can't, Watkins," she remarked sharply. "I'll have to find a man who can."

"I've been married myself and divorced. You don't need this explanation. I'm not yet free of feeling—"

"That's okay. Good boy, good boy."

Let her hit him all she liked. "I'm not free of some wounds myself—"

"You said that already."

"So nice to see you again," he murmured, showing her out. As he followed her to the open redwood stairway leading down to the courtyard of the Pacific Heartland Mall, he touched her elbow and shouldered next to her and tried to take back a bit of control. "Elaine. I would like to offer you some sage fatherly counsel from an old friend and acquaintance. Perhaps you should try your best with the husband you have, since—"

"Shove it."

"It must sound silly when all you want is severance and freedom. But let me quote a wise person. Keep what you have, this person said, because it's no more better than what you used to have and no worse than what you're going to have."

"Can it, freeze dry it, compost it."

"Well, that's a natural reaction. Sorry. Wait a second." And this time some urgency in his voice made her turn to look into his face. "You don't, Elaine, you don't ever put ads in the paper, do you?"

"Huh?"

"I mean, for a lover or a friend. I mean, for loneliness and the blues?"

She gazed at him as if he had taken leave of his senses.

"I guess you don't then," he said. "What kind of a remedy is that? Insane to do a thing like that, also, either."

 **7**

Nevertheless, it was important not to be distracted, not even to give up. He owed it to his hopes and dreams and . . . and . . . to accept Aviva's generous offer of forgiveness, which might not be repeated.

He hoped he was not being a good old puppy just because Bethany asked him to. How excessive to find his salvation only for Bethany, even if it suited her convenience and conscience. By rights it should suit Watkins, too. Damn right. Tell 'em, counselor.

After a couple of days, during which he hoped the impact of flowers, candy and a bottle of white wine would sink in, along with whole phrases of apology, he called Aviva again.

"Aren't you nice!" she said. "A rain of keepsakes! Makes me feel you're ashamed."

"Shame starts us off on the right foot, doesn't it?" he asked. His loins sweetened with the thought of an Iranian stranger, related to Zoroaster or the Pahlavis. Perhaps strangers are the key to familiarity. What is closest should be most distant. An Iranian sociologist might have all sorts of wonderful data to share.

But he forbade himself to do too much thinking. He had reached the other side of his age, where God had blessed him with health and desire, misery and loneliness, and now he should just coast with God's blessings, plus Bethany's.

Since the gift of intelligence hadn't sweetened life for him.

Love is a warm blanket. Pull it up to the head and it exposes the feet.

So he said he would go to see Aviva anyway and this time he

did, feeling the guilt of not really wanting to, yet really wanting to, thudding in his middle-aged heart. He was healthy; good Kaiser Plan physical—passed; this was not a warning. He was thudding along with everyone else who dreams of love and thuds scared he might or might not find it. Hi, Aviva, he would say, I'm Watkins, you don't look so Persian . . . No, better fix that one: I never went out with a Parsi lady before . . . No, How about just, Pleased to meet you at last?

He fulfilled something like these plans for the opening felicities, and she said, "I'm a woman, not a lady. I'm Iranian even if you don't know what we look like—you expected a veil? a mustache? I'm from an old Maronite family, if you've heard of that. Super French. Really awfully Gallic in our traditional vibes."

"I'm sure," he said politely.

"My father and brothers would take you down to the wadi, tie you to an olive tree and castrate you if this were home sweet home," she said. "I've been somewhat Americanized, however."

"I sincerely hope so," he said.

"Do you like the Platters and the Coasters? I collect oldies but goodies. In my country, as a girl, I used to adore them . . . I can still smell the sheep, and hear the doo-wee, doo-wah of some of those dynamite hits. Dusty diamonds were my favorites from the beginning—the Eberle Brothers, too, come wailing over those stony hills. In those days we weren't a backward country. We had our own Christian pirate radio station. That's what got me interested in American sociology and why things are as they are—societies in transition—am I talking too much?"

"No," he said.

"Neither are you," she said. "We're each nervous in his or her own way."

"Bethany!" he cried, raising his eyes to the blue sky of Iran in the form of a stippled plaster California nonearthquakeproof ceiling.

"What's that?" Aviva asked.

It was a prayer for mercy. "Song from when we were little tykes," he said.

"I don't remember that one. Who did it? Maybe it was a number they didn't play on Christian Pirate Radio. Bethany? How did it go?"

"It went," he said. "It just went. I don't remember except how much I liked it."

"Too bad," she said. "I like to listen to the oldies but goodies, especially when I'm lonesome for my country, which some Moslems call Eastern Iraq. Somehow when you hear them later for the first time, it isn't the same. In sociology we call that the nostalgia effect. Time gives a certain resonance. It gives a certain thickness to history. Do you realize these things in California as an adult?"

"I do," he said.

"My students don't, they lack the depth, but I'm so glad you do. Shall we be friends?"

Confused, he answered. "Of course. We are."

He looked into her eyes and she smiled. There was sadness in her gaze as she took him in through the eyes—an erotic taking-in. She expected a mountain prince or bandit captain, with treasure in caves and gold-flecked Crusader eyes, the tawny skin of an Arab wanderer and a darting hammer-headed fish for a penis. She expected Swiss bank accounts transferred in time from Teheran, a darting hammer-headed intelligence. She expected a wild chap with a knife in his boot and a calculator for a heart. Instead, there was this longing middle-aged chap with the remnants of marital fleshiness not quite jogged off. And because she was good, she was a good person, she had responded to his advertisement, she had gotten herself into this, she was determined not to disappoint him and, more important, not to disappoint herself.

She was ready to go through with it.

To Watkins, her voice was red silk. It rustled like red silk. There was a quality to it beyond her education. Of course, these days it wasn't racial. But that red silk, it was there, rustling.

He was ready to go through with it.

Neither was sure they *would* go through with it although both were ready. Perhaps both were merely half ready. In the mind,

89

ready. In the heart, ready. In the body, ready, but not quite.

"Pardon?" he asked.

She was reaching for his fly with her right hand. "I find this the preferable way to be friends," she said, unzipping, exploring, beginning.

He said little. She brought both hands into it. Was this another California fad, sweeping the state? This grown woman, too?

Later she said, "Now we work backwards through time to discover our own radiance. Let us visualize together, Watson."

"Watkins," he said, gently correcting her without asking if Aviva was really an Iranian name. It sounded almost Israeli to him. Perhaps, in the fullness of time, better he shouldn't ask.

What they had done they had mostly done standing up, only toppling together at the conclusion.

" 'We had fed the heart on fantasies; the heart's gone brutal from the fare,' " he remarked, quoting Yeats.

"What fair?" she asked. "The Yolo County? One time I bought this chocky cake from a farmer, his wife made it herself. I adore your folkways, Watson."

He endured this conversation with Number Two on the list, Aviva, but what he thought was Bethany, Bethany, why have you forsaken me? Sacrilege it was; sacrilege, too, to refer to God when he only wanted a woman; he would do with the death of God, the killing of God, the torment and torture of God if only he could be restored to Bethany, have his love again close, warm and silent, even a few hours in the afternoon and on a rare evening of Dental Society meeting, periodontal subsection; no, he wanted her for himself, only her, living together with him, married to him; but yes, he would accept the old terms, waiting in his cold and womanless house until she called, came cheerily from her husband and children and many family and athletic duties; came to him, came to him, came to him, but wouldn't anymore.

And Aviva had been so good to him. She had met him more than halfway.

"Your heart's gone brutal from what fair?" she asked. "Is that country punk? There's this kind of lyric's coming in now, sort of Dylan gospel pure, but mean, I'll bet you dollars to doughnuts."

"Would you like to make something hot to drink?" he asked.

"What are you doing?"

"Biting your neck." He decided it was incumbent upon him at this time to behave in a playful, relaxed and perhaps a bit romantic manner. Therefore he winked and pressed his teeth, sheathed by lips, against her country-loving Middle Eastern throat. "I'm after blood," he growled.

She handed him a plum and laughed. That's the ticket. The nice fruit, tart and sweet, distracted him for a millisecond. Then he returned it to her, and she also bit, saying something about its being refreshing, and his lips were sliding down her body, his hand sliding up her blouse, both his hands seizing plums; his lips and hands were sliding and tearing down her body, peeling off silky red things, his mouth fastened to her and him wondering what she'd say now in her red-silk voice: "It's refreshing"? And he was crammed into her, his fat fishy thing, his fingers, her fingers, the small death momentarily achieved by specific plan and design. He wondered if he shouldn't take up drinking.

She gave him a moment of rest.

"You're phallic," she remarked. "That's a macho stage among middle-aged men in my country, too."

"Thank you," he said. Why not insist it was a compliment? Better than treating it either as an insult or a topic for discussion.

Oddly enough, he felt her heart beating hard, hectic in light panic, like sand kicked and scattered.

The sweet world, Watkins thought, is soaked in hope. And trust. And expectation of the future. There are babies sleeping with night-lights and smiling parents who tiptoe in to peek down on them. Beyond my travels here and there, with women who cause parts of my body to act alert, some great happiness is sulking because I haven't yet discovered it.

Happiness, I'll find you!

My mother, despite everything, yes!

91

My father, despite everything, who waked me gently by touching my forehead with his stiff fingers, yes!

My wives! Whom I comforted, whom I comforted, who comforted me in the middle of the night, and who then learned not to love me, yes!

Happiness! I'll surely track you down!

Aviva's gaze was fond. "You're an odd person, Watson, which is about what I should suspect from the source. You drift in and out. I mean mentally, you have so much on your mind. Yet don't you know what socialization really is, my dear? You must. Else you would not have placed an advertisement." She stopped and took his head between her palms, warm palms, almost tenderly. Yes, tenderly. Yes, regretfully. "I too," she was saying, "I too, coming from an obsessed people and an obsessed part of the world, divided as we are, divided as you and I are, know what you know. I know what obsession is, but it doesn't help."

8

He woke the next morning with the burnt-rice smell of fertilizer blowing over the entire world from the farms around Davis and Woodland, and then he heard the hoot of the train to Sacramento, that small-town-lonely-for-elsewhere sound, and the scrape of a branch outside his window. He lay there till the train was gone. The branch scratched, scratched, to be let in. He had often thought of trimming it a little, but he liked something green and growing out there by his condominium town house window, no matter what troubles grew on the other side. He would let it scrape and never trim. And as to the burnt-rice smell, perhaps his nose was more selective after sleep.

It was a morning of meditation for Watkins. Poets might write poems on such early hours of smells and dawning light and calmly troubled world view. The problem about lyrical release was: Watkins had some difficult thoughts concerning himself which seemed to come from afar; that is, his needs were vivid, but the judgment of his desires was harsh. As he stared at the new light, heard the branch, he made cool afar appraisals of Watkins, as if he were someone possibly to be taken on as a client.

Aviva was right and Watkins believed it important to do something about errors in character which were evident even to an intelligent horny Iranian social anthropologist. Whether it was Bethany he sought or true love in general—another mother for himself at this late date, or devotion from his faraway children or revenge for past sorrows—he was seeking what he should not seek. Something about being Watkins, a man, was in undersupply with him these days. If only it were hormonal. But

Watkins felt, sighing as he pulled on his pants, that his moral being was on the wrong goddamn track.

Pete Positano came to mind. Pete did look young and wired and sure of his games. If his ways of ripening character were not a solution, at least they were something to do. They tried. Watkins wondered if he shouldn't make contact again—old Pete, whom he had been glad to avoid. It wouldn't hurt to try.

It was a morning of meditation. On a day of earth smells and the sounds of good America, Watkins felt judged by his own bad choices. The searching out of one woman after another seemed almost promiscuous to him, no matter how serious his purpose. If someone else did it—definitely dumb. Postcoital *tristesse* haunted him ten hours and a sleep after coitus. It wasn't fair, but maybe it was just. Another deep effort should be called forth.

It was time to follow the road always pointed with such enthusiasm by his fellow professional, Doc Pete Positano, B.A. Brooklyn College, M.A. (Psychology) N.Y.U., Ph.D. (Counseling and Psychology), University of Southern California. Skilled Interpersonal Groups. Industrial and Individual Restructuring. Day & Night Service.

Watkins retrieved the card from his desk, and the advertisement inserted in the *Pacific Sun,* "as a probe," Pete said, "to see if there's a needful and aware public out there. I don't give a fuck what they think at the med school, I've got tenure." During the convulsions of the late sixties, Pete had been taken on by the medical faculty to teach Interpersonal Relationships (one of his grandparents, he said, was black, although no one could prove it); through an apparent blip on the screen—be fair, Pete did publish a lot—he had been granted tenure, although his course was no longer required for entering first-quarter freshperson family care students.

Dr. Positano was the last individual on campus to wear tie-dyed tee shirts. He had cured himself of strabismus by Flutter-Touch Aura Self Therapy (planned masturbation). He was no longer cross-eyed except at moments of dudgeon or repose, when his left-brain-controlled right eye tended to turn inward toward the Spirit. He had recently launched his Thirty-fourth

Lightning Campaign to expand his psyche.

In the 1980s Pete resembled the California condor, a licensed and attested Endangered Species, a survivor of the Summer of Love. But he moved as if he still sensitively and caringly owned the entire "goddamned beautiful fucking world."

For Watkins, in this small town, it came with his life's program to be on first-name terms with (intimate with) a professional tenured licensed revolutionary. While students sometimes revered him, and other people thought him silly, Watkins did not exactly revere him and thought him not merely silly. Pete was unpredictable, conventional, backward in his forwardness and a distraction to the routines of a high-achievement campus. Watkins had kept his distance lately. He was aware of divorces, marriages, ever-increasing mental health. He remembered when Pete lived in a commune—that long ago.

But they were still colleagues. They had both lost wives, although Pete referred to the women he lost as "lovers . . . I lost my lover again, Wat. I've got to face the fact there must be something in me that wanted to lose my lover. I chose defeat in marriage, Wat, just as some choose to starve in Africa or flake out in DC-11s. But there is something in me that feels, I don't know, yes I do—a period of mourning and regroupment coming on. You know, when I wake up on Sundays, alone, which I did last month, the thing I had like a big take-on is: Suicide as a Viable Alternative. I was thinking of writing a piece for *High Times.*"

"And then what?"

"And then I thought you could want to join my specially chosen, but it's not elitist, group of fellow sufferers, Watkins. A nonsexist men's group. Are you up for dealing with our problems, and only faculty or administration allowed? We'll have to keep it secret or the *femmes*'ll demand representation."

"It's a men's group then," Watkins said.

"You hit the nail on the head. But nonsexist."

"It's time," said Watkins.

"You mean you'll try anything now?"

"Almost. A few exceptions."

Pete sighed. "Me too. I too have had failures although I'm in the Success Mode, a creative time of solidarity with my being. It raises all the issues. For example, what success has done to my relationships with a kind of fresh young thing I used to like. Let me go into deep background on this. I always know when it's about to be over. My lover says her birthday's next Wednesday. So I get the birthday present. And on Friday she breaks up with me. Once I got back together with a *femme* who broke up with me in March and now it was December and she said her birthday was two days after Christmas. So she got the Christmas present, the birthday present and boom. If she had so many birthdays she'd have to be as old as Adele Davis was, but she's only twenty-eight. My luck."

"That kind of problem I never have," Watkins said. "My ladies never have birthdays at all."

"That's your problem, Watkins."

"They're married. They can't bring strange presents into the house."

"It's worse. I call that predatory."

"Yours is not predatory, Pete. She's just grasping is all."

"*I* said it. Don't accuse me. I'm a man of power and I don't take to accusation." He made a motor-running, purring sound, like a sleeping cat; a jungle cat, king of the Coop coffeehouse. "Playing with ourselves in that cozy room," Pete said, "we'll get to be like boys before they're ruined by masculinity—"

"Rah rah, we'll have endless hours of delight," Watkins said.

"Yeah! Yay! We lay it on the line in there, Wat. We stop at nothing. If you want results, that's how it is. Do you want results?"

"That's what I seem to be into, Pete."

"And there's the trouble with you, Watkins. No patience. No hanging out."

Watkins wondered if his methodical voyages toward Bethany's pen pals was a sign of not hanging out and of being impatient. He decided not to defend himself.

"We live in the microchip world," Pete was saying, "but we must cling to our instincts. They are telling us something valid.

About love, someone was right when he said it. If it's not easy, it's impossible. So what we've got to do with great effort is learn to take it easy."

Watkins sighed. Whoever said that bothered him.

"I only emit what I feel," Pete said. "The truth."

Watkins met his friend's eyes, although Pete was better practiced at this. He could turn his left eye inward at will and still meet Watkins's eye with his other. Where the anima was located. Through which the karma was transmitted. In tune with the radiance. Pete winked and Watkins was suddenly, God help him, filled with the hope of male fellowship. He said, "You might even be right, Pete. Didn't you just say the truth will make us free if we don't work too hard to find it? I'll bet it's worth a try. When do we gather together in the search for truth?"

Behind HumanHouse, formerly CUC, Campus Understanding Center, formerly the 4-H Club, a garden used to grow. Now it had gone apocalyptic—shriveled vines, brown stalks, crusted lumps of soil and footprints hardened into Paleolithic relics of scampering nonsexist ravagers. It was supposed to be French Intensive, but when Ronald Reagan was elected, the gardener decided to switch over to Business Administration. Instead of the eternal vegetable cycle, modern life was being redeemed indoors. Watkins studied the notice stapled to the kiosk and wondered if it applied to him:

MEN'S ANTI-SEXIST POTLUCK

BRING FOOD TO SHARE, IDEAS TO DISCUSS,
AND TOYS TO PLAY WITH. BRING SONGS TO
SING. BRING HOPES AND FEARS.

Before trying radical psychic surgery with Pete, he thought he might explore his destiny in the Campus Fellowship Circle. He needed to get used to unprivacy. He browsed among the materials on the battered kitchen table at the door: to know himself as a man today, in this troubled world which consists of men, women and sometimes children, in this difficult place of ambition, hope, dream, desire and yearning for calm, where it is so difficult to find significant nonsexist, nonracist, nonelitist, nonageist, nonweightist, non-IQ-ist, nonfreewillist connection. . . . The reason for the kitchen table with the chipped zinc was that a wooden one had been unilaterally liberated and nonconditionally expropriated by the Native Americans for Justice Commando Braves when they raided HumanHouse one night in search of typewriters, photocopiers, desks, coffee machines, dope and miscellaneous office supplies to furnish the new Native American Tribal Center. The HumanHouse folks had delegated the Sisters of Perpetual Indulgence, an order of male nuns, to dance over to HoganHouse to try to reason with the Native American rip-off folks. The Sisters, garbed in peaceful black robes with white cowls and lavender headbands, were held off at the culvert by bows and arrows. Because they were willing to share nicely with palefaced persons, especially male sisters, who came calling with peace in their hearts, the Native Americans did not shoot either the arrows or their backup shotguns, nor did they seize them for prison-style, underprivileged, class-oppressed, rear-entry gang rape. (Sodomism was not their thing. They called it Palefaceism, and they preferred corn bread.) Sister Darrell of the Order of Perpetual Indulgence returned with the terrific idea of using Goodwill kitchen tables for furniture instead of that greasy old mahogany stuff, indicating acceptance of women's formica world and repentance for all the shitwork which went into deforestation activities. Darrell's proposal passed by unanimous abstention.

Watkins wondered if he might not be a little old—not old, just mature—to be hanging around HumanHouse. But this was an ecumenical drop-in world, where faculty, graduates and even retired industrial farmers from Woodland occasionally passed through to refurbish their interpersonality. Watkins did not put himself above any younger frayed souls. The man that advertises must learn to conceive of himself in a new way. Watkins could not yet conceive of advertising for legal clients.

He was too old to be doing what he needed to do, which was to hang out in HumanHouse. Yet in HumanHouse Watkins stood, by a chipped Goodwill table, where others also browsed and poured from the coffeepot.

A sturdy young man in Levi's, boots, beads, undershirt—one of the generation which has never worn a jacket without snaps or a zipper—began to argue for casual sex as a nice way to say hello. "I have sex with certain people, I call them up, they want to, also—it's nothing heavy, it's not what you call exploitive or traumatistic. We relate. We sip a glass of something, we relate before and afterward, catch as catch can. What's the big deal? What's the evil here?"

When no one replied, he offered a possible answer: "None that I see."

A group had sprung up in the room where men waited to sign up for groups. Watkins didn't mind. He wasn't planning to give his name or share his life, but he didn't mind waiting for Pete Positano among these honest avowals.

The sturdy moral person was brooding. He had discovered thoughts on his mind. "I'd like to find a real woman," he said, "a weight lifter who is really beautiful is what I'd like and we can really be together. Is that too much to ask?"

"Really," said another butch young man. "We're all kind of peergroupy as far as that goes. We want to get together with somebody in the cold, cold night."

Watkins tried to remember his cold, cold nights in Davis, California. Well, it got chilly sometimes; damp, quiet and lonely for sure, and the branch scratching at his window. Again he wondered if he was too old for this sort of thing. And now he answered the question: Absolutely.

On the Native American Memorial Formica Kitchen Table a container of potluck stew was congealing. Waxy white stuff on top. When it was heated, the fat would melt, grow yellow and friendly. The coffeepot was spitting hot water and coffee over the formica. No one paid any attention. Finally Tony, a young poet, grabbed a towel. "I like to feel like your traditional woman sometimes, activating the mother-space in me, to maximize the

99

femininity options of my being." Then he wiped.

"You really dig wiping, don't you?" the man in Levi's asked. "You got a thing for cleaning, don't you?"

"I acknowledge that which you just uttered," Tony said.

"Hey, Watkins?" called the youth at the switchboard. "Are you Watkins? Tallish guy with gray hair, gray eyes, quiet vibes? Pete just phoned and says he's sorry, he'd like to reschedule, there's an emergency. He hopes you'll understand. He's giving comfort and support at the crisis center—I think it's a little Big See problem."

"Big See?" Watkins asked.

"Cancer," said the duty man at the switchboard. "He was asking your forgiveness and he'll reschedule."

For potluck Watkins brought an appetite. For talk he brought words. As a beginning of the joyous inward struggle toward truth, he brought this little bagful of problems all clanking together in his head. Well, fellas, here he was. And he was ready to help others if they could help him, please. It was not that he was another lost soul. It was merely that he had not yet been found.

"I hate clichés and jargonist expression," a young man said over his knitting as he personed the reception desk. He was talking straight into the telephone. "Why can't people just tell it like it is, instead of always trying to interface with their projections?"

Another young man was working his crayons in an Oriental rug coloring book.

The man on the telephone was saying, "Peer pressure is some of the heaviest peer pressure going down these days. Personally, a feelable option for me might be the example of a respected East Bay mystic—you know, the guy who might or might not be the son of Shiva—you know, the laughing one—"

The warm sun poured through the windows. Greenhouse effect in the California dampness always made Watkins sleepy. "I feel, I feel . . ." the young man with a weight lifter's torso was declaring, "if you could do away with the whole erection-ejaculation trip, I call it the endless software loop, you could have many multiple mental orgasms in sequence. An erection is *pain*, you know. It hurts and a person craves relief. Pumping iron is more like a pleasure, if such there be. Personally, sex is a power trip they laid on us for their own purposes."

"To propagate the race?" Watkins said, feeling he ought at least try to contribute. "The gods? Or women?"

"For whatever reason," the hefty young man said. "I don't want to get racist about it." He almost smiled.

"I appreciate your response to a stranger."

"I've got nothing to hide," said the weight lifter. "Are you waiting for someone?"

"Pete Positano."

"Doctor Positano has a tardiness syndrome. The doc'll be here. Pete usually shows up if he's got an appointment."

There was silence in the room as the young men and Watkins contemplated the karma of chronic lateness. It brought temporal power to a spiritual universe. Pete Positano, the Sacramento Valley mystic, was at least as much the son of Shiva as anybody in the East Bay. Give him that.

9

The Sacramento Valley therapist, Pete Positano, son of Shiva, ex-husband of Elaine, hadn't shown up but offered an explanation. It just didn't want to happen. Pete promised to organize his anima for their next meeting and get the show on the road, since caring men can truly help each other. Shiva and Elaine don't qualify.

Watkins wondered if he was becoming a fanatic. Finding a woman to spend the years with him was not the answer to worldwide inflation, depression, unemployment, terrorism, depletion of resources, overpopulation, the threat of nuclear accident, totalitarian regimentation in half the world and weary drifting in the other half. True, he wasn't capable of single-handedly solving all these matters, but surely he was capable individually of doing his best. During these mature years, had he suddenly stopped doing his best? Was he turning selfish? What if the answer wasn't really an answer? And didn't he know this already? So in addition to all else, was the greed for love something that not only did not work but also made a man stupid?

While he added judgment of himself to his other problems, the office required some care, even to coast along; a friend's will to be probated; the dentist to be visited; his quarterly income tax payment to be filed and paid; also bills, after the checks were written by his secretary, Yorda, and signed by him; the fridge to be defrosted (a mess on the kitchen floor, which the cleaning lady, Dolores, would wipe up); letters to his grown daughter in New Orleans, mild paternal ones—no telephone calls now because he didn't trust himself to sound mild and paternal; a friendly note to his former wife, amicably rejecting her suggestion that he help her out in a difficult moment with her new lover, just temporarily pressed a little—his even pulse rate and blood pressure while replying to her merited a celebration but he didn't bother and not bothering merited a little celebration, too; tune-up on his Saab, a car which was built for rough wear in Sweden but got it in California, although there was never any salt on the roads unless someone was crying, and then it was generally self-pitying salt; his colleagues to placate, although they seemed willing to let him play Menopausal Statesman, at least for a time—he would not go so far, so lazy, to have them gossip about whether early retirement could come at his age; a stress test, the best exercise of the year, which ended with his doctor saying he had "the heart of a much younger man," and Watkins said that fellow certainly had a busy heart, because all his friends seemed to use the same one, and the doctor chuckled; his stockbroker to tell to hold, don't buy or sell, I'm making no decisions right now; his dentist to tell him the X rays showed no new cavities, they stop at a certain age, then it's gums, periodontal, that's the problem; the newspaper to be dumped in the garbage with its rubber band intact around it, the news not even unrolled, the television untouched, even *Newsweek*, his usual bedtime browse, piled up by the lamp . . .

So was he a fanatic about something which the normal healthy seventeen-year-old begins to find himself too mature to bother with?

Both the Sacramento *Bee* and *Newsweek* brought the usual kind of news to Watkins—what he didn't want. Victor Lonkin, a classmate at Stanford Law School, had been appointed to the State Supreme Court and died, like a pope, within a few days of taking his oath. Watkins regretted he had delayed writing his note of congratulations to good old Victor. The note hadn't arrived before Vic's death because Watkins had not mailed it. But then remembered he had made a joke about stress tests, and hoping Victor did well on the treadmill, so perhaps it was just as well.

He dreamt about Vic that night—a funny clever graceful boy

who learned without sweat and spent a lot of time in a wet suit at Monterey, digging for abalone. Watkins had a snapshot of the two of them, each with a wet-suited girl (each became a first wife), holding snorkels up in a toasting gesture. That was before it was illegal to pry abalone off the rocks with tire irons in Monterey Bay. They had slapped the rubbery flesh till it went silly, and then fried it on the beach, with a driftwood fire flashing and spitting dampness underneath, and drunk red wine, white wine, and from each other's dreams; the white foam of water margin glowing in the starry dark, and they hugged the girls, they hugged each other; and then they went back to adjoining rooms in the Tortilla Fisherman's Motel with the girls they later married. . . . Watkins felt an itch behind the eyes about Vic. It proved he could dream about something more than himself. He would have preferred not to have this proof.

At breakfast, wide awake, he felt saddened—in addition to depressed and sorry, which normally should have been enough. He was a bonny lad with leathered forty-four-year-old California skin. He was an adolescent with fine marks on his stress test —age twenty-seven by the treadmill. For years he hadn't seen Vic except at bar association meetings. Yet he missed, oh he missed his old friend from McAbee Beach at Cannery Row, where they had eaten abalone, their own, beaten it till it relaxed and then cooked it near a wharfside hotel while the girls drank white wine and wondered when the boys would make their move . . . Poor Vic!

He decided to telephone the next woman on Bethany's list, Marjorie Atworth, as he remembered Victor, briefly a state Supreme Court justice. He saw him in a snapshot one of the future wives had gotten off. Vic was clowning around with his snorkel, pretending to suck it like a boy sucking his thumb . . . Watkins was telephoning, he was wondering if Marjorie Atworth might be the sort of woman who could put something in a pan, put butter in with it, make something sizzle and brown, giving off that nice sizzling, browning smell, fish or potatoes or onions, some good quick old tasty things like that. Swiftly this homely dream of a lady in a kitchen was overtaken by another of his fat one-eyed engorged self staring her in the mouth as she smiled and decided to take it. Because oral sex was a more likely hope these days than the offer of a delicious pickup meal in the kitchen. Because dinner in the kitchen was a dream of jokes, ease and comfort, but the other was what he could more likely, as a practical matter, expect if all went well . . .

Later he might write a note to Vic's wife. When Vic proposed, had he thought to ask, *Will you be my widow?* And he would contribute a small sum to Neighborhood Legal Assistance in Sacramento in Vic's name. Later he would do both of these things, and also throw away the rubber-banded tubes of last week's newspapers. Opening one of them had been his mistake. All about Vic on the front page and a photo in his robes, not his wet suit.

Her phone was ringing. She lived in Dixon, Area Code 916, and maybe Bethany had factored in the advantages of not too long a commute. "Marjorie Atworth," he said, "this is Watkins. From the advertisement. Your nice letter. I'm getting back to you."

How shy they both were mumble mumble. How strange this is but what an adventure mumble mumble. How they might as well just mumble mumble.

He drove to Dixon.

One of the better things, he thought, looking for Scrim Street, intersection of Rice Avenue, is the lack of resonance in these meetings—it was also one of the worse things. (Then why was his heart thumping?) The lack of danger and the danger, the indifference and the need, the distress and the stunned curiosity were part of it, too. The path of true love crossed many means of transportation.

The town, with its well-kept ramshackle houses, nicely painted, dogs roaming, dogs growling and huffing on the backs of pickup trucks, had the look of a child's version of New England. The houses just fell down on lots. Some of them were add-on houses, a fix-it granddad spending his retirement years joining a railway car to the original barn. As he drove up, sharp-eyed Watkins saw a mouse in the street. In Dixon, nice Dixon, it wouldn't be a rat.

The air was sunny and warm. Gnarled fruit trees dropped plums on chickens which grew fierce on a diet of prunes and snails. Neighbors shared eggs and traded breads, occasionally a prune pie. Much might be wrong in the world, but paperboys delivered on time, and kids walked to school, and families lived near the grandparents. But even here, in Dixon, a young woman named Marjorie had taken pen in hand and been selected by Bethany.

There's Scrim. Now turn left. A cul de sac ending in a dirt turnaround. Her directions were clear. No, the thumping in his chest didn't mean he was in love with someone he hadn't met. It only meant he was a bit apprehensive, a tiny amount of bleakness lay in there; he was terrified. The late afternoon sun and the air were as clear as good directions.

He sat a moment behind the wheel. He rejected the teenage temptation to comb his hair. Carefully he closed the door, not slamming it. Good solid Swedish economy door clunk. She would have heard; she knew the time had come; surely her heart, too, was foolishly jumping.

The act of will that had gotten him near the top of his class at Stanford Law, along with Vic Lonkin, now brought breath deep into his lungs. What a victory, not to pant like a dog! Watkins moving from triumph to triumph. He tinkled the bell on the gate as he strolled so calmly toward her front door, which was ajar to catch the sunlight—a long laser burst of glare on a worn carpet with a figured design. "Hi yourself," she said before he had spoken a word.

"Thank you."

"I haven't done anything yet—Watkins? Is that really your name? I just want to make you feel welcome."

"Thanks again," he said.

Marjorie Atworth had an inexperienced California face and experienced buttocks, it seemed, when he took a first look at her; clean blond young face and slow deliberate walking motions.

But then he took another and the eyebrows were too thin and dark for her hair. Her behind was thin and narrow. She had an experienced face, a jaded face, but an innocent, virginal, kindly, spinsterish ass. No, that wasn't the full story, either. Oh, it's hard to get to know a woman in first-meeting safari snapshots.

He suspended judgment. That would be the prudent man's thing to do. At times Watkins liked to emulate a prudent man.

"I never did a thing like this before," she said. "I mean the use of media to facilitate such a personal, uh."

"Neither did I," he said.

"Have you ever? . . ." she asked. "I mean, have you ever made a friend through an advertisement?"

"No, of course not. Would anybody in his right mind? Do you take me for that sort?"

"Nuh-no," she said thoughtfully, trying to be a judge of people who were not rapists, ax murderers, sneak thieves or failed husbands and lovers.

He believed he was evading a bona fide lie. Surely none of the women he had thus far seen had become a true friend. Considering that he had advertised for love and was just now chatting with a woman who had answered his advertisement, both their denials that they would do such a thing showed advanced possibilities for the leap of faith. In this, human beings were different from whales and dolphins.

"I had a longtime lover," he said. "A woman, of course. She let me down."

"We'll do that sometimes," Marjorie Atworth murmured. "As Freud asked, what on earth do we ever want?" She winked conspiratorially. "I also had a longtime lover." She winked once more; it was a separate wink, a separate conspiracy. "And she also let me down."

"Oh," said Watkins.

"I thought that ought to be upfront," she said. "Does it distress you? Have you ever, oh my? with a bisexual? before?"

"I'm sorry, no," he said, "to the best of my knowledge during the past seven years."

He invoked the Statute of Limitations.

She smiled without winking this time. The broad fair face seemed winsome and inexperienced. "I believe you'll find me quite feminine. That's how I am with men. If I didn't see myself as a lover of the wrong sex sometimes, why would I bother? With so many options, it means I make a real choice to be a man's woman when that's what I choose, Wats."

He winced. "Watkins," he said, "or Wat. Otherwise it's like kilowatts."

"Or voltage," she said. "I'm handy around the house. Plugs, small repairs, even sewing—the *femme* side of Marge. Once we lay out my past, how I might, could sometimes trip away to a butch with a sunburned neck and that American smell of diesel on her collar, we are both free to choose. As far as you're concerned, I'm just the girl who married your dear old dad. I've turned over a new page. I'm playing the other loop. Hi there, Voltkins."

"You're telling me, supposing you and I . . . you're telling me you might suddenly decide no, so now you need a woman?"

"I'm not telling you that, not at all. I'm only telling you that's what I've done in the past."

"But you haven't changed everything in your character, have you?"

"Not necessarily. But I haven't *not* changed everything, either."

The lawyer in him was interested. He was confused. She sought to be perfectly clear. She believed in both honesty and clarity, and if possible, those two qualities brought together again, as in the old days.

"I've not altered my druthers, yet I'm sure I can live in the moment, Mr. Voltkins. I've presented myself as I am and as I hope to be. If that's not enough—"

"Oh, it's enough."

The prune trees dropped prunes, the chickens pecked at prunes and snails; the neighbor grannies traded breads; the sleepy town of Dixon dreamed on, safe from the university confusions of nearby Davis, the political and urban riot of nearby Sacramento. Marjorie was proud to embody, in her own

person, the small-town virtue of frankness about her bisexuality.

"So having laid my cards on the table, I want you to know,
Volt, at this very moment I absolutely do not have a vision
of some muscular, strong, insightful, slightly matronly
young toughie, what I used to call a toughette because she was
so firm, so decisive, so divine. Instead, I'm focused entirely
on you. I'm not thinking of a sun-smelling tractor mechanic
named Peg. I'm thinking of a tweedy small-town attorney-at-
law called . . . Are you sure it's not just a *nom de fuck*? Really
Watkins?"

"Really Watkins."

"Today, you're my tough but gentle," she said. "You're lithe
for a man of your age. You're graceful in your walk, a true
dancer. You smell sweet with some sort of soap I can't quite"
—sniff, another sniff—"identify."

The air was clear and silvery in there, like a closet full of
knives. Reassuringly she took his arm and matched his step to
hers while she gave him a little tour of her house, chattering
encouragingly. She had given up cigarets; the cigarets she had
given up were Tareytons, if he wanted some; now she chewed
but she never smoked; she . . . What she was telling him, very
nicely, was not to worry, he was safe in her house, even if not
a soul in the whole wide world had a clue about where he was
and she could bury him in the backyard with the chickens, snails
and prune pits with nobody the wiser. Well, perhaps Bethany
would come looking for him in a few weeks.

Nice lady. Considerate about a fellow's doubts. Timidity was
not a moral flaw any more than baldness would be.

"Look, my skylight," she said. "A gift from my ex-husband,
inadvertent. Income tax refund we shared. Honor to him for
sharing. I energy-saved with thermopane, plus got this cathedral
ceiling."

Watkins craned his neck. The light was warm and amber,
cathedral, but the thermopane itself was peppered with dead
flies, fried in some previous sun and drying there. There were
edges of rust on the industrial prefab windows. Think of it as

oxidation, he decided, natural, organic, mineral. "You've found a style for yourself," he said.

"Everyone must, Watson. Else your style finds you. This is a small town, but I've traveled. Also I subscribe to magazines."

He paused and waited. She refused to do all the work. He had to contribute, too. "Skylights are great, I truly like them," he said, and he truly did. "The sky out here especially, always changing."

"We're not unique, Volt." She bobbed her head rapidly with appreciation of his taking part in the conversation. "Other skies are not fixed, either. In Paris for example, or in Palm Beach, they are ever-changing. Boy, are you nervous."

There was a glint in her eye. Was she onto herself, not only him? He began to fight back. "You're pretty naughty," he said. "Matronly toughies! I'll bet you're putting me on."

"Maybe I'm only mischievous. I do have this desire to correct people, don't I? Men notice this about me, though women don't so much. Mr. Lawyer, you misunderstand me perfectly."

"I do what?"

"It's a pity. Because I want the same soft sweet cozy help in getting through the night you want, sir. Shall we continue the tour? Be gallant. Take my arm again."

Her house in Dixon, which she at least once called her pad, was larger than it seemed. It was furnished in Huckleberry Farouk style, a grandeur of hanging macrame ropes, low gleamy couches, lace and gilt and paper Tiffany lampshades, one of which had shredded from age and heat. In a cozy corner she used a post-World War II red nylon panty to filter the bulb with unnatural glow. A Zodiac poster. A Grateful Dead poster. A low table, paisley pillows and slim throw-pillows in various spots in case of an emergency languor of the limbs. On the low table, luncheon meats, cheeses and chocolates in a blue glass dish with Shirley Temple's profile etched into it. And an actual French brandy (Remy Martin****) bottle, recycled with peach liqueur.

"I've a lot of Oriental in me," she said. "I've been to India. I've trekked in the Nepal. I discovered my Eastern side. That's what

III

I've found. These are my collectibles. Some, of course—flea markets."

"They're more than an investment," Watkins said, "they're a way of life."

"You said it, I didn't. No one else but us is to know what happens or occurs in this *maison*—a word I heard in Katmandu. Would you like a bath?"

"Or a shower?" He was getting an overdose of tubs.

She made a face. "In the East, bathing is a ritual, a ceremony, it's almost mystic or religious, not just some hurry-up scrubbing-away of the day's accumulations."

She had thought ahead. The tub was already filled. The mirrors were steamed. A tiger-striped beach towel lay fetchingly on the floor to absorb any wet from between the toes after the ritual, the ceremony. She was slipping out of her caftan and warning him to step *up* into the tub, since it was already on legs —fox paws, by the look of them—and the Detroit industrial-design people who make modern tubs had spoiled people into stepping down. Undressed, her lower regions had a more mature look than her bland, bright, blond expanse of face. There was darkness below.

"Do you mind joining me for a bath?" she inquired.

"Pardon? Do I mind?"

"Don't offend, Watkins. That's not what I'm saying. For ordinary social interaction you're okay. But if we happen to begin a little foreplay and it seems destined . . ."

She paused shyly. She too was timid. She blushed.

"It seems destined to go in the direction of ying and yang, do you mind being squeaky clean?"

"Not at all," he said. "That's what I prefer."

She sighed. She stood there, lifting first one foot, then the other, getting used to the thermal extremes. "We don't have to predict," she said. "We don't have to make preconditions. But on this one matter, I like to make it perfectly clear. The smells of men, you know, I'm not so used to them. The tight musky reek of crotch. The excretory . . ."

"I understand," he said hastily. "You're a poet with words."

"And I'll scrub myself good too," she said. "What's sauce for the gander is sauce for the goose."

Should she really have been placed among the top five? Watkins wondered. Had Bethany made an error of ranking? Was there something in Bethany that sought to play tricks on him? Or to make it clear that true love was not all that simple a matter?

The sound he heard, as his mind raced toward various alternatives, was the sound of a tidal wave from the bathtub heaving over onto the floor. It happened because they were both lowering themselves into the hot water. They both thought Ahhh. Watkins did not ask to play with her rubber boat. No jokes. Meditation was the ticket. They sat and let the heat do its consoling work. He didn't touch her, not with his hands. His waves touched her waves. He smiled and she smiled. He believed she was beginning to approve of him. Splish, splash, they were taking a bath. She sniffed steam up her narrow nostrils. Perhaps soon they could take bars of soap and wash each other in the crevices that sometimes offend. But since he hardly knew the young woman with whom he was bathing, and he was her guest, he would wait to be served. Vic Lonkin would have made faster moves.

She exhaled. Her sinuses were in order. She said Ahhh aloud. She reached for the soap dish. When she handed him the bar of soap (he to go first), she held his hand a moment, the hard soap beginning to wet down. With only soap between them, she had another confession to make. "It is a terrible, terrible thing," she said, "to be smarter than the one you love. I hope not to be in that fix with you."

"I'm only a moderate achiever," Watkins said, "but I have a high IQ."

She put on a trickle of fresh water. Maybe she liked splashing sounds. "And besides, I'm not in love with you, am I?" she asked. "So I don't see any further obstacles."

10

"The heart is deceitful above all things, and desperately wicked." It wasn't a good day for Jeremiah when he announced this opinion.

Better Watkins should look on a brighter side, such as what does that *desperately* mean? That he and Jeremiah were trying to be *calmly* virtuous? Pete Positano had views on the subject. His career as therapist-prophet in the med school was the fulfillment of a motto he had developed as a young counseling genius: Physician, you can only get others straight if you get yourself straight. The same for lawyers. He had a little take on Watkins, too. It was never a jury trial with Pete—prophets cut right through the red tape.

Overhead, the rice-colored clouds floated listlessly across the delta, ready to dump dryness on the flat valley. Pronged metal irrigation twigs sprayed water on the fields from deep wells and from the brackish Sacramento River; no one was deceived by clouds anymore. The puffs of grayness in the sky bluffed and hovered and turned sullied from overuse. The sun was constant these days—a worn yellow veil of haze. Watkins thought maybe his heart really was deceitful. . . .

He had never fooled Bethany. It was one of the good and bad things about her. She was on to him. He supposed it was a thing in his favor, in his own eyes and in the eyes of God, that he liked her intelligence about him. Of course, it was also inconvenient, but he had learned in his life with wives that convenient women weren't necessarily the best. They didn't necessarily work out. Bethany interested him and delighted him, and she even liked him personally. And was inconvenient because she wasn't polite about his secrets.

Even now, she seemed to know where he was, at least when she wanted to know where he was, and he was just sitting at his desk at home, knocking paper clips about in a little magnetic box —a poor substitute for Latin music, staring at the white plaster of the twin condominium town house next door (poor substitute for the mountains of Nepal, the church of Saint-Germain-des-Prés), watching the unmoving branch at his window, which after all was a nice miniature world, budding, leaf covered, with a green eraser tip of life where it touched the glass, when the telephone rang and he had no doubt about who it would be.

He let a whole discreet Bell Telephone interval resound. He thought he let it ring, but his hand reached out against his will. It knew and he knew.

"How are you, Wat?"

Of course, often the telephone rang and he was sure it was Bethany and it was not.

"Wat, are you there?"

But this time he forgot all the times he was wrong.

"Wat? Hey? Answer please, Wat."

"I thought you weren't going to call. I'm glad you're not perfect."

"You mean I can't stick to my resolutions? I can. But I miss you, Wat."

"When can we meet?"

"No, no, I just miss you. This is just a little blip. I *can't* see you, Wat, because if I see you—"

"Why not?"

"I might want to see you again. And if I see you again, there we are." Her voice was low, although surely there was no one in the house to overhear. As clearly as he felt his own sweating body, his anxious sweating hand, he could imagine her curled up on her knees on the couch, whispering and murmuring and laughing into the phone. "So I just want to know if you're okay and anything else you might want to tell me."

"I miss you, Beth."

"That's true, that's true. We don't need to tell each other that, Wat. Anything else?"

His dream of love was to tell the truth and not to play tricks, games, strategies, tactics. What Bethany was asking was about Adela Jenkins, Aviva, Ms. Atworth, Linda King and whoever else might be filling his time. But Wat would offer nothing, he would make her ask directly; and when she asked, he would think how to evade the answer.

"I've been running a little more. Lost a few pounds. Some flab you might have noticed—"

"I never noticed, Wat. I liked it."

"There's a fuss going on in the faculty senate. I told Frank not to get me involved. Adjunct prof doesn't have to take a position. My friend Vic Lonkin—"

"Who?"

"An old friend of mine. I guess I didn't tell you about him . . ." She was curled up on the couch for sure, she was giggling for sure.

"We hardly had time to reminisce about old friends from the past, Wat. It was the nature of our . . ." Her voice trailed off. She wasn't giggling after all. "Our afternoons together. Our time together. Our . . ."

It was hard to talk on the phone with her. She wasn't giving way at all. She was just talking on the phone. He couldn't mention Vic without causing a justifiable impatience in her. Vic wasn't relevant here. Vic didn't die to be used by Watkins to soften the heart of a woman.

"Tell me about Mr. Lonkin, Wat. I know that name from someplace."

"We went to law school together. We used to go prying abalone off rocks. We studied for the bar together."

"You've been seeing him again lately, two bachelors on the town?"

"No," he said. "Beth, what are you doing with yourself?"

"You mean have I found someone else to be a Wat for me? No,

dear. You're special, Wat. It was special, Wat. I guess I want to tell you that. This is the time before carpool when I think about you every single day."

"I really . . . like you, Beth—"

"I don't know why. I don't know why you like me. I don't know why I think about you every single day. It's stupid, Wat. Don't tell me what you're doing about those women. I don't care. I only care for what I'm losing, not what they're getting —I only care because I'm trying to be sensible and a good mother and a loving wife and, if I can, a grown-up—"

"Bethany? Beth? Beth?"

She had hung up. He knew enough not to call back. It would be too hard for her to try to say more. It would be too hard on him. He imagined her way of saying, as she sometimes used to, These are only selfish tears. You have no right to feel sorry for me. These are only tears for myself.

It was what she always said; as, for example, last year, when the family went away for the summer. "These are selfish tears because I miss you. These are only selfish tears for myself, poor poor little dumb Bethany. When we have fun and laugh and feel good, because that's what it's about with us, Wat, then it's for both of us. So don't let me dump these moods I sometimes have, not on you, Wat. If I'm selfish and these are big fat ugly dumb selfish tears, that's not your business, Wat."

Okay, what could Pete Positano do for him? Along the line of keeping busy and solving the problem of being alive when some good people were not and the woman who might redeem the facts of life for Watkins, or at least endorse them properly, was busy with things that mattered more to her. Things which, in fact, were rather more important, once a person granted that Watkins was not the most important element in the world or even in Bethany's world.

Pete thriving in the helping trade, what did Watkins want of him? Sexual help? There was so much of that. It was a drug on the market. How to be "better" with women friends, men friends? Oh no, not more American government. Not more improvementism. How to live with failed marriage and love? How to live with kiddies far away and busy with their own growing up? When he was doing about the same things they were, only with a bit more disposable income?

Pete liked full disclosure. That was the deal with Pete, plus straightforward honest male grief about the catastrophes and tragedies, all gathered together about the camp fire. Let's see now. Bethany needs to simplify her sunny days; his married Bethany won't meet him afternoons, after tennis, sometimes even instead of tennis, anymore. That's pretty dim in the tragic dilemma line. It wasn't even totally pathetic, except he felt it so.

Did he love his grown, moved-away daughter and son? Yes. They looked good to him. Sometimes they met on national holidays or when the Bar Association had a meeting in the East.

Did he quarrel with his former wives? Not very much. No. The one he might quarrel with if he could find her, he couldn't find. And he wasn't looking for her. And he wouldn't even quarrel with her. He was comfortable with her running away from him without quarreling with her.

Vic Lonkin? He only thought of him when he read the news. Afterward, true, he remembered their friendship like a series of postcards unfolding—McAbee Beach in wet suits, sweating the Bar Review course together on Golden Gate Avenue, smoking meerschaum pipes like genuine grown-up country lawyers, the first attempts at married palship, four people who didn't match anymore. They went their different ways. Vic was a friend from days gone by. A lot of beer had foamed under the bridge. Still, an erratic echo in his heart, a beat of the wrong octane in the machinery, different in degree but maybe not in kind from what stopped Vic's reciprocal recollections of old what's-his-name, the guy who settled in Davis, Watkins—that pang was a preview of coming myocardial attractions for Wat, too.

Pure self-indulgence and please say good-bye to that. Still, poor Vic; good-bye to sympathetic knockings in the chest and good-bye to Vic.

So was he comfortable?

No. Bethany's plan was symmetrical and sensible. She scattered loose temptations around his feet to distract him. He could think of them as loose desires. All he had to do was bend a little, and he was willing to bend. Bend and pick them up. It wasn't as easy as all that.

Striking a blow for balance on his own, it seemed he was looking for a guide, a community, a leader of men, a sharing and an instruction. He was looking for a philosopher and a creature of nature to help him stay alive in this unraveling portion of the century. That's how the times and himself felt to him—needy, distracted and unraveling. Watkins, the man who had everything.

"Have I got a men's group for you," Pete Positano said, and shifted gears. Everything in his mouth and throat altered. It was not a question. "Come on in. Do. You're welcome. Please do come to our group, Watkins."

Dr. Positano's, Pete's, the voice of the man troubled Watkins. He really didn't know him. He wasn't really a friend. He was on campus and they had met was all. When he was married to Elaine, they had dinner together a few times. The wives didn't pursue the acquaintanceship, and then the wives disappeared and nobody pursued the matter. The voice, talking over the phone, maybe it was his professional voice. All at once there was a slightly prissy offshore accent, as if he had studied English from a pirate radio station specializing in antique Donovan and classic Beatles and a lot of Destroy and Shark and Dead Kennedy punk. But that wasn't Pete's South Bronx in-person voice. And in person the head was strong, bald, with a long fringe of brown hair and tufts in the ears. Over the telephone he sounded as if he had a shock of white hair he kept tossing out of the way of his forehead. The voice was breathy. The voice had met Mrs. Jacqueline Kennedy Onassis during some previous incarnation. It didn't breathe all the way down. It wasn't quite a drawl, though surely there was a little whine in there someplace.

The making-an-appointment voice might be different from the actually talking-together voice.

"Would you have a cup of coffee with me?" Watkins asked. He

hated the querulous in his own plea. "Let's just meet on campus at the Coffee House. Maybe just a few minutes. Just to check on each other, it's been a while—"

Chuckly, confident, in-charge Pete. "You're really in trouble, that it, Wat? Been a long long time no see no hear no touch. Sure, I can give you a moment of my valuable hanging-out time."

Wasn't it kind of Pete. They sat under an aluminum umbrella outside the Student Union. Their voices racketed off metal. The sun had disappeared behind the building. A group of Chinese students at the table nearby was working little calculators; no, it was Rubik's Cube. They were learning to hang out, too. Pete was so happy with what duty bound him to say, even if it hurt: "Your problem, my friend, is what we used to call anomie, we got better words now, which you don't need, all the head trips you take yourself on anyway. Let's zap you with the classic diagnosis: anomie. Anorexia nervosa of the spirit. Wat, you are skinny in your soul."

"Nice to be slim someplace, Pete."

"See? Jokes and headtrips when I try to offer you a frank, fraternal and brotherly brief diagnosis free of any charge. I try and I succeed, but what good is it? What I don't understand, further, is what gives you the right to disdain, if I may use such language, campus chicks? Snobbery? Are you that religious? Don't you have tenure? Are you so choked with principle"—the prophet boomed triumphantly—"you can afford to be an arrogant headtripping mindfucking loser?"

"I can't answer all that yes or no," Watkins said.

"And what about androgyny? I found the truth of androgyny when it was still called bisexual. Are you too arrogant? Don't tell me it's a matter of taste, Watkins."

"It's a matter of taste, Pete."

"Headtripper. Mindfucker. I'm only tentativing out a little diagnosis, a probe."

They fell silent together. Thanks would be superogatory; silence was better. Two old acquaintances perhaps doomed, in middle age, to become friends or enemies, through no fault of their own, drinking coffee in the late afternoon while the rest of the campus made love, studied for exams, solved Rubik's Cube. The flat gray rice-colored clouds would wait until tomorrow. They wouldn't rain tomorrow, either.

Watkins continued to be troubled by the voice of Pete Positano. That soft purr after the South Bronx success snarl. Well, everybody works out a manner. Pete, who clawed his way around campus as tiger with tenure and official med school firebrand, had the right to play Jacqueline on the telephone, Abbie at the Coffee House, if it worked for him. Pete's style was not the problem.

They agreed about the objective problem, the one outside themselves. It was how to deal with what the world wanted men to be (men in trouble living up to it) and what women wanted men to be (what *do* they want men to be?) and what men would like for themselves (unfearful, unmiserable, even brave and happy if such is possible) and what Watkins *thought* he wanted (to be the lover of Bethany or another woman who could make him not love Bethany). Without giving her name, Watkins mentioned how those afternoons after tennis—the bath together, the murmuring and cuddling—had saved his life from itself. No names, please.

That silo visible on the rise of the hill beyond the flatness of campus, it was as far away as the smell of grain and fertilizer when the wind blew across the fields, and the night burning of the rice wastes, and the bluffing clouds that brought no rain. It was right here in his nose. (He was evading the subject.) The subject: Maybe if he were a proper man instead of a middle-aged boy, an old child, a viable presenile codger, then he could tell why he was still looking for another woman to give him the comfort he didn't get from his previous women, who were mostly forgotten, or his wives, about whom he cared little now, or from Bethany, for whom he longed beyond good reason. No explanation. (The burnt rice and silo were replaced in his head by the recollection of light-limbed Bethany wrapped about him, heavier-limbed hairy Wat wrapped about Bethany; her smells of clean, light, exercised, fanatic-about-exercise bones—fizziness of Bethany—this was no explanation, either.)

Why not learn to be a man instead of this needful lover? Oh my. He had enough trouble getting to be forty-four years old as a boy. The shelves of HumanHouse were filled with books about unleashing, unlocking, dechaining, how to become more fully something else, something better. The Male Dilemma. The Male Machine. The Liberated Male Personality. Beyond Male Masculinity. Saying You're Sorry and Male. All those apologies and resolutions seemed to be for others, even if they happened to be aimed straight at abject Watkins.

He understood there was a problem and that's why he was dealing here with Pete Positano and his fellow men. Couldn't deal anymore with Victor Lonkin. Watkins in pursuit of help and the truth. Watkins not giving up.

They met in a carpeted encounter room with fat pillows in HumanHouse across the California frontier as the sun was going down over Interstate 80 and Western civilization. Troubled men, uneasy men, fretful men, men in disarray is what they were—that sort of men. Modern Man. Watkins wondered when Pete Positano would show up and if this lateness were some sort of traditional dating drama he was putting out. But then Pete showed up, and Watkins wondered if his anticipation of Pete's tardiness was some sort of complaining drama *he* was emitting. No time for futile introspection now; they were called there to be with each other in truth, love and self-help. In fact, where were they?

"Where I'm at," said Pete Positano from his land of shared pain, "is I want approval, I don't want any more negativity shit, I want to be accepted for me."

"Uh-huh, uh-huh," breathed Rod, the convening host from HumanHouse, a Universal Unitarian Humanist minister who had gone into the helping field because he craved something more nitty-gritty. "I'm not exactly ordained anymore, Pete, but I accept you. That's a start. Now, gentlemen, as your facilitator, let us proceed."

Shoes off, toes wriggling. Two or three half-lotuses, the rest sprawling. Watkins was the only one with black lawyer socks stretching up the calves; well, he was the only lawyer. Evidently

Pete felt harassed inside, where reality began, and felt like taking the initiative: "I don't want any mindfucking psychobabblers here. I take enough poopydoo already. I'm a man of power and if you can't stand my power, stand away. Power—" he frequently made a two-finger quotation-mark gesture around the strong noun or verb as his words flowed on; at present there was none of his whispery Jacqueline Bouvier telephone voice; he underscored an aria against mindfucking with a mighty repertory of gestures and intonations which called for the raising of the voice. "—my power, it's too hot for some people. I turn up the burner. If it's too hot for you here, a bunch of academic types except for Watkins and he's just an academic lawyer, don't ask me not to be Me, Myself and I, Pete Positano from the South Bronx who got his Ph.D., if it's too hot for you, move away from the stove. . . ."

Rod, the helping professional, opened a window onto himself. "I seem to need to be professional about everything. I'd like not to be so obsessive-convulsive. Gormay chef, cabinet-maker, humanist, even when I was a former Man of the Rational God, I had to be tops, but now I've got two kids, a boy eight, a girl five, I really love that boy eight and that girl five is so sweet, I don't like things to go wrong. My wife, uh, I guess I still have a wife, but I'll fill you in later . . ."

Now it was Pete Positano's turn to say, "Uh-huh, uh-huh."

Chuck, a bearded scientist, asked: "Is there some reason we're not telling our last names?"

"Let's stick to what's relevant," Rod remarked briskly. "Is your father's name relevant? What about your mother's?"

The scientist nodded. "I don't have male friends to dialogue with, that's how ignorant I am. It was my lab all the way. Since I came out here to California, got taken on by the lab out here, research grant, I realize there's more than work, the golden carrot, the big-time reputation. For example, there's fun, I want some of that, plus there's, oh—"

"Getting into yourself?" Pete asked. "Just a probe."

"Something like that. Maybe some good sex, if it involves honesty on both sides. I don't have a formula." Chuck didn't want to finish. Watkins felt the witness might have said more if Pete had not supplied an answer.

"I hate competing," said Fred from Poly Sci. "Sometimes I find myself breaking pencils and hyperventilating, I need to express myself so much, but then when it's my turn I can't speak. Pete, you have a lot of power, just like you say you do, but you tend to interrupt a person's thoughts and then—"

"Oh, man," said Pete. "I hear you. I want you to truck right on down with me. I can give you a lot of comfort from my own distress. I can help you center yourself, Fred."

The group was looking at Watkins. Their centered eye boiled into him. Pete's eye demanded the confession of failure, the only road to honesty and sharing, Watkins wanted company. He was here, wasn't he? He said, "I have wives and memories of wives and grown children moved away and a woman I love and other women—" He wasn't going to tell about Bethany's advertisement. Honesty was okay, but not handing them the knife and showing his belly. He was willing to share the private, but not the secret. "Some of my relationships," he mumbled, "are in varying degrees of disarray."

"Oh, man," said Fred. "Pete?" Chuck and Rod also looked to Pete for a response.

"Man, I hear you talkin'," said Pete. "We're with you, aren't we, all? Watkins, *we are with you all the way.* We're on your side. Now, that's straight? Okay. So what this group can do, it can give each other support, it can give love, it can give..." He tilted his head, commanding his followers. What comes after love in the giving department? "It can give *love,* not that poopydoo, that *shit* we have to take from the world. Man, just like Watkins, I'm angry, I'm mad, I'm plain pissed—"

Watkins wanted to raise his hand to say he wasn't angry, he wasn't mad, but teacher wouldn't call on him.

"—I've got to express my power they're all stopping me from." Pete tugged at his earring. "That Blue Cross Plan don't work for me. They keep shooting my bills back at me, plus the doctors don't know shit from penicillin—I'm in a position to tell. Just shows how the machinery has gone nutsy, my friends.

125

Isn't that what's on your mind, Watkins?"

Pete was crowding them a little. He was experienced, knew how to live in groups, darting about like a pilot fish. Watkins decided calmness might resist Pete's power—he thought of it as fever, hysteria, powerlessness.

The communicants offered their bad news about wives, children, onrushing age, sex, work, miscellaneous night distress. Pete kept saying, "I hear you, I hear you," in a rush to get to the important things on his mind. He nailed the decade and America as an Ageist time and a Sexist Society; no one disputed him. Like Watkins, they were preoccupied with men and women being together. Maybe they were better than he was. They also worried about ambition, competitiveness, compulsions, about health, money, jobs and Achilles' tendons. At first they didn't talk about the love of any individual women. But of course Watkins didn't, either.

"I want to be understood," said Rod. "I understand, so why can't I be understood?"

"I hear you," said Pete. "They give you a lot of shit. That's what I'll call it. Man, you got a right to be mad. I'm mad. I'm getting into violence, man. That's getting to be my new thing."

Watkins worried that Pete might, with force and violence, rip off his earring. At the same time he was learning something about himself, and about himself with this old friend Pete Positano, who was rapidly becoming a mere acquaintance—that a certain kind of competitive, talkative, deeply resentful man was . . . a menace? No, a difficulty for him.

Was this because he was competing with Pete in the mind-fucking game? (Pete's word.)

No, Watkins decided, willingly answering his own question. I dislike Pete because he's dislikable. He's trying to be one on whom nothing is lost. He is one who finds nothing but his own need. For Watkins, this also seemed to be a warning.

While he was studying trivial matters, such as whether he did or did not need to like his old colleague, Pete Positano, the group as a whole was learning something else. They had superior activities. Watkins wanted to join. Sounding-off was fun. It was pleasant to exchange remarks, a sort of energetic loafing. Confidences and doubts, consolations and angers, without the help of a screw-top bottle of Chablis, this was advanced behavior for advanced thinkers about themselves. Complaints. Confessions. Phrases. Something like basic training was taking place. Even the new recruit, Watkins, felt a warmth in the chest which he identified as the beginnings of comradeship. The news about Vic Lonkin had rocked him a little.

Chuck, the bearded engineer, thirty-three—the age when Christ was crucified, Watkins noted unaloud—and married eleven years, two children, separated for a time from his wife—during this time he had his first affair—was now happily, he announced resentfully, back with his wife. They had a few problems, that was all. She was, uh, angry. She wanted to be, uh, herself. He was grunting like a wrestler. In fact, he was wrestling. This time Pete did not interrupt. All the fellows waited.

Chuck said in a low voice: "Hard to open up sometimes." Uh. Uh. "I'm not an Eyetalian, a Jew. I'm used to being, uh, too careful. In my group we call it dignity, cool. My group makes a lot of trouble for itself is why I'm in this group."

"Go on, go on," said a bunch of Jews, Italians, Undignifieds. "Get down to it."

Chuck was gasping and flipping his hands in his lap. "Well, my wife. She. Well. She wants to *initiate* sex."

Oh, boy, what whoops of pleasure and congratulations. Chuck looked blond and bewildered. A fringe of working blond beard. Watkins and Pete did not believe Chuck had told the whole story, but in the meantime, everyone asked what's wrong with that? It's great if you finish dinner, maybe a take-out pizza, maybe somebody even cooked tonight, and the kids are tucked in, the boy eight and the girl five (but that was Rod, not Chuck), and now Chuck and Mrs. Chuck are sitting in front of the teevee, and now her soft hand goes creeping up your thigh. Oh, boy.

Well, no. Chuck was the only man not enjoying this. What was wrong? "Well, she wants control over her own body. Well, she wants the decision about sex to be hers. Well, that macho male thing pisses her off."

Well, what's wrong?

"Well."

"So she's initiating sex, isn't she?" Pete asked.

"Well, no. She wants control, she. She wants to initiate it, she. But she never does. Well"—he was stammering—"what she really wants is to initiate nonsex, no sex." His voice rose to shrill: *"No goddamn fucking at all!"*

Whew.

But it wasn't a total surprise to Watkins or, he suspected, to Pete.

Chuck, this sweet muscular young blond engineer, with a wrestler's compact bulges, also had a purple, congestive heart-failure face. "She's mad at me. She won't. If I try, she's dry. She's mad and stays mad for a week. I think that's when she's happy. Nothing!"

Pete Positano studied him. That face of Chuck might have been called blushing, but it looked more like congestive heart failure, and Pete squinted against the pain. At first Watkins thought Pete would stroke, make nice. Instead, he grinned and said, "Does she let you grab yourself?" (Pete seized his own crotch. He wasn't pretending. He did a South Bronx hustle of his balls.) "Does she let you play with yourself?" (Pete rubbed his hand over the fresh bulge in his jeans.) "Does she let you jack off?"

"I suppose so," said Chuck. "I don't ask her."

"Well then," Pete said with a purr and a hum, "well, then she's pretty good to you, isn't she, Chuck? She only wants to control her own body, right?"

"Yes—"

"No. She runs yours too."

Everyone waited. Rod lifted his hands to his ears.

Chuck lowered his eyes. "Well," he said, "if I had an affair now that we're back together, that would hurt her too much."

Oh God. The fellows sneered. None of this was Universal Unitarian Humanist fellowship. Because Chuck's wife was mad at Chuck, she declared no sex for her and none for Chuck; those were the rules. Even Rod showed a momentary nonfacilitating aversion to Chuck by holding his nose between two fingers. The little gesture came back to him from when he was eleven years old.

"But, damn it, I *like* her," Chuck said. "She's my best friend. Does marriage have to include . . . I mean, after eleven years and the kids five and eight? . . ."

"Me too," said Rod.

"If you feel like it," Pete asked, "why not have those noonsies, those mad bad afternoons on the floor of your office with the graduate student?"

Chuck shook his head. "I couldn't do that."

"But if it's not important?"

"I couldn't do that."

Everyone—Rod, Pete, Fred, Watkins—was yelling and laughing and pushing at him now, but oddly enough, despite the sudden noise and disorder in the room, instead of keeling over with a burst of anxiety-clogged capillaries, some kind of moral sneeze cleared Chuck's plumbing. He looked into each shining furious face. The stream was gushing with freshets of comradeship. He was interested and touched by logic and illogic, and defending himself, and even seeming to listen to their abuse of him.

"I only brought it up because it wasn't settled in my mind," Chuck said.

They heard. They waited.

Watkins said, "Why not just have that affair but not hurt her? Don't tell her about it. Pretend you're a Frenchman."

Fred said, "You could have it with a man."

"Wuh?" Chuck asked.

"Well, me. It's only a probe." This sort of thing had not yet come up. They were about to quit for the day, and here Fred was throwing this monkey suggestion at them. "Me, sometimes I get bored with my wife, the kids, they get on my nerves, so what I like to do once in a while, maybe the Christmas letdown or around Halloween, is"—well, he wouldn't stop now—"is a little male scene. Just for relaxation. For a new option when the going gets rough."

Rod stared at his watch, confirmed what he read with a brisk nod, stretched, started to put his shoes back on. As he laced, he looked up winningly, facilitatingly, and asked, "Next Wednesday, same time, same place?"

Watkins was slow with his shoes. He was trying to lace up his thoughts. Yes, male friends, he liked these fellows and some of his colleagues, he was charmed by intelligence, cleverness or even good looks. He wasn't jealous of them. Vic Lonkin and he used to camp overnight on the beach in Monterey. So was Fred just being more available to the world? Was Watkins's pursuit of understanding from a woman just a way to avoid what Fred was more open about? Is Open what it was about? Is that why he suffered such choosiness, such a stupid refusal to accept anyone but the tennis-playing wife of a dentist?

Watkins finished his shoes. He was sure he liked women more than men's rooms. Nevertheless, he brooded on the implications of Fred's solution to the problems of Chuck's wife. In Human-House on campus, he sought to be united with how things might improve in a better world.

Stubbornly Fred continued. He had the courage of a mild and thoughtful hero. "When you come right down to it, to the basic meaning of things," he was saying softly, shyly, "I mean when you analyse it in depth, Chuck, you're really kind of a gorgeous hunk."

11

The kinds of help Watkins was seeking added up to trying to tell him something. He was crawling toward the edge of brink. He stood on all fours on the green growing tip of decay. Contradiction was his crystal-clear method to resolve his lack of clarity. Even his grinding students at the School of Law were surer of spirit.

Damnit, he was distraught. It occurred to Watkins almost every day that what he was doing might not be the way to climb back to safety. The reminder did not put any caution into his behavior. *Go back!* was not useful advice to the man who was already careening backward. He was looking for true love; trying to win something; he was being crowned with a dunce cap. When he taught his classes, and lectured about precedent, about how morality led to rules and procedures, and thus to the rights of even the wicked, he was thinking about running his hands on Bethany's thighs or dying, like Vic Lonkin. His eyes dimmed, his students took notes, he almost said, *And when she comes, she giggles.* Instead he said, "Even the guilty deserve the best defense they can be given. Generally, of course, they don't get it."

His mistake might have begun with putting so much need on her slim unwilling shoulders. His mistake might have come from confusing pleasure with peace and justice. His mistake started long before he knew Bethany.

She was a symptom, what she had planned for him was a further symptom, and what was happening to him as he shambled about the state of California was an elaboration of both of their symptoms. Distractions were not true love. A life of vain hope was not a true life.

Now that he had all that clear, which woman on Bethany's list should come next? He studied the sheet on which she had typed names, addresses, box numbers, telephone numbers, zip codes, area codes, brief notations of personality and references to filed complete letters. In the main, their character was: Available. His own character was different, but also available. The hunter was only following orders.

Then all by himself one day, with no preparation from Bethany, while peacefully engaged in getting a refill of his antihistamine prescription and questioning the very basis of his existence, Watkins happened to meet a woman he liked. She was a meter maid giving him a ticket for overparking in the little stretch of redwood downtown which had recently installed meters—a big-city refinement. He dashed under the stained redwood overhang, past the country mural and the beer-cool swinging door of Punk in the Night, and said, "I'm here, I'm here!"

"I'm writing," said the meterperson in her unfaded blue uniform of honest workingperson polyester. She had a wide short plump body. Her three-wheeled vehicle was humming. Her face, heavy in the jaw, was dappled with some sort of fleshy excess. She was amused by the smartly dressed lawyer frantically protesting his five-dollar ticket. Why did they all do that?

"I was *here*," he said.

"I can't stop writing," she said, "and you know I can't tear up the ticket."

"But I called to you—"

"But you're a lawyer—aren't you Mr. Watkins, sir?—you know once I've started writing . . ."

Impasse. He stared.

"You can just mail in the check. You lose a morning by going to court," she said.

"You know I'm not going to do that."

"Mr. Watkins, I shouldn't respond to your shame and anxiety, but I'm human too and I'd like you to have a nice day. I just finished my LifeSpring Seminar. I know I can handle aggression, but I'd like to learn to handle corruption and generosity."

"Wonderful," he said. "How much?"

"I still have to write the ticket. It's free of any charge. So what I'll do is here I'll change the one to a seven on your license plate, well, to make sure, also the five to an eight, see? And now the computer can't pick up whose car it really was—"

"Thank you . . ."

"Only following orders. I've got to write the ticket. When I do my graduate training I'll have to figure out how to adjust to not following the regs." He started to reach into his pocket. "You're not going to offer me anything," she said, pouting. "I have to chide you for attempted bribery. So far I'm into generosity, I haven't started corruption yet."

"No, no, no, of course not," he said. "I was looking for my card. If you ever need anything—a divorce, a will probated, maybe a little murder defense . . ."

"I know," she said. "I'm amenable to all the passions, Mr. Watkins. Perhaps some evening when I'm free and you're free and we feel like it because we're both free, and you have a six-pack, or I have a six-pack, we can sit in my kitchen, Mr. Watkins, just person to person, and shoot the shit. I don't use the hard stuff. In LifeSpring, for instance, we even try to get over the lesser addictions, such as nail-biting. The hard stuff—vodka, gin, heroin, excuses every one of them—interferes with the conduct of my professional duties."

Watkins was remembering the silly moments with Bethany and driving toward the public courts where she played tennis at this hour. He should not be doing that. He should be doing something else. He shouldn't be in his Saab and driving just now past a gaily decorated VW with Cinzano traced on its doors for a payment of fifty dollars a year. Students got their coke money the oddest ways. Some cleaned apartments, some managed condo complexes, some stenciled their wheels with tricolored bottles. The high price of coke was also stimulating individual initiative (Watkins felt sorry for addicts and wondered if he was a certain kind of one).

Some worked in cancer labs, forcing monkeys to smoke. Some installed wood-burning stoves and solar-collecting greenhouses.

133

Some were adjunct professors of law, a useful job within the system, but gave their strength to inappropriate notions of justice. Felt they were entitled to love.

Sometimes Bethany had made him play games. "Let's play Kansas City," she would say.

He used to do that for her.

"I'm from Kansas City, Missouri," she said, "and I make up jokes. Would you like to hear one?"

"Okay," he said.

"Okay. I take that as a go-ahead. Why is there both a Kansas City, Missouri, and a Kansas City, Kansas?"

"I don't know."

"Because Missouri loves company. Would you like to hear another?"

"No."

"I take that as a go-ahead. There are a lot of Chinese folks in Kansas City, Missouri, named Wong. If they have a child, what do they name it?" She waited. "White," she said. "Because two Wongs make a White."

When she tired of these games, and of being unafraid of her big bad high-IQ lover, her favorite lawyer, she found a game of her own. She had chosen Watkins to play her game and he was doing so. But probably she hadn't planned for him to park among the trees as he was doing now, and sneaking about to watch her in her regular-as-clockwork thrice-weekly tennis workout.

Three times a week on the Davis public courts. She still wore whites—old-fashioned woman. From a distance she could have been a college girl. It didn't make any difference that, up close, the sunlines and laughter lines and slightly hardened lines were slicing up the skin around her eyes and mouth. Or yes, it did make a difference. He loved her more for her determination and experience. If she didn't know she was suffering, that was merely a semantic problem. Watkins believed the body knew.

Parked in the shade, he watched her game. She was matched against a short, intense, skilled player, Marvin Ellis, a lobbyist in Sacramento for the rice growers. He returned everything she

134

sent his way. He was stubborn and careful. She bent and touched her knees before she served. She wrinkled her nose. She slammed her serve at Ellis, she chortled with laughter, she grunted a little on a strong forehand.

From his car he couldn't hear her grunts. But he knew that gesture around the mouth and eyes, and those grunting rutting sounds.

He wanted her. He couldn't have her anymore. While she waited for Ellis to serve, she took two excess-energy leaps into the air to keep warm and moving, lubricated.

He started the motor and drove away. He slammed the wheel with his fists. Now what good did that do? No one was watching to approve of his passion. Bethany was as concentrated as a monk on her tennis religion.

His fantasy of informing her husband: but Watkins was civilized, he was not a brute, and that would only retroactively demolish everything between them. The lady was inventive. The best solution was to do as she said. In such cases a negotiated settlement leading to submission was in order.

He drove and he didn't stop thinking about Bethany. He made a solemn vow to stop as soon as he got to his office. By the time he reached for his briefcase. By the time he finished parking the Saab. By the time he locked the door.

Although he was tallish, heavyish, but running twice a week, middle-ageish, lawyerish and accustomed to estimated tax forms and contractual provisions, he felt like a child in his own bed. He felt like a lad, a boy-in-waiting, a page in gusts of carnal expenditure. She had been waiting for him, it seemed, through several years of her marriage.

Love was sometimes as light and quick as tennis, and sometimes a lot of brawling and thrashing. They were animals in deep grass; the arms and legs flew their own needful ways—highly untechnical, Watkins thought. That was even better.

Bethany blared when she came, if she didn't giggle like a girl. If she was pretending, it was still a mighty energetic noise. She *couldn't* be pretending. Not that honking. No woman would.

Afterward he felt tired, warm and easy, and awash with con-

tentment. He asked her if she felt okay. "I'd like," she said.
"What?"

She was asleep. He thought it was the most wonderful moment without consequences in his whole life. There may have been consequential moments which were just as fine, but he couldn't remember them.

A bird sat on the condo sill, tilting its head at them through the window. It might try a tentative peck at the glass and then again it might not. It was a robin with what seemed to him a white breast. Perhaps the red had been bleached out of his vision by the brawling and thrashing he had just undergone. The tilt of the bird's head reminded him of a youngster bored on the telephone. But Watkins was not bored. The bird was. It departed in a flick of feathers.

"Your breast is so white," he said aloud, and the lady smiled in her sleep. Sometimes inadvertent communication was the best.

She slept for twenty minutes. At home, hamburgers to broil for her kiddies; her eyes fell open, clear, not needing to be wiped; she dressed; she was gone. . . .

He stopped remembering her when he parked his car, just as he promised himself, just as his solemn vow stated. It was an oral contract which had not been spoken aloud. Then, an hour later, why was he telephoning her at home? She would have showered by this time after her tennis with Marvin Ellis; hamburger-patty time.

"Hello?"

He didn't know what to say.

"*Hello?*"

Could he say it was Watkins, the crank caller?

Gently he put down the telephone. He wished to apologize to her. There was no way to do so. She would be shrugging and not too disturbed. After tennis or love she felt at ease with her body, ready to handle craziness. She would be making the salad for her loved ones. She would be dusting the hamburger patties with spices. She might even, in the miracle inconsequence of such things, be idly wondering how her old friend Watkins was

136

doing in his investigation of the women out there who longed for the love of a sensitive, lonely, healthy prof. mn.

He would not think about her. He left her imaginary body in her imaginary kitchen, and only allowed himself one more question: Would she be resting her eyes from her contact lenses just now by wearing the oversized amber horn-rimmed glasses that made her look vulnerable, so young, easy to hurt, as she was not.

Her kitchen and her body were real to him. Only Watkins was imaginary.

12

Chuck's battle with his wife went on, charted in the Male Peace Room at HumanHouse, although as far as she was concerned the war was over and she had won. Someday, perhaps, she would "initiate"—her word for leading the way to sex. Someday, perhaps, she would forgive. Someday, justice would be done in the universe, and more important, injustice would be repaired by oblivion. The group helped Chuck in his chosen fate, which was to wait and wait for kindness.

Fred's confession hung from the conversation like cobwebs. Okay, so he enjoyed a lad now and then. These were postcontemporary times and such was man's endeavor in his confusion. It had been shocking to some, but wasn't that part of the deal? Now it wasn't shocking anymore.

Rod explained how and why he was in the helping field. It put him at the mercy of smoothing the way for others. Since people who suffered seem to develop strong smells, it was not always easy. Uh-huh, uh-huh, said the others. "If I'm boring and it gives you someone to look down on, that might help," Rod said. "On the other hand, that might be *your* problem if I'm boring. Think about it."

Pete thought about it and Watkins thought about it. Pete said, "I'm into power, as I've said. I'm a vital person. I'm aware of my problems, but I'm too strong for this goddamn world. The bastards won't get me, because also I know how to bend, I know how to yield, and then I know how to come back with my teeth bloody."

"Whom? . . ." Watkins asked. Pete was just getting warmed up. He was racing his motor. Murderous statement was a means to scare the other motors to the side of the track. "Whom," Watkins asked, "were you biting with your bloody teeth when you were yielding?"

"You, mindfucker," said Pete, "you've done nothing but lie to us. You think this is a liar's game?"

There was some truth in Pete's jab. Watkins decided to throw him off balance by a quick dodge in the form of a surrender. "I've got some sadness in me. Probably a lot. I'm willing to talk about what's past because it doesn't matter anymore. My parents maybe. My wives."

"Your kids."

"Even that. Though it matters. Though they're grown up and they got their own things now."

"So what the mindfuck are you doing with yourself, Wat?"

"You've got some ideas, Pete. I'm not ready to say."

"Then I'll say," Pete announced.

Watkins looked away indifferently. He looked at poor, lost, muscular, good-looking Chuck, weary and blank Chuck. Watkins looked weary and blank himself as Pete blabbed excitedly, confessing on behalf of his friend: "Watkins went to see a woman he met by mail! Someone who advertised for him! He answered her advertisement in the *Reader's Digest* or something! He actually couldn't find someone for himself and so this mindfucker who comes on so strong here with being calm and snotty and everything, this *lawyer* with his lousy marriages which didn't succeed, I happen to know he got himself a mail-order fuck! This mindfucker!"

Watkins was amazed at how wrong a man with an alert listening face could be. A man whose profession was sympathy, understanding, empathy and insight could achieve such rotten witness. Watkins was amazed and not at all perturbed, as detached as if he lay on a battlefield and the shells were whistling and he was already dead. "Pete," he said, "you nailed me. I confess. I avow. How could you retain so much?"

"Mindfucking again! Sarcastic! His line of defense!" Pete said.

"You said you're a man of power, Pete. You're a man of hysteria, is what I see. Sort of womanish even."

"And sexist besides. He thinks hysteria is feminine! Not only he can't live with my power because I'm Italian and loud and came up by my own bootstraps, but a goddamn macho male chauvinist, in addition, too—"

Rod loved it. This was breakthrough.

Watkins had broken out in a faint sweat, a nice feeling, like after the first seven or eight minutes of a run. It smelled good to him. He felt ready to move and lightened. He didn't mind that it wasn't the sweat of running but of mental strife. It was combat, not anxiety. Evidently he was ready for the fray.

"Pete, you want to be anchorman of this little network, don't you?"

"No, laddy, anchorman of the whole poopydoo world! If folks would only listen, I could tell it straight."

"Ah," said Rod, coughing, "ah, Pete, I feel this should stay with the valid personally meaningful, if you'll allow me—"

"All is allowed, Rod." But Pete seemed to accept the rebuke and sank down into his aura. He was gathering his power around him. Back to Chuck and Mrs. Chuck.

Fred looked hurt. People seemed to have forgotten about his bisexuality. No one was caring. What was the point of coming out?

Chuck also felt discouraged. He had a problem which was real. Did these others think theirs were more real? Wasn't it obvious they did, and wasn't it obvious they were wrong—his was the most real?

Watkins cast his vote for Chuck. What could be realer than Mrs. Chuck? But Watkins seemed to be the only one who was willing to pass the torch of suffering to another. He credited Chuck with Chuck's misery. Was this interest in another a kind of—what Pete would call—mindfucking? The expression was getting on Watkins's nerves.

"I wish you'd stretch your vocabulary, Pete," he said.

"No violence!" Rod warned as Pete half rose from his half-lotus position. "Hit the pillows if you have to. Scream and smack the pillows."

Pete murmured Ommmm briefly, like a small boy playing

141

with his toy truck, then closed his eyes, his half-lotus the envy of the masses; he invited peace into his soul; then he said, "I pass."

"Thank you, thank you," said Rod. "We're learning and we're getting to be much better friends. But do we pay sufficient attention to each other? Anybody remember Fred came out of the closet a few mere minutes ago it seems? Anybody care to remember I said last time there was a measles epidemic raging in my personal family? What about Fred and me?"

"Calamine lotion," said Fred.

"That's for chicken pox. Measles is a different virus, scientifically related to shingles and other kinds of measles. But thank you for your contribution, Fred. And now I have a question for you: Is it anyone at all you happen to meet in the men's room when this thing comes on, Fred, or is it someone special, or something special about a certain someone?"

"I'm a chicken hawk," Fred said.

"Sir?" Rod was puzzled by vocabulary other than his own. Perhaps he was thinking of a virus, a pox. He sought to probe more deeply. "Fred? You said?"

"Chicken hawk. Rice queens such as Chinese boys. Dinge queens such as black boys. I like kids, real young ones. Chickens. When I'm in that mood, I'm a hawk, I pounce," he said bitterly, eyes downcast, eyelashes fluttering. "That's when I'm a man of power, too."

No one wanted him to cry. "Nonsense," said Chuck. "You've imagined all this. Do you ever suffer blackouts, sleepwalking?"

"Only when I'm sloshed to the gills," Fred said, "and my wife has to wipe me up and put me to bed. But I remember everything. *Especially what I wanted.*"

He added shyly, "That's where sometimes I'm ahead of you fellas."

Everyone wished Fred didn't make it so complicated for them. In his shy way he leaned on them. Pete said, "You're open, I'll say that. You tell what's in your mind, heart and pants. You're not like Watkins here, the mindfucker, who doesn't want to talk about his mail-order brides—probably poor Korean girls or farm runaways."

Rod was pulling his toes through his socks and making them crack. "So how does everybody feel today?" he asked. "Is everybody all right? I feel kind of peaceful and relaxed, except I wrote to General Motors to tell them how I feel about their cars, domestic production, is that how everybody sees it?"

Chuck perked up. He knew about production problems and American assembly lines, the competition from Japanese engineering, even if his know-how stopped at his wife. He had participated in a statistical study of how many automobiles put together on Friday tend to have errors in them; about the same as on Monday. And the Tuesday, Wednesday and Thursday U.S. cars weren't so good, either. Sunday they made no mistakes, but they made no cars. "Personnel is going down," he said. "Pride in workmanship. Even Canada."

"And your wife isn't," Pete cried, cackling, "she isn't going down."

Watkins gazed at Chuck. He was trying to remember the marriage in which Chuck dwelled, and to fit the sober former wrestler's body into the problem of the sober former wrestler's distraught mind and fretful soul. Is sex essential to a happy marriage? Is good engineering design sufficient to make good cars? Chuck wanted to be told. Why did the answer have to be yes, no or maybe? It had to be one of them. Or maybe it didn't. Tell Chuck. He wanted his wife to be right, but he wanted to be right, too. He wanted his history to be cleaned up. General Motors couldn't do it all by itself. He wanted to be comforted in his distress and they weren't doing it. "Empty heart is like an empty life," Watkins said.

"The Stones," said Chuck, surprising him by knowing the words. The song dated from that time long, long ago when Mick Jagger was young, not yet skeletal, hammering at the eminence of the Beatles, and Chuck and his wife used to grab at each other in a car at the Sputnik Drivein in Washington, Iowa, and gasping and coming with sticky fingers and they loved each other.

So he remembered that song. Long long ago, when a full heart was a full life, long high-school years ago.

"Yeah," Watkins said.

Chuck grinned. "Say, don't you have grown children already? And you're here?"

Doing a child's work, he meant.

"Yes, pal."

Chuck squirmed and wriggled; his plump thighs strained the seams of his pants. So needful of love—being called pal by a middle-aged man made him blush. A nice letter from a GM vice-president could make him warm all over. The pleasure and pain of clashing emotions, the pleasures of pain, reminded Watkins of something. What was it? Oh, of course—appetite. Not the need for food, more complex and mysterious than that. The appetite stirred by an upward rounded head with straight fair hair hanging and flying in the excitement of talk. Bethany laughing and pulling her knees up in bed and saying, "Ooosh, it's warm, I'm so prickly, look at those freckles." It was not the dream of pleasure which flooded Watkins's body as he looked at Chuck. It was the reality. It was desire for a specific living creature, it was Bethany. His ambition was to clasp a cloud in his arms.

Everyone was watching at him. Had he said something? Even Pete was silent, eyes wide and expectant. This group of boys was filled with desire; lust fueled the sarcasms, groans, laughs, whispers, shouts. Shadows of bicycles passed outside the drawn curtains of the windows of HumanHouse. The reflection of a bird or a Frisbee dove down the glass.

No wonder Watkins felt light and hungry afterward as he headed out across campus, and had indulgent and friendly feelings even for Pete Positano, and cozy warm ones for the other sufferers. He wasn't ready for work; not ready, either, to write to another box number. "Chuck?" he asked. "You want a coffee?"

"Sure thing," said Chuck, whose wife never asked him to sit a while over a cup of coffee. And as if continuing a conversation in the Engineer's Club: "Chrysler's no better. Ford is losing it. Toyota and Datsun, they're on track, especially Toyota. Do you ever do class-action suits, Watkins? I mean, a bunch of consumers who got a lemon get together? . . ."

Watkins was on a coffee date with a nervous, talkative young person. They sat in the student coop, amid all that delicious flesh, and Chuck was babbling about design defects, production defects, as if Watkins hadn't heard that his wife never put her product on the line. A girl in a gray velveteen running suit kept glancing over her French grammar textbook at Chuck, not Watkins. She liked hunks. Chuck didn't notice, and anyway, he wasn't involved in French grammar. That wasn't his field; he didn't care about Renault, Citroën or Peugeot. Watkins could learn to love French grammar; but of course he was too old for her, and that's a decisive accident of destiny.

13

Most of the women who reply to your box, Sir, must be freelance hookers. I am not. I am a blackjack dealer at Caesars Palace in Las Vegas, U.S.A. I am employed. That's my living. If I wanted to be a hooker, I'd hook, but instead I came here from Cambridge, Mass., to burn out my sinuses and find the money and time to do what I really want to do—translate the poetry of Tristan Corbière, who was a hunchback who died before he reached my age (I'm not old), and also to run on the desert. It's one of the few fashionable things I do—you might name it so-called jogging. The desert is lovely in the very early morning.

I am able to do these things, yet I am not happy. Content, yes; happy, no. So therefore if you wish to take a chance on a non-hooking poetry-translating blackjack dealer, I can get you a deal at the hotel and you can look at me at my table (Station 8) and no harm done if you just move on to the slots or the hookers and never even say hello. . . .

Her name was Linda King. The elements interested him—French poetry and blackjack in the Nevada desert. He imagined a skinnied-down, melancholic young woman with a falsely superior smile playing at the corners of her mouth. He could put up with that. He was interested.

He got a deal on the flight. True to her word—cool ironic regretful voice on the phone—she arranged a High Roller's Discount for him at the hotel. She sounded so greatly regretful that he said, "Look, I'd like to see the new electronic slots, anyway."

She laughed shyly, charmingly.

"You have no obligations at all," he said. "We'll just have a meal at some odd hour."

She laughed again and said all the hours were odd in Las Vegas, and wanted to keep him on the phone a while.

"Let's chat then," he said. "My nickel."

"You understand me," she said. "I'm worried about this whole thing."

"That's the first thing we have in common. We're both thinking: Is it a creep? Is it a crazy?"

"I don't know about you," she said, "but I have some doubts about me."

"Well, are you psychotic?" he inquired.

She considered the matter while they both heard dim cheerful voices from long-distances calls bound to them on the circuit. "I think the short answer is: not psychotic."

"There are—" he began, but she wasn't finished. She wanted to be fair.

"If you're quick, you can hide a lot. If you're troubled, as I am, you have reason to hide everything."

"Thank you for that," he said. "I appreciate. I started to say there are slow insults in all our lives. For one thing—attrition."

She listened in silence. He liked the fact she was paying attention, and hoped she would do that in person. "That's not quite what I meant," she said. "I hope you're not making this trip into the desert to have a discussion. Are you?"

"Whatever's right," he said. "I'll follow the leads I get."

Her laughter was nice and antedated the attrition she had suffered. It might be important to let her know he too was terrified about what he was doing, they were doing, but he was going to go ahead and he hoped she would too because if a person didn't go ahead he or she died a little. The way to say this by telephone did not come to him. He had the time and the money, but he didn't have what it required. It wasn't just a matter of sorting out the pronoun references. He was quite confident the way to say this in person might very well not come to him, either. Sometimes the gesture of a hand and the look of an eye helped, sometimes the heartbeat, sometimes even the will to be kind helped. Sometimes nothing helped. Knowing what he knew, and feeling Linda's distress even over the long-distance wire, and also feeling his own, he made a best effort.

"I can't be any weirder than what you meet there," he said.

"I meet nobody if I don't choose to meet him or them. But if you pass by Station Eight and want to leave a message, maybe we could"—her laughter was very shy and nervous—"we could have the special steak-and-eggs breakfast, served between eleven P.M. and seven A.M."

"That gives us a lot of time selection on the special," he said. "I'm a big spender. We can have it any time."

The night before he flew Frontier to Las Vegas, insomnia knocked inside him like the wrong gas in a motor—snarlingly protesting what was going on. It could be about Linda King. He knew it was about Bethany. Perhaps he didn't know.

Morning came and an airline ticket flapped in his hand. A commercial on his car radio repeated itself into his ears as he rode the short flight. The Electrojet bucked in a desert cloud-storm, befitting a western airplane. *How do you spell Relief?* the voice asked with rhythm, resonance and confidence. The answer would come very soon now.

With the weight of another, he thought. That's how you spell *Relief,* not *Rolaids.*

This city of Las Vegas was about planning to be a winner; as dangerous as planning to fall in love, all hope and dream and actual loss. People kept coming back for more. Was he planning to fall in love? No sir, just here for the fun of it, your Honor. Genius may be the art of taking pains—being a lover required taking not too many pains.

This is worse than tennis, Bethany.

He wished he could sleep better alone.

In the lap of the airport the electronic slots blinked with their compressed radium glow. He blinked back in a swelling desert heat which struck him in the face like a magic pain wand. His cab was air conditioned. Caesars Palace greeted him, a tape loop sounding at the entrance from speakers hidden in cement seashells. *"Welcome to Caesars Palace, Thy Pleasure Dome! Thy show in thy Showroom tonight is Cher, her Revue, her Band and her Charm. Thou must enjoy thy stay or discuss with thy assistant manager. Welcome to Caesars Palace, Thy Pleasure Dome! Thy show in thy Showroom tonight . . ."*

He checked in and reported to thy desk clerk that he didn't need a porter. A man in a shiny black suit of the sort worn by Frank Sinatra's non-show-business friends circa 1960 stood watching at the desk clerk's side as he registered. His room was in Thy Swimming Pool Access Section. A guide past the acres of slot machines, row on row, might have been helpful. He found the room, touched flocking on the walls thick enough to break a fall, lifted a hand to the air conditioning, abandoned his clothes, ran barefoot to the pool. Ah, nice. He swam and quieted the jangle within and without.

Watkins lay by the pool, three-quarters in shade, tanning only his feet, and listened to the gossip of two pretty young ladies with two hefty older men who kept answering telephone pages. "I met one of those photographers, pepperzinis, you know, chase a person to Dieseldorf or wherever you're going if you're famous, get the shot. The guy I'm with this time isn't in the celebrity business, hopefully. He's a big real estate mongol—complexes."

"Builds them or sells them?"

"Hopefully both. For senior-type citizens. No kids, all the pets your heart's desire. He's a famous biggie in that line. And there are more senior-type citizens every day. It's a growing field."

"Has he got the time of day for you?"

"Hopefully. He says he wants to rest in the warm, mature but not fat like his ex—in the arms of a twenty-two-year-old who really understands him."

"With me," said the other woman, "it's somewhat similar. Only I'm twenty-six."

"You don't look it."

"Neither do you. It's choosing carefully, isn't it? When I was in Beverly Hills this producer guy I was breaking up with, it was more a trip than a worthwhile experience, I went to this free-lance lesbian mystic, sort of holistic, and she said not to bother getting any older, nobody would appreciate it . . ."

Watkins dozed. His feet grew pink. He was comforted.

He woke with a start and it was no more than ten minutes later. Linda's letter had seemed a little stiff—uneasy—but he could understand that. He took a quick splash in the pool to chase away the shadows. He came out, stood in the shade and blotted himself with a towel. The two non-twenty-two-year-olds were now exchanging their life's stories in whispers, probably had come to the intimate stuff. A man nearby—narrow chested, in a flowered shirt, with a gray tan and a pinched face—noticed that Watkins was alone and said, "Here we are at Caesars Palace, one of the top hotels. I never take her to the Best Western, and like Rodney Dangerfield says, my wife don't give me no respeck. I should live so long. She wouldn't even come to the pool with me."

"I understand, I understand," said Watkins, and dashed across the cement, hoping his wet feet would protect him from the radiating desert blaze. The man in the black suit, not looking hot at all, the one who had stood by the desk clerk when he registered, moved out of his way slowly so that he could enter the hotel. The moment of blocking him made his heels and toes burn. The man was wearing a black silk suit that needed a tie, not a gold chain. He was wearing a gold chain.

Linda had given him her hours and her station, and he decided to follow her instructions. He would watch her dealing at blackjack for what that could tell him. He would not run away. He did not know what he would be staying for. Let it happen, he thought, however it happens. It doesn't happen when I work at it.

Position G, Station 8. She didn't know what time he would show up. In any case, programmed to deal with snap the cards, watch and rake the cards and money, there could be no exchange of shy greetings on the floor—maybe not even a sign of heartbeat or interest from her. The pit boss, if that's what he was called, a brown and curly refugee from some war-torn Middle

Eastern nation, viewed the action from his orbiting space satellite behind the dealers. Dead pans were the smart facial attire on both sides of the tables.

Linda King. Her face looked a bit greenish under the forever-midnight glow. Too much makeup. Perhaps that masklike greenishness was part of the modus operandi for women dealers; no clocks and no time allowed on this flesh. Although trial work wasn't Watkins's chief interest here, he approached with the creepy sensation of plea bargaining. Why was he guilty of having written to her? He had only replied to her letter, which had replied to his advertisement, which Bethany had placed without his knowledge—he was framed! He was innocent! But then again, he would have to take the rap. Even a man struggling for a merciful verdict recognized that to pass the blame to Bethany—and therefore to Linda—was the coward's way. He was not sure he wanted justice. He just wanted to come out of this tunnel.

Linda didn't recognize him yet. At her table a lonely young gambler, soft, plumply pretty, with cowboy boots, Indian shirt hanging loose over his jeans, gold chain with some sort of medallion—a crucifix, by God—bouncing on his chest hairs, sat brooding in front of his chips and cards. Linda was raking them away. Jesus had turned His back on the blackjack cowboy.

As he watched, it suddenly occurred to Watkins that Bethany regretted what she had done—Bethany was jealous—Bethany knew he was having marvelous adventures with ardent and adventurous women—and with this junk thought to give him a quick rush, he approached Linda, muttering, as if in English and by phone, "Watkins here. Hello. What now?"

Through whited lips—well, the climate was dry—she said, "I'll ring your room at midnight when I get off. A half hour after. I want a swim first, get the smoke and air conditioning out of my face. Now scoot, there's no socializing across the table."

Kind of neutral, Watkins thought.

As he pushed through the rows of clicking, swirling, tingling slots toward the wing of Thy Palace where his room lay, he was wondering if Linda King was a true American woman and would be twenty minutes late. Making a date at ten to 1:00 A.M. might change the rules. Or if she was really a miracle person who could swim, wash the distraction away, take care of her hair and hike to his wing of thy money-extraction maze by midnight and a half.

A man in a teal blue coat tapped him on the shoulder as he turned the key in his lock. "Sir?" the teal blue person asked. A photograph was pinned to the badge on his lapel. "Sir?"

"Yes?" Watkins hadn't stolen any chips, picked a purse or left a drink unpaid for.

"Sir, she says make that one o'clock. Thank you, sir."

Watkins lay down for a nap, gazing at Thy Ceiling. The man in the uniform jacket might have been a vice-president of Caesars Palace (well-tailored jacket) or a Thy Bus Boy (it was a uniform, after all, with security data). He dozed. It didn't matter. "May Thy Dreams Be of Gain Beyond Riches," the tape had said. His dreams were not of those.

Watkins dozed, but anxiety continued to knock inside him, protesting what was going on beneath the hood. He lay among the monuments, chapels, tombs and crematoria of Caesars Palace ("Thy Better'n Ever"), and it seemed his toes could sense the reverberations of the Circus Maximus show with Ann-Margret, or maybe it was the Cleopatra's Barge Lounge, with Bruce Westcott, Continuous, 9:00 P.M. to 3:00 A.M., or the action in Caesars Bar, where the B.S. Trio was Ultimo Tasty. Thy Glitz, Thy Funsies, Thy French Chicken-of-the-Sea Dining, Thy Pinkie Rings.

Bethany had only meant to help. Convention City and slots and the pickup trucks and campers roving up and down the Strip, the drivers carrying paper bags around their bottles— what did she have in mind for him? Or did she only want to free her conscience, off-loading Watkins, and did she think a fearsome triviality would do it?

Although sure he couldn't sleep, he woke with a start at twenty after twelve. Probably Linda was making long sweeping breaststrokes across the pool. He was taking a shower. Linda was brushing smoke and chlorine out of her hair, since she

153

didn't have time for wash and rinse. He was tying his shoes. It was nearly one. He opened the door and saw a man in boxer shorts putting a room-service tray out into the hall. In the hall, smell of dead cigarets and air conditioning. No footsteps clattering toward him.

He sat under the lamp and read *Thy Personal Guide to Caesars Palace* and wished he had brought something else to read and remembered he had. He went to his bag. There were two shy light knocks at the door.

"Hi."

She entered and seemed to glide around the room. She was not so tall as she looked behind her table of green baize. Her hair was wet from the pool. She wore white jeans, a filmy white Indian blouse over some sort of shiny silk; she wore low-heeled sandals. She wore a little lacework of been-around, been-around-in-the-desert lines around her eyes and mouth. Smile lines, one could call them. He turned, watching her as she measured his room.

"Nice place they gave you."

"Aren't they all basically the same?"

"Yes. But I never visit the gamblers' rooms."

"I'm not a gambler," he said.

"And I'm visiting your room," she said. "High roller, aren't you?" He ducked his head winsomely. "So am I, but it's between us. No house take on this deal."

She studied a scene of Montmartre which someone had copied from Utrillo. "Thine own Utrillo," he said.

She sat down abruptly, patted the chair nearby and said, "I've got it. A terrific idea. Let's agree, okay? No sex."

"Uh."

"This has nothing to do with any inspection of you. You look clean and attractive. But obligation is making us crazy, Watkins, so if we just—"

"How about," he said, "to keep the romance going, why don't we just say no obligation?"

"That's better. I like your language. Just one further codicil: on your part or on mine."

"Signed and attested," he said.

She sighed and looked relieved. She said, "If you can afford it, order a bottle of champagne from room service."

He moved to the phone. "Are you hungry?"

"Not necessarily."

Champagne and little sandwiches, Thy Assortment. Later he too could shove a tray out into the hall.

When strangers meet, powerfully mauled by expectations and events, they might either make love or tell their life's stories. Of these two choices, they were now doing, alas, the more intimate thing. "I can see you like my looks," she said. He nodded, *I do.* "Neat, tidy, clean and I move well." He nodded. "But I don't like to swim in the daytime. I don't sun. I have this incision from a ruptured appendix." She considered, then offered the truth. "A cesarean section. They can make it fine-line smooth sometimes, but it got infected, fingernails, I was crazy, no, distraught, but it's like a spiderweb—"

He didn't ask whose fingernails. He didn't ask where the baby was.

"So I'm like a tidy pretty woman who knows she's ugly inside. I'm a neat, clean, tidy one who knows, soon as a man looks at me, I'm messy and . . . They call those scars that stick up 'proud flesh.' "

He heard himself uttering words which surprised him. "Let me see."

"Are you listening, sir?"

He shrugged. "That just came out. I'd like to suggest I was just expressing sympathy in a peculiar way—"

"To show you don't mind. You sure it doesn't turn you on?"

"I don't think so."

"Off?"

"I can't judge in advance."

She began to unloosen the belt of her white jeans. And then she stopped and began to laugh. "Let us stipulate, Watkins, one important matter with one less important submatter. We are both embarrassed. It makes us kind of funny with each other."

"Not easy," he said, liking her a little.

155

"And ease is what we have been aiming for so long and not getting at all."

He liked her quite a lot.

She rehooked her belt, showed him no proud flesh just now.

He urged her to go on with her story, her turn first before his. He promised he would not find her unfeminine or whining or egocentric or anything else on the minus side of the universe, but very, very interesting. And his turn would come. So she said she had gone to college in Connecticut, but not a famous college, a branch of the state university. And since she was discouraged by the class, charm, wealth and confidence which surrounded her, and wanted some, she dropped out. Never mind the logic. And then since she was pretty, she took a job near the money, in an art gallery in New Haven. But that was dumb. A receptionist, and it was one of those tourist decorator galleries. You know, Indians in full headdress and cows flying around with violins. Real Schlock plus imitation schlock. But she got the idea of selling paintings. And this man suggested she advertise a few prints, a few oils as if she were a private party, sacrifice, must sell, personal reasons, and when the suckers came to her house explain they were an inheritance from her dear grandfather— wear black for the occasion—and just wanted them out. . . . Incidentally, by this time she was living with the owner of the grief-infected artworks. She despised Salvador Dali, melted or stiff, real or fake.

Through him, she met a hotel executive from Las Vegas.

When she got tired of being a private, low-overhead art dealer she accepted an invitation for a trip to a warm dry climate.

That broke up rather quickly. "Not till after my birthday," she said. "I waited till I got my birthday present from him."

Her birthday present was the tuition to enroll in blackjack school. "It's a mechanical thing. There are a few mechanical and moral aptitudes. The rules weren't beyond me. You need an IQ of one hundred ten, of which I have much better, and no prison record, of which I don't have any. I cleared. I got this job at Caesars Palace."

She stopped.

"That's not really a life's story you're telling me," Watkins remarked. "That's a few selected scenes. It's barely a short subject drawn from the basic life's story. You're holding back."

She smiled. "A Tall Tale and True, from Legendary Time Past. Think of me as Tinkerbell, Watkins. I sure am holding back—damn right. Won't you, also? Okay, holding back, but no lies. Somewhere in there, not necessary to tell how or why, there is also a child. *Ex*-child," she said. "I'm going to see her again Christmas, I think, maybe next summer. Her father kept her because he loved me so much."

"That must hurt."

"Revenge is sweet. Now about you, I'd prefer if you don't give me the gore and pain because I can guess it from here—your face, Watkins—without you saying anything. I can *see* it, man. It has to do with women, your mother, your wife"—he was shaking his head—"or some other women."

"All of the above. Of course you're right. But since I obviously am not out of a job or paralyzed—"

"You can be a philosopher about it. A scientist. You're *interested* in your own love life, which doesn't happen to be the case with everyone, Watkins. It's rare at your age." He felt his eyelids crinkle. It wasn't fatigue. It was itch from something that got through the barrier of the air conditioning, or maybe just the late hour. "Grief has made you thoughtful," she said, "but jeez, maybe it's only thoughtful about *love.*"

"Thank you."

"You're a love pervert."

"These errors fill the world," he said.

"The cracks widen and that's what it is, Watkins."

She was plainly delighted with her suitor, her gentleman come to call with conversation in Caesars Palace. "So after all that former disappointment, we say it's not a bad life!" she cried. "Are you unhappy? I'm not. I swear by all I hold dear—I'm not! Of course, I hold nothing dear anymore, Watkins."

He squirmed. He had always drawn the line at discussing happiness-unhappiness with strangers, and even, in fact, with friends. With Vic, he had talked some nights through, but that

157

was a long time ago, student days. He wasn't going to change now, just because he was in a hotel room in Las Vegas at 2:00 A.M. with a new stranger, one of his best strangers. She surely had a man in Las Vegas, maybe someone right here in Caesars Palace, but she wasn't telling because it was none of his business and if she wanted to tell him she would and, he decided, if it mattered at all, he wouldn't be invited to visit her, would he?

With an uneasy sense that logic didn't logically apply everywhere, he turned these thoughts away. There might be someone she did not hold dear.

It was his turn. He mentioned his marriages—not bad, not good, although the divorces seemed mostly bad. He mentioned his law practice and hastened to add he was not a really *rich* lawyer, in case she thought she might have a birthday coming; a prosperous small-town attorney, which is another matter. Since she came to Las Vegas from the East, she might not know that Davis—solar Davis, bicycle-riding Davis, university Davis —was one of the small boom towns in California. He didn't want to seem a sugar- or even a natural-honey daddy. He mentioned that he carried no herpes, no high blood pressure, no outstanding physical defects—hobbies were running, tennis, swimming, Vivaldi, Bach, Couperin and a social conscience. "A typical California upper-middle person," he said glumly. "Now I have no secrets from you."

Yet he did. He might have been able to tell her about premature ejaculation, if such had been the case; about bankruptcy, disbarment, child-murdering, if such had been the cases. Such were not the cases. But he could not tell her the name Bethany. He could not say that Bethany had written the advertisement and picked his possible future loves for him. All he said was, "A disappointment . . . she wouldn't leave her husband."

"I won't ask you more, since it's obviously a tender subject," said Linda.

Watkins worked at it, trying hard, and finally broke the silence. "Patricia Ann," he muttered, "was her name."

The heavens did not open up and strike him dead. The truth is not possible, he thought. It is not always even necessary.

Linda King's gaze upon him seemed to waver a little. "This kind of conversation," she said, "I mean talking about everything is what I mean—it's tiring. It's not negative, but is it really positive? I wonder if it's too much, too soon."

"Too much what?"

"Usually people just goof around and play and that's so *easy*, Watkins. Courtship, you know—modern courtship. But this telling so much truth, little broken pieces of the truth, it's worse than tiring. Aren't you exhausted?"

"I thought it was the desert, the traveling."

"It's the tension, my dear Patricia Ann's friend. Are you sure you don't have active herpes and that's why you're so amenable? To talk?"

"I'd know if I did," he answered. "I take Vitamin C."

"So do I. With rose hips. The natural acerola. I'm a native-born health person." She held up her hand to silence him. Just because she was talking nonsense, and they both knew it, was no reason to interrupt. "So are you native-born to health, I suppose. Look, have you been to Veronica Velveeta's shop in the mall? Get some natural vitamins, validate your ticket? I need to sleep on things for a while, Watkins. It's been a long day. Why don't you get oriented? And I'll sleep and get myself oriented, would that be satisfactory?"

She smiled into his eyes and looked away. One of the things he had begun to like about her was how she looked into his eyes and smiled, and did not bite the smile off when she looked away, but continued to smile as if some mist of him still commanded her attention. One of the things that also worried him about her was how the smile continued, a vagueness, as if the person did not know he was no longer there. Well, he was there, but she was looking at the wall and she was still smiling.

"I'll go easy on you," he said.

"Yes, please do," she said. She showed her nice even teeth, California teeth they even had in Nevada these days. "If I give you the chance."

It was confusing. He was hard to please, he knew. He had been punished and he was needful and suspicious. Something

159

about her smile was reassuring and something was unsettling. Something was vague and something was almost as sharp as Bethany. Maybe it was just her sending him away for a while and he didn't want to go. At least she didn't test him on Tristan Corbière.

Night plus day, he thought, equals sunrise, and day plus night equals sunset. And this lady is ambiguous about me.

"You visit the town a little," she said. "We've gotten sort of acquainted, which is strenuous, so let's rest now."

"It would be easy to rest together," he said clumsily. Little-boy wince pretended it was a joke.

"So much sex comes from embarrassment, you know? I mean, people can't think what to do or say next, so they—"

"Don't I know," he said.

"We'll do it differently. Maybe no better, but since we're doing everything differently from real human beings, why not this?"

"I'm real!" he said. "I'm stupid but real!"

"And you're nice, too. I mean it. If you weren't, maybe I'd just fuck you good-bye and disappear, but don't we both know about that? I really do kind of like you, Watkins," she remarked, and it was almost like a puff of smoke as she disappeared. A throb of neon. A pulsation of Las Vegas middle-of-the-night glow.

He continued his night's sleep. When he woke, the day was blazing. He could visit Veronica Velveeta or put on his Saucony shoes and shorts and work out the craziness by running along the Strip. In this heat, this fierce oven, run? That would be crazier than the craziness. In this heat, this oven, visit a Veronica Velveeta, a woman with a name like that whom he didn't even know? But she ran a travel agency and he needed to postpone his departure by a day or two. She could endorse the ticket. So it was almost sensible.

In the Desert Mall, down Las Vegas Boulevard from his hotel (taxi, white-flecked lips on the driver, too-small tip for a short run), he found The Trips Agency, Veronica Velveeta, Manager. It was a long narrow room papered with posters depicting Maui,

160

Tahiti, Acapulco and Nice, all featuring the same all-purpose native maiden, her breasts, her nipples. Beneath the posters a row of heavily mustached ladies answered phones and swung on their rotating chairs. It was not so much that they had mustaches, actual hair lying slickly in place, as that they were dark and heavily made up and their skin glistened and the shadows above their lips shone like cat's whiskers in moonlight. They talked quickly and confidentially about rental cars, three-day weekends with double-occupancy, free tokens for slots and drinks and vouchers for lounge shows. A crew of hookers undergoing recycling as telephone solicitors. Watkins didn't think too deeply on the subject. Which was Veronica?

From an inner office came Veronica Velveeta, also dark, slender and rakishly mustachioed, greeting him in an accent of some borough of New York which was not Manhattan. Watkins was ready to contend that neither her maiden nor her married name was Velveeta. "Linda King sent me," he explained, "and said I should ask particularly for you, about changing my reservation—"

"Any girl here can validate," she remarked, "it's a talent they all develop, but did Linda say *particularly*?" She beckoned him behind the counter. "Come into my office, Wat, the air conditioning is mellower. What she meant"—closing the door—"what Linda means is clear. And she might be right, but we can't be sure yet."

Why does this always seem to happen, Watkins the Lamb asked as he was being led into an *abattoir* of the Desert Mall, when you think you don't want it to happen, and not happen when you think you want it to happen?

He was thinking these thoughts because the well-creamed dark lady of the upper lip was kindly making a sandwich of his light poplin pants between her two well-creamed bunlike hands. Impatiently, compassionately, she unzipped. Of course he could resist. It might have been proper to do so. But adrift as he was, and not so sure of himself as he used to be—and the nice smells of the velvety lady, and the yielding of the wide leatherlike couch, and the softly creamed hands . . . He let it happen. Oh, oh, oh, and it happened.

She smiled at him. "No obligations, no quid pro quo asked or expected. Absolutely not any reciprocity intended. You don't have to think you owe me anything, Watkins, that would spoil my trip. Just go down on me a little."

Why, he hardly knew her. She was only the friend of an acquaintance. But perhaps in Las Vegas you don't need a long period of precunnilingus sharing and trust. He said: "What I'd rather do, if you're a runner, is we take a run together."

She perked up. "You said runner, not jogger. I like that. And the truth be told, Watkins, I'd like that better myself."

"Thank you."

"A person can get oral sex any time, but try to find someone who's into health and running in this town! I mean, if they are, they're also for Jesus." She was slipping into neat little shorts, a little terry halter, Nikes with those feminine little neckless socks. "*Voilà!*" she said. "Let's do it. I'm blushing already. I've got the measles all over. Running really arouses me, Watkins, puts the gurr in me."

"I appreciate, but I'd like to run with you—"

She looked at him, aghast. "My God!" she cried. "My God! How inconsiderate of Veronica! Why didn't I think of *you*, only what *I* wanted? Dressed in resort wear, not running! Oh, my apologies, I'll drive you back to the Palace and you can get your gear. And we can talk."

What she liked about Las Vegas, she told him, chattering happily as she steered her air-conditioned Impala, is that it's not the scene of the crime. That is, places where people are raised always seem to reproach people. You can't help being reminded of your parents and all they did wrong, and of your marriage or marriages and all you and the other concerned parties did wrong. But in Vegas, well, it's not home. It's like living in Paris or Rome—she bet Watkins had never considered this—it's like being an exile, you know, an escapee, you know, an an, an—

"An expatriate."

"That's it! An expate, and you're fresh, you're free, everything is how you want it, plus there is real money to be made in so many different ways—a dear close friend of mine invented a whole-grain honey-yogurt Shampoo of the Stars—"

"I can see why you're a friend of Linda's," he said.

"We talk too much?"

"You're both thinkers."

She smiled brilliantly—the mustache less gleamy in the bright sunlight—and said, "Plus doers. I probably won't tell her what we did, or more precisely what I did to you, since I gather you're interested in her."

"Thank you," he said.

"Veronica won't tell her," she said, "because Veronica probably doesn't have to. She knows. She's like a little psychic, too, where all the bodies are buried."

He didn't thank her for this information.

"Aren't we women full of surprises for you men?" Veronica asked. "That's just because we're unpredictable."

"I brought shoes and stuff. These days I have to take care of myself."

"Make that your personal choice, Watkins. You men are just as wild for me, too. I figured you for a golfer and cocktails, not a runner—surprise!—even though there's a nice hint of leanness around your jaw and thighs."

"Thank you," he said once more.

"You'll have to stop saying that," she advised him. "I'll get conceited. But it's just another of those Paris or Rome things I was talking about in Vegas—a kind of natural Old World European courtesy. It's how we make it in the travel agency, too, plus a little Teamsters business."

She offered to keep her motor running and wait for him in the Impala while he changed into running clothes because she hated the plastic greediness and the recorded voices and clangs and bells and shrieks of Caesars Palace. ("They make Ex Thou a minute, but who needs money if that's the price?") Or maybe she would just park the car and they would start running from the Impala, down to the MGM Grand, past the memories of terrible fire, where so many died and the insurance was such a bitch, across the Strip that direction—"Go get dressed, darling."

163

He hurried, aware of all the gas she was using to keep the air conditioning going. But she was doing stretches in the blazing sunlight, waiting for him, and Veronica Velveeta was saying, almost as if she were talking to someone standing in his spot on the Caesars Palace parking coliseum just an instant before he arrived to stand in it himself, his feet sweating already in his Sauconys: "I'm not homesick here, *unh*. Homesickness is a longing, *unh*, for something you don't have in yourself, something Veronica is missing in her own being. I used to think a husband, a stall shower, a microwave oven would stop the homesickness. *Unh*. So we use sex for that purpose, but of course." She stretched on her toes and reached for the sky. "Running really sweats it out—you want to run?"

He nodded.

They ran.

"It's an attempt," she muttered. She was finishing a thought. Probably it was the one about making love.

Watkins understood why Veronica Velveeta was a good friend for Linda, but he did not understand why he was running with her, and why he had done what he had done with her, since he really liked (was attracted to) Linda, unless Linda planned it that way, to test out the attractiveness in some manner he didn't understand very much or sympathize with at all. Nevertheless, just as he really liked Linda, he also enjoyed the freedom of running with Veronica Velveeta after they had sweetly made a kind of love which had little to do with her pleasure.

He decided she had developed an unnaturally close and precious relationship with herself. "You are a liberated woman," he said.

"Don't talk. Breaks breath. Some people say you should only run hard enough to keep a good conversation going, you know what I mean, not too hard, but in this heat, in this heat . . ."

He kicked a pebble and she winked at him. "Concrete," she said, "not even a real rock. You know what I mean. Even the natural desert stuff comes from man-made materials. Lost Wages, Nevada. The real desert's under Caesars Palace, all that

Old World charm and blackjack tables, but you'd have to dig through the chips to find it."

"Interesting," he said.

"You can talk. I guess you got a good wind for a guy your age. Let me give you an example . . ."

To give him an example of Old World unreality and inflation in the desert, she told how many thou it cost to lease her narrow shop in the Desert Mall, where all the ladies with dark upper lips took orders for air travel both in the sky and on the ground by luxury Trailways. He forbore asking why she considered luxury Trailways a form of air travel. One foot ahead of the other. He forbore asking how she could come out with a profit and she appreciated his discretion. So she told him. "I have this associate. The deal works for him. Laundering some money he handles." She was breathing regularly and deeply, but due to the running, the sentences were coming more crisply. "Good friend. Few years ago. Killed you. Would have killed you for what I did to you. An hour ago."

He was grateful for this posthumous warning.

"Mellower now. Good friends and business associates. Wouldn't kill you today. Doubt even check up anymore. How little he cares. Just close friends and I launder his money. Is all," she panted.

Something in the peaceful mood of this roaming along the gritty road, with the desert sun beating down on the giant poured concrete and glass toys which money had transported onto the sand, with the friendly Mafiosa chatting comfortably about getting into health and murder and her affection for all people, especially androgynous young men, not counting Watkins as such, of course, neither particularly young nor particularly androgynous, especially since she had done her time with the strong-smelling cigar-smoking macho sort—something in the pleasant exertion and the feeling of strength and release which came over Watkins made him feel he was running along a cool river, a kind of babbling at his sides, his lungs bombarded by the proper sorts of ions, negative ones, emitted by the babbling lady; he was feeling good; it was the high of the runner. He was grateful to Veronica, to Linda, to Bethany, to the complex luck of life on earth.

"Maybe the only skinny kid who got real close to Howard Hughes in his long-toenail phase. Not a Mormon. That's not his religion. Teamster was his religion."

Like many young women who have been hurt, have overcome the pain, once Veronica began to talk about a former lover with an understanding older man, a person with distinguished gray at his temples and firm thighs suitable for senior half-marathons, she sought to be complete about it. Not that love was ever complete. Even at the crest of mystic feelings of wholeness during the runner's high, one still had toes, one still might sense a drop of sweat tickling someplace.

"Howard thought he was a comer and so do I, but he came already. So now it's launder launder launder, Wat, all the livelong day."

It didn't seem like the time and the place for mystic feelings of wholeness with the universe, but who was Watkins to look a gift in the neck and deny it?

About this cool mental valley with its cool river shedding waterfall gusts of delightful ions over the embankment: In real life, Watkins and Veronica were now running past two hookers in hot pants, one black, one white, the black one in white satin pants with a gold chain loosely falling over her hips, the white one in black satin pants with a silver chain which was the twin of the gold one. The tight lines of their buttocks were pinched by the fitted costume. They strolled arm in arm, elbows linked, swinging along and giggling at the sight of the runners. "Hey man, look at them *crazy* dudes," said the white one, and the black one said, "We could compose a good combo," and the white one said, "Hey, you need somebody, it's a job for two, lick that sweat off you guys?" and the black one said, "You chaps use a little Clark County massage, get that hardworking salty feeling off you? . . ."

And they were still chattering, first one, then the other, taking turns, as Watkins and Veronica ran by. Evidently they had

166

enjoyed a prosperous morning already, or perhaps they were high on coke or some other girl's helper, because the invitation was offered in good-natured fashion and rejection of it was accepted in the same spirit. "Hey, bye now, babies!" They went on giggling and clutching each other, elbows linked, gold and silver chains clashing in the sunlight. "See y'all now!"

Veronica ran Watkins safely back to the hotel. The greeny glade of ions and vale of mental cheer tended to fade, but Watkins still felt good. "You'll have a nice shower and rest. You'll sleep. Give all my love to Linda."

She unlocked the Impala and said, "Whew. Car heat."

And she was gone, waving good-bye and leaning so he could see her darkly mustached face in the rearview mirror.

An Eldorado pulled into the lot with two old friends delightedly waving at him and making laughing motions with their mouths and sticking out their tongues, too—the Clark County girls in hot pants. A chauffeur sat in front. Between the two women perched a hunched and sad little man, not yet cheered up as he soon would be, surrounded by Clark County vistas everyplace he looked or reached. What need had he of negative ions?

The stall shower is truly one of the great American inventions, assuming it is truly American, Watkins decided. Needles tingled over him, hot, then cold, then hot and cold again. He dried himself with a towel the size of a blanket, and then dropped naked into an acre of bed. It was no trouble to sleep. Thank you, all. He thought not about Linda, not about events of the recent or distant past, not about Veronica Velveeta and his good run and his practice of law; he concentrated, as if some fever were receding, on sinking without a ripple. Oh, good. He slept.

Linda must have known one of the maids. Perhaps she had a master key. She was sitting on the bed and studying him when he awakened. He seemed to come awake naturally, not to be awakened. "Like a baby," she said. "Even the grossest men sleep like babies—you're not gross, however."

His mouth felt as if he were. He wouldn't tell her this, and he wouldn't be kissing her until after he brushed his teeth, if then.

"How was Veronica?"

"Wuh?"

A trill of laughter. Lightly she touched his shoulder; a familiar caress it might have been. He glared at her, sitting up in bed like a patient looking at the doctor who has come with the news that from now on his temperature will be taken by the nurse in the way *she* prefers. His knees were pulled up under the sheet. He was protecting his modesty as she went on being happy.

"You're nice," she said. "Who could resist Veronica? I just thought we might put that whole subject behind us for the time being. For your sake. Veronica offered to help. The other person whose ad I answered—you're not my first love, dear—was as nice as you but a little, oh, I'd call it feeble. He didn't get any respect from his wife, he told me. He raised three kids, a boy sixteen, boy fourteen, girl twelve, but never any respect. When we had coffee, uh, afterwards, he counted out some *dimes* for the tip. And he kept his eye on those dimes when he asked me, down in the coffee shop, if it had been satisfactory for me on a scale of one to ten. You know? Was it *satisfactory*? Can you imagine? As if anyone knows, anyway? I think he wanted me to tell him about my kid."

Watkins glanced up sharply. Before they reply to my box, they reply to other boxes.

"Used to live in Washoe with her dad. He's married to a girl who has everything—young, good-looking and stupid. Which is how my daughter'll grow up. But what could I do better for her? Maybe I could see her way to be smarter, but what good is that, Watkins?"

"That's a difficult question. You've had a hard time to be so, well, cynical. It's not necessary."

"While you were sleeping," she said, "I looked in your wallet to see what your real name is, your age, whatever I could find. I didn't touch the money. Didn't lift a credit card. Thanks for telling the truth as far as you went, Watkins."

"You're thoughtful," he said, and feeling kind of good all at

168

once (compliments helped), just lumbered out of bed, his dong hanging, his sinewy behind as visible as it might be, and ambled across to the bathroom, where he shut the door but did not lock it. He peed. He brushed his teeth. He gave special attention to the gums.

When he returned, she had laid out his clean clothes for him.

"You're okay," she said.

"So are you."

"When it comes right down to it . . ." But she didn't finish this sentence. He didn't know what happened when it came right down to it. When he was nicely covered, she said, "Is that it for now? You've had your adventure?"

"I'll go," he said. "You've had yours."

She watched him pack and told him her story. She was a reader of the *National Enquirer*, Guillaume Apollinaire and Tristan Corbière. "Those French writers of sixty years ago are *really* sexy and dirty," she said. "They're so suggestive, I mean. I mean Turn of the Century. *Après guerre* is sort of what I mean, too." She had also had a daughter at fifteen, and the child was not really a child anymore, and after a few years in Washoe, now her parents were raising Elise, Lise, as their daughter in San Diego. The kid's father needed to devote all his time to the wife who had everything. "When I go to see my kid, I'm like a big sister, a sort of half sister."

"Must be difficult," he said.

"I don't have maternal feelings for her. I like her. I feel like a big sister."

"You remind me of someone."

"I know, I know. Your old ladyfriend who did you wrong, Watkins."

She smiled. It must often have been the case for Linda.

"She's also funny," he said.

"They do a person wrong, the funny ones."

"Explain that to me, please."

Instead, she told him more about herself. Blackjack dealer; he knew that. Former French student with Aid to Dependent Children plus scholarship to help support her kid; he didn't know

169

that. Now sometimes girl friend of a certain prince in Monaco. "Not an Arab, I'll give you a hint."

"Rainier?"

"I only give one hint."

She lived in the asphalted heat of the desert here. The Clark County cops waved to her from their Fords and Mercurys. She was a native-born accountant at heart, she said, although she fucked up and that's how she got into poetry and gaming instead. She thought she might make poetry of the save-up-for-holidays, pre-honeymoon-test-drive visitors in Las Vegas. The ones who browsed in the Nieman-Marcus or the Bullocks at the new mall. The timid animals and the rough ones. "I'm good at dealing cards for the same reason a paraplegic is good at having no use of his legs. I can't do anything else." And then she added with a winsome smile: "You think I might be compelled to imagine you with Veronica, as if I'm jealous, but I can't. I can't possibly imagine it. It's as if I can't see sex as a movie or jealousy. But when people lose more money than they can afford, at my table, I mean, I always know. I think I can imagine the pain of others. Am I correct in thinking I can do this? I see them creeping off to throw up in their rooms, or to tell lies to the person who came with them, or to themselves. How come I'm such a freak, Watkins? And did you realize you laid yourself open to a freak in the columns of that newspaper?"

He looked at her and confessed that he too wrote poetry. In times of need, he did. It was someone to talk to. He apologized for mentioning it. He paused.

She said she wanted to hear a poem. He said he couldn't recite them, he could only remember the idea. She asked him to tell her the idea. As best as he could remember it, he said.

She stopped. She was waiting.

"A woman's body is like the sea," he recited. "It holds the heat at night, it holds the heat in the winter . . ."

"But a person can drown," she said.

"How did you know? How did you know?" he demanded angrily.

This woman was dangerous. He wondered if he had enough

hope remaining to get interested in an intelligent woman with no manners.

"What's your idea of being married, I mean being good-together married, Watkins?"

"Should I tell you?"

She had asked, she said, did she have to repeat herself?

He stared into her eyes to let her know he'd not say another word if she started to grin at him.

To get up at dawn in a warm bed and go look out the window at the pink and purple of the not-yet-visible sun. Then to do bathroom things, rinse the mouth, brush the hair, scrub the face a little. Then to go see the first yellow of the rising day. Then to crawl back into bed and cuddle against the spine of the sleeping, murmuring wife. To feel the warmth come back. To scratch her shoulder blades lightly and patiently, to rub patiently and lightly as she murmured and wiggled. To put himself between her. To wiggle together like two happy worms.

She sighed.

"What's the matter?"

"Me too," she said, "I'd like something like that, a poetic husband who likes to look at the sunrise. But maybe I could wash my own face and brush the teeth, too, being married, while you did that. But I'd be back in bed, pretending I was asleep when you got there. And I'd manage to be warm."

They gazed tenderly at each other. They had lived through a long marriage and were proudly looking at the debris of their golden wedding celebration. They had lived a long hope together in a short time.

"That's nice," he said.

"Too damn bad," she said.

"Why?"

"I'm a vagabond." She sighed and spread her legs and flashed a bit of thigh and ran her fingers up the place between them. "I wrote to you, didn't I? And invited you so nicely to come visit Las Vegas? And arranged for Veronica to give you a good time? And fool around with you?"

Her fingers were playing; her eyes were wet. Her fingers were poking. Tears were falling. "I must be a bum. You're a small-town lawyer-vagabond and I'm different. I'm a player. Now go home. Go back to your nice little town. Your garden. Your dream of cuddling with someone. *Leave me alone.*"

"You brought me here to tell me to leave you alone?"

"Watkins: It's not a movie, there's some killings, blah blah blah, things finally get resolved, fade out as you walk away tall. It's not like that. I want you to leave Clark County."

"Would you care to explain? Why don't you just stay here a while with me? Maybe you have a friend, but you must have been interested, so what if we just go on like we are—"

She glanced at the phone by the bed and the pressed-sawdust lamp with its painted knothole protuberances. "If I stayed here with you," she said, "well, you would have a marvelous time. I would like that. For you, I'm clean and nice, and for me, I like you. That's the plus side. The minus side is you'd never see the Las Vegas airport again."

He waited. Perhaps she had more to say.

"You have a kind of mean or vengeful friend, Linda?"

"You would leave town for the desert outside, that's all. Gophers would make little holes in the mound. No trouble for him, and I suppose he'd want to have a little honeymoon to celebrate—probably South Lake Tahoe."

After a while he said, "That seems to be a threat. I don't suppose you're talking about the fellow from Monaco."

She did not say.

The phone began to ring. She raised her hand, indicating it was not necessary to pick up the phone. "It's a sign of craziness not to take me seriously, Watkins, unless you just want to finish with this vale of shadows. Didn't you meet him at the desk when you came in? Silk suit? Ferde? He doesn't necessarily have an outstanding personality, but it would have been smart to notice him, or at least notice what I left out. Sometimes he's dormant, Watkins, but then he's malignant."

"Okay."

"I served your purpose. Some excitement, a couple of modern American adventures. And you served mine. So I'm grateful and

I want to give you a chance." The phone was still ringing. Her hand was on it. "It's for me," she said.

The phone was still ringing. She shook as if in chill night winds from the desert.

"Get out before I pick this up. Your clothes will be downstairs at the desk. You probably won't have to pay. Compliments of the house, my dear."

14

Velvety wolf-headed violets grew in a low row near the stairway
to HumanHouse. Someone sought to bring beauty here. A
breeze ruffled their small faces as Watkins tramped up the steps
toward the regular meeting.

"You used to be first one in, Wat."

"I'm not late, am I?"

"No, but almost."

Then Pete wondered how Watkins's nose happened to appear
to be so sunburned and Watkins said the appearance reflected
a reality, nose left out in the sun, and Pete wasn't satisfied, in
general, with Watkins's answers. Pete Positano was doing his
best to make this group work, even if certain members had no
sense of what it meant to be twice-born and they kept their
character armor on and they sneered at true seekers of the un-
shelled magic in all of us. All of us except the mindfuckers.

Rod, Fred and Chuck were willing to listen. The moral pressure was global. Pete counted on the group to help save any
soulless souls which happened to find themselves on site. If they
could be saved, the group inspired by the fire of Pete Positano
was here to do it. He understood that appearances were a meta-
phor for reality; that's how profound he was.

"You wouldn't believe what mystical science is giving us
these days. You try listening to me, Wat. Recently I discovered
you can have a thought caused by something that hasn't happened yet. This is because time is *bent*. It's *curvy*. Not many folks
have caught on yet. For example, I'm working on equipment to
send messages faster-than-light backward in time. Well, not the
equipment, but the basic theory. You think this doesn't explain

all the prophets? Sure as Delphic Oracles it does. And the DNA code, too. Plus how the KGB is plugged in to us, and why we're gonna have a high-octane earthquake pretty soon—*willed,* this time. This is state-of-the-art stuff. You think the CIA got an answer or even a second-strike capability—black holes? tidal waves? spirit drills? Shit no. We're defenseless unless we wake up from our long slumber!"

"How do you know?" Fred asked. "Give us some evidence, Pete."

"I'd like a few details on the physics side," Chuck said.

"It's a good probe," Rod said. "One thing we all got to know about the right-brain side of us is keep the feminine left brain in mind. Or is it the other way around?"

"If you're really powerful," Pete said, "you get these takes all the time. It's simple. It's only the new postmodern physics. Tell me if I'm wrong, Chuck, but doesn't laser theory bear me out in a small way even if some legalistic mindfuckers doubt my word?"

Chuck frowned. Although hefty, muscular and physically powerful, he liked to think things through. He didn't have a quick answer to the apocalypse.

"Thanks for the tip, Pete," Watkins said.

"Thanks for the tip! Thanks for the tip! That's how all the prophets got turned off. Thank you very much, and climb up on that cross." Pete paused. He knew that a soft answer sometimes turneth away wrath. "I don't want to go that far about me," he said softly. "Anybody who thinks like that has got to be a little paranoid, except if he's not. So instead let's talk about our friend the mindfucker. Wats is so sure of his hang-ups he can leave them festering. He can run away and have fun in the sun and exploit some poor lonely woman and come back to find his grief waiting for him like a pet dog. Goddamn you, Wat."

Watkins held his knees and bided his time. He was not exactly in a position of strength with Pete. Pete was right that he could not outrun his griefs.

He regretted a certain snottiness that gave him an advantage on nobody, and didn't help with the griefs, either.

Pete frowned jovially; it was another talent he had. He could also lay it on the line deviously, sneakily upfront gut-level, because of so many faster-than-light laser crosscurrents in his soul. He was angry, but he was all-forgiving. He contained multitudes. This was the 1980s, when microchip refinements to the 1960s were finally coming on line. The 1970s had been a holding pattern. Even Pete's clothes didn't wear out in the 1970s. Now all Pete asked was the largeness of soul to submit to him. "You know how some cops are on the take?" he asked. "Well, I'm on the give, man. Help me give to you!"

And what if Pete were right about Watkins and women?

"So I'll continue," Pete said.

Rod, Fred and Chuck looked at Watkins. Watkins noticed that the hands which held his knees were losing a bit of circulation and if he didn't want this extra tingle he should ease up. He eased up. He offered no objection.

Now that Pete had disposed of the relation of international thought control and curvy state-of-the-art time geography to the new physics, he could get back to something nearer and dearer —Watkins's love life. His receptors picked up static in Watkins's aura. Wat was AM when he should be FM. He was still playing Top Forty when the world had moved both forward and backward. "You're really, really," said Pete, "into life-size sex aids, aren't you, Wat? I mean women."

"I never heard them called that."

"Now you did. Think about it. They breathe, they wiggle, they heat up? Is that all they are to you?"

Watkins was the last to disagree that he was having troubles with women. Yet he disagreed.

Crazy Pete. There was this shrewdness about him. Watkins hadn't thought of himself as merely a careless mourner, employing anonymous persons to make memorial sounds, cuddling to melancholy and loss. But if Pete were right? Was he smug in his yearning for Bethany? Were these women just appetizers to create a tastier sorrow, this chase after the box numbers, this consciousness raising with his fellow lads at HumanHouse? One day he was running along the Las Vegas strip with Veronica

Velveeta, and the same day he was thinking about poor sensitive Linda with the disturbed family arrangements while she was asking him to hurry up and not get killed in Clark County, and two days later he was discussing the Word of Pete on paisley pillows in a psychedelic rumpus room.

He was putting his own life into night court and touring it with a bunch of nosy paralegals. By this time his education should have progressed. He had paid the penalty of loss. He had served his parole in the custody of Bethany. She informed him it was time to move on. She was right. She had helped. He was busy trying to move on.

Then how to explain the night sweats, the lurch in belly, the ceaseless imagining of Bethany's light wet slippery flutterings as she lay beneath him and her legs flew up to squeeze his shoulders? And how her hands pressed on his behind. Her fingers dug. How she wanted to extract every drop of him. That fizzy scent. How he couldn't stop remembering even when she no longer wanted any drop of him . . . "Wat, are you paying attention? Do you care what we know and decide about you?" Pete was asking.

When she said to turn away, he turned away, just as she commanded. He hardly thought of her husband's heavy thrust in her. He simply turned away.

Smug, was he? Smug in his grief?

Goddamn mindfucker Pete.

"I'm listening," Watkins said. "Did you happen to say something I should hear, Pete?"

Pete had a good karma catered by Werner Erhard, Baba Ram Dass and Joia, a really boss mystic lady from the east; Brooklyn, that is. He was authentically derived from many quests and therapeutic breakthroughs. His smile was beautiful. His teeth were an authentic miracle for a man of his age who used to smoke tobacco and still smoked controlled substances for purposes of enlightenment only, or maybe getting it on once in a while. He was hopeful and brilliant, a boy whose smile declared, *I'm centered,* and whose nervous eyes asked, *What's centered?* Recently the new physics had given him a whole new line on things.

So today he wanted to work on Watkins. He went to work. The rage was rising in him—a centered, peaceful, affable rage. Watkins wanted to say Brother to Pete Positano because he also felt that good-tempered desire to kill. There was a slight locker-room smell to the room with its pillows; this wasn't just stocking feet and shoes lined up in a corner. It was Pete and Watkins getting something on, and Fred, Rod and Chuck were alert to their own expectations of some kind of trouble. Oh, good cheer on its way! War can be such fun, when fought with intergalactic metaphysical missiles and submarine ego digs in the encounter room of HumanHouse.

"Let me ask something," Pete stated. "What kind of a lawyer is it that stalls all the time?"

"It's called asking for a continuance. No special kind of lawyer. It's part of the legal process."

"Do you think you're a kind of philosopher, Wat?"

"I think. Probably think too much about myself."

"Oh, boy," said Pete. "You want a continuance? You'd like to stall a little? Or would you like to get right down to it, Mr. Watkins Old Pal Good Friend of My Ex-Wife?"

Watkins was weary of hunting down the ladies Bethany found for him. Las Vegas had taken some of the starch out. If this was the quest for true love, he was ready to try for a little brotherly hate. He met Pete's bright and boyish eyes and raised a hand in a pupil's gesture: "May I inquire something? Just asking. Why is it the one who talks about mindfucking always comes in late, as if he's too busy to waste his time but wants everyone else to waste ours waiting for him? Could I have an answer to that, please?"

Pete was taking little gulps of air. Watkins liked that. In battle, he also made little gulps of air when attacked where it hurt.

"Please don't tell me," Watkins said, "not again, it's because you're so powerful and I should stand away from the flame."

179

It felt nice to swing away, even if only with words. Hatred made revenge a happy experience.

Pete too was filled with joy. "That's a high yoga, man," he said, "a boss boogie. I enjoy you, Wat, I sure do. I was with Werner the other weekend, a whole weekend with Werner, and he said I had the power. Man, you *give* me the power. 'Cause I can deal so good with mindfucking folks like you, man."

Sixties jive gave the fallen Catholic, fallen Italian, fallen Kaiser Plan therapist with the new earring in his ear the authentic power. The power the canary flower child and Harvard psychologist, Timothy Leary, a personal friend of Pete's, had lent him—some of that authentic white-teeth force. Pete took the power from all sides. *I am myself if I am somebody else.*

"Have you done est?" Watkins asked him.

"Man, you're mindfucking again."

"Did you do est?"

"What does that have to do with it?"

"Did you do est?"

Chuck and Fred and Rod looked interested. They tapped fingertips, they pursed lips, they nodded encouragement. "Well," said Pete, "I spent a couple weekends with Werner . . . you mindfucker."

"Uh-huh. Well, it would save some of the time you say I waste if you just said yes. I mean, if you have the power through est, you shouldn't be afraid of a yes answer in the affirmative mode."

"Lemme lay a personal hang-up on you," said Pete. "I'll show how honest I can get. I take responsibility for myself. I'm not chicken. I'm committed to change and growth, my karma is on the line. I'll answer your question, Wat. The bosses in my department don't hassle me so much, but my fellow wage slaves do, and then the bosses get involved and *they* hassle me. It's my ideas, my growth, my power. I got a good job, bro, I'm fuckin' good at it, so they can't fire me unless they moral turpentine me, tenure is *freedom,* man—but I ain't gonna do nothin' harms me, not this sister, no messing around illegally. I'm just gonna toast on my own flame. I acknowledge that. I live a peaceful but warlike life. They can go fuck themselves." He leaned back, crossed his arms, put on his Indian inscrutable mask. "Is that a yes for you?" he asked. "Wat, now you see how a man of power responds?"

Chuck, Fred and Rod were trying to figure out what they had just heard. They were running it through the computer. Watkins agreed that Pete had won a round of camouflage from him.

He had thought the group would dilute some of his worries about true love and digging into his soul and not just being so longing and in dearth and need all the time. Oh, that's not clear. Fuzziness isn't necessarily sincere. Try again. He wanted to be more contented with his lot with women, or with his lack of lot, or to discover how the lack was in him, or if it was just fate, or perhaps just merely his own inefficiency as a coveter and cuddler—oh, it keeps coming unclear. But that was why he tramped longingly past the wolf-faced violets into HumanHouse. Pete, you're changing the rules. I know these are changing times, but I want the old rules back, Pete.

Watkins decided to try for a comeback. Pete presented himself, preening over recent triumphs. Watkins remembered the trick of a low voice that made juries lean forward to hear. "Sometimes I think," he began, and Rod, Chuck and Fred leaned forward to hear, "sometimes I think you think you're looking in a mirror, Pete, and you see a lot of hair and dirt and interesting darkness. But you're not looking in a mirror. You're bent over to look up your own behind."

"Haha. Haha," Pete said. "Self-involved, am I? And you're not, Watkins? Proctologist, heal thyself. So you're here just because you like to sit on the floor on fat pillows?"

Watkins gave Pete another victory. He could tell because he suddenly felt tired. Lip-curling insult wasn't his best shot. "I'm a bit bent over these days, too, Pete," he said. "I think I better take responsibility for that."

Pete looked at him shrewdly. "You're saying it. I'll give you credit. But only for saying it, pal."

Watkins had noticed that women did not turn out to be the main business. The program in HumanHouse was the raising of men's understanding. The opposite and often opposing sex was not his friends' chief worry. Perhaps theirs was the correct way to proceed. Watkins was willing to grant that Pete, noisy Pete, might have a point. This anger, suspicion, mistrust and boyish optimism about changing everything through love might be buried balls-high within other concerns—power, ambition, work, even connections with other men—yes, Pete, okay, I concede—there are different loves and connections among human beings in the world where everyone is born to die and let's not forget it. Why do I keep remembering Vic Lonkin, diving in our wet suits for abalone, and I only found out because I happened to look at an old newspaper in the kitchen? Okay, Pete, you serve the time and you're right to do so. For purposes of comfortable argument.

Watkins knew from experience that he could think anything he liked and even if people were watching him shrewdly, as Pete was now doing, they wouldn't necessarily read his secrets. This was one of the things adult life had taught him; not an awful lot, but a help.

Probably women also entered groups with the hope of fretting over men and ended with other concerns. The lads at HumanHouse had even turned away from Chuck's problem with his wife. Chuck seemed easier with no attention being paid. Watkins forgot to worry about whether Chuck and Mrs. Chuck (Anne-Marie) were having fun together. Rod, Fred and Pete were not worrying. Perhaps Chuck had found that his brief ventilation in this room—his fibrillation, his hyperventilation—gave him the spasm of relief he required. (On his way in, Watkins heard two undergraduates discussing Greek myth: "Hera changed into a duck, so Zeus had a spaz.")

Pete had his spaz over Watkins almost every session, but without relief. Something in Watkins nagged at Pete and something in Pete Positano wanted to nag at his former friend. Thanks to open, frank, honest sharing and caring, they had become former friends. Pete was beginning to work on family problems. He was a helping professional with two ex-wives and three ex-children; a free spirit with tenure, and the pleasure of not having to keep up an office or pay malpractice insurance; a devoted observer of Watkins, whom he was jovially asking: "Why aren't you a together person?"

Watkins knew this question from the law. It was a helping version of *When did you stop beating your wife?* Watkins gave it a D-minus and a shrug.

"Liar," said Pete.

"I didn't say anything."

"Yeah, but I can read your mind. Your mind is an open magazine."

Asshole, Watkins thought.

"And in your head," Pete said, "you just called me mind-fucker."

Goddamn if this frantic wiseass couldn't read him sometimes, not so well as he thought, but sometimes and well enough. And nevertheless, for reasons which came of the intimacy of abuse, of this sprawling male abusive camaraderie, of this freeing of spite and the spirit of destruction, Watkins now began to be fond of Pete once more. Pete had a way of keeping things moving and alive. They could bounce off him. He was a kind of barrier with his own built-in bounce to transmit. And he had been right about something. Watkins admired him for that.

"Let me inform you categorically," Pete said, "let me stipulate this. Unlike some mindfuckers I happen to know, I'm not stuck in the past. Whatever my own opinion might be, it's a probe. I don't necessarily agree with it."

"You don't necessarily agree with your own opinion?" Watkins asked.

"You see? You see? He's doing it again."

Suddenly Pete slid forward without standing up. He propelled himself with his hands, like a legless vendor. He wasn't finished with astonishments. He threw his arms around Watkins, who struggled manfully against the smell of male armpit soaking through turtleneck and the shell necklace cutting into his cheek, saying, "Hey! Hey!"

"You're a mindfucker," Pete panted, "but I like what you're selling! I'm buying!" Watkins extricated himself and crouched in semikarate position to repel further assault. Chuck, nearsighted, was peering intently at these men who seemed really to have a life together. They didn't have wives. Pete was advancing toward Watkins again.

"Let's boogie, Wat. I get kind of pissed, but your aura, it's magic. Hopefully, we can be buddies again when all this shit has gone down—you know what I mean?" He slid back with adroit hand propulsion. He tightened himself into a half-lotus position.

Wary, Watkins would not commit himself. English was his language and he wasn't sure he understood Encounter. He sat back down.

Rod relieved the problems of translation and response by rapping softly with his fingernails at a worn place in the carpet where he could get a crablike rustle against the wooden floor. Rod wished they might return to business—not in an elitist way of insisting—he just declared that he wished it. "Love," he said, "is the original question that brought us together. Love of women, love of each other, love of the eternal principle of righteousness which we call"—and he blushed for using the dirty word—"which we call Supreme Being. Do I have the sense of the group that we could—?"

"Can a truly great humanist be smug?" Watkins interrupted.

"*What?*" It seemed as if everyone asked at once.

"Just wondering," Watkins said. "You may proceed. I didn't mean to break the spell. Pete, go ahead. Tell us about love and how you manage it."

"Love? *You* fall in love, Wat, *I* don't fall in love. You got it all wrong. The love is *in* me. When you realize that—*if* you do, fella—you're home free. You don't fall in it, you bring it out 'cause it's already there. The toughness is in me, too, and I like it that way. I'm proud of how strong I am, my sacred fire. Listen, I won it the hard way. I have a little saying about that: I paid my dues. That means, well, you can figure it. When my first wife left me, Elaine, you remember, Wat—I stared at the wall for a fucking year. No, nine months. Just catatoned. But then at a Laundromat I met Laurie. She told me about fabric softener and it was great. She said Washeteria. She was a wild and crazy, well, wow. A High Yellow. I guess it's true what they say—the Kama Sutra Kid, I called her. And then it unraveled, she was too flippy, flakey, so I met Jennie. We both felt the same way—zap! Love again! There it is, a sociological fact. Jennie wanted the child trip, the marriage trip, that's what she thought. But like I explained to her, the love is in *me*, it's all got to be really mine. So then I met Stanley." He looked each of them in the eyes before he continued, Fred last. "And just a week ago I met— after all these sessions—I *really* met Fred."

"Pardon?" Chuck asked.

Fred looked downcast and shy. He plucked at his socks between his toes.

"Which doesn't mean," Pete added, "I don't really get my rocks off with women, too. And Watkins was a friend of mine before he started this mindfucking routine of his, which I fully understand comes from all his own sadness he can't really share with us yet because he's not capable."

Fred said, "Which doesn't mean I don't still have my wife and kids, that's my main thing in life also."

Pete and Fred gazed tenderly at each other. It was deep male understanding between these two, not just what other people might think. The matching earrings—left ear for Pete, right one for Fred—caught the light like a whisper. This makes no sense, Watkins thought, it's just an unnecessary complication. Fred and Pete beamed. Watkins knew he was uptight. Fred and Pete were happy. Despite his earnest efforts, Watkins was not. The world was a song and a festival for Fred and Pete. Watkins thought: Ick, back to the pay toilets in Sacramento.

Chuck said, "I've been thinking about a vasectomy. Of course, in your case, it's not necessary. Anne-Marie thinks it might be a good idea for me to take responsibility for the damage I do to her body. Of course, that's just us—"

Watkins wondered if Chuck saw revealed a new solution to his problems.

Rod said, "I feel sleepy. I don't think I'm out of touch. I'm here. I'm centered. But maybe this room is kind of stuffy and we should open the window more. I feel kind of logy."

Watkins understood Rod's drowsiness. It might be nice just to curl up and doze off. He too felt outnumbered by the announcement from the new couple, Fred and Pete. It had not been a part of the plan. In the years he had associated in the faculty Senate with Pete Positano, he had not suspected how open he was to the solution of problems. Well, if it works, it works; if it happens, it happens; that's the American way. Pete explained it happens in women's groups also, which he knew because many of his best lovers were feminists.

"I'm a feminist, Pete," Fred said. "Don't forget me."

"You're my best friend, too," Pete said. "That's the love that's in me today."

Rod declared their time up for this session. He hoped everyone had gained something to think about. Watkins was thinking about Fred and Pete, not Bethany. Well, he had gained that much.

A few days later they were burning the rice fields again. The acrid smoke drifted across town as Watkins strolled toward the campus, and grew stronger among the green quads and bicycles and rangy California young people as he strolled a curving walk toward HumanHouse. The scorched rice husk smell reminded him of coal dust, odd in this fresh dry air. A law student in a vested suit, success-bound, tipped his hand to his forehead in a downtown-styled salute as Watkins passed. "Sir," he said. In his own private ledger of the steps to achievement, he gave himself another check mark. Watkins nodded. The student saw a distinguished adjunct professor who could soon be asked to write letters of recommendation. Watkins was heading toward Pete, Rod, Fred, their session together.

The little row of velvety, wolf-faced violets nodded continually in the breeze. Tough stems and persistence, tough velvet; this was a reassurance for Watkins.

The fellows removed their shoes at the door and lined them up neatly, like the kids of Watkins's childhood leaving galoshes in the cloakroom. They sprawled against their pillows and Pete said almost immediately, "Do you love me? I've been thinking and I decided I've got to get it straight with you guys."

"Uh-oh," said Watkins.

"Do you love me? I want to be accepted for what I am, not this not that, but *me!*"

Rod finally spoke up. "Well, I accept you, Pete, I really do. But your aggressiveness—your fire and feistiness, Pete, which I truly admire—"

"I'm not a cafeteria, you can take this and not that! I'm whole or I'm nothing! And I'm something!"

Rod nodded. "I do," he said. It was easier, it was also more *facilitating*, to agree.

"Look here! I'm into my yangness. I love Freddie over there." (Fred was fingering his earring and blushing.) "He doesn't play macho games. He does his thing sweetly, with kindness in his heart—"

Fred whispered, "But I wish I had some of your power, Pete."

Pete burped. In passion he swallowed air. Flesh and blood have habits; this was his. "I'm not arrogant, I'm me. If you perceive me as threatening, like the mindfucker over there does, that's his problem. I'm me, you're you. One thing I can't stand is pigism, sexism, racism or elitism in any form."

"Or jargonism," Watkins said, and then hastily added: "Right —I'm a mindfucker, Pete."

"You said it, I didn't." Pete momentarily looked shy and puzzled. He was searching for another way to say it. He didn't find it. Silence surged softly over the five men struggling in this room to refresh their souls. Five grown men, Watkins thought.

After a pause, smells of anxiety and feet, distant taste of burning rice husks, Chuck said to Rod, "Where are you today? I don't *feel* you, Rod."

"I'm fine. My sinus. I think I'm allergic to rice burning. My wife says it's house dust and I should vacuum more. Just coming off some heavy antihistamine is all."

"Thank you for that report on your domestic sinus arrangements," Pete said. "Do I have to spend my time on this shit?"

Rod said, "Thank you for sharing your impatience with us, Pete." He blew his nose; how fast the cavities fill up again. "As a catalyst, you are outstanding. I agree with your input that the sinus is an extension of the brain both biologically and psychologically—science teaches this."

"My kids," Chuck said, "they're feeling the pressure. I think they feel something about their mother, Anne-Marie, and me. I feel they kind of feel the lack of feeling, not the lack of feeling exactly, but the lack of . . . feeling."

"Let's talk about vasectomies," Pete said. "For example, sex is never better. You're not laying a trip on the lady." (Fred looked hurt. Pete shot a warning glance at him—no sexist jealousy allowed.) "She doesn't have to take responsibility, and that's courteous of the man, *he* takes. You tell her up front you're not interested in babies. Zero population blah blah blah. I think you'd like it, Chuck, and then you wouldn't have to deal with your kids, your wife's resentments—"

"It can't be retroactive," Watkins remarked. "In this country a kid can't get aborted at age ten. And a vasectomy is about the future, not the past—"

"You're still in a linear time frame, aren't you, Wat?" Pete inquired with rare sympathy for Watkins's limitations. Fred must have been contributing a measure of dampening peace to Pete's fire.

But now Fred was hurt and taking the line of not being interested. He was staring at the paisley pillows with his eyes rotating slightly to give him a kaleidoscope sensation. He was emitting interest in his experiment. Or maybe he just felt blank and uninvolved after his twenty seconds of intense, illegal and forbidden jealousy.

"Well, if I don't stay with my wife," said Chuck, "just assuming, I might meet a girl and we might, who knows—"

"Man, sex is never better. I had mine at the beginning of that last horrible decade, man, got myself cut and trimmed, and it saved the seventies for me. Just pulled it right out. Man, it doesn't reduce your sex drive, Pete Positano here to certify, man —it takes you right back to the Summer of Love, just turns it around and—"

"I know, I know the engineering of it," said Chuck. "It's physiology, though."

"If you have any doubts, then don't do it."

"I have some doubts."

"Well, I'm telling you where I stand. That's my input. Trust me. Just do what I say."

"Are we statistics?" Watkins asked. "Are we decades? If we're into natural human relations, this two point eight kids is just another idea. How about my brothers who don't have any kids? Do I get to use their quotas?"

"You have brothers?" Rod asked. "What kind? I mean, how old? They're younger siblings?"

Pete was squinting winsomely at Fred. He was making amends for talking about women to Chuck. He was ignoring Watkins.

Watkins looked at the earring in Fred's left lobe and asked, "What does that mean?"

"It symbolizes I'm different, a gypsy, in my heart a gypsy even if I got tenure here at UC-Davis, it reminds me I'm not like everyone else, I do things my own blessed way."

"It's multipurpose, isn't it?" Watkins said. "Anything else?"

Pete and Fred gave each other a long gleamy sea lion stare. Then, to Watkins, Pete directed a half-lotus-based marine salute, snapping it off. They were supposed to tell the truth, and yet Watkins was a mindfucker who only deserved loving, caring, I-and-thou put-downs. "It symbolizes," Fred began again, "well, okay, I'm not only making it with Pete, I'm open to my bisexuality. But I also dig my wife and kids, whatever kind of pain they bring me. Okay?"

"Even if they're a drag," said Watkins.

Pete, smiling, tanned, loose limbed, gauze shirted, hate filled, stood up and snapped off another marine salute at Watkins. "I'm a violent man," he said. "Do you know how close you are to getting a paste in the mouth?"

Watkins stood up and said, "I know how close I am," and waited.

Nothing.

Rod spoke in a droning voice. Probably he selected this voice carefully. "It's been a good session. We got some bad shit out. I think they got another group coming in to use the room, so see you next time."

As they left, Watkins wanted to express fraternity with Chuck by saying, "That Pete, he . . ." But Pete's gleamy eyes caught Watkins. It was permissively forbidden to carry resentment out of the room in which they were wrangling and creating intimacy. Resentment was not the goal. This was a space shuttle in which they careened. History had launched them on simulated space travel, but the queasy weightlessness was real. Watkins had no right to nip at Pete outside the sweaty place of confession and what Rod called "support." The fuss of their dealings had grown as busy as family: "Do you *have* to smoke?" "Do you need to stick your bare feet under our noses?" "Why do you always pull back and then make us repeat what we said, you deaf, are you getting deaf or dumb?" "Why don't you sit closer, are you separating yourself from the rest of us idiots?"

"I guess I should sit closer," Watkins had admitted.

Watkins guessed this nagging and fussing was a part of their business together. They huddled. He was waiting for true love in a group which was asking, Are we afraid of dying, is that why we don't manage age and disappearance? Are we afraid of women, is that why we chase true love?

Is that what the group was asking? His colleagues here were nattering and babbling and putting earrings in their ears and words in people's mouths.

Watkins had nothing better to do. He would wait to see if something came up. Without Bethany, without true or false love, time stretched over clarity like the burning rice fog. The women who replied to his box were each some kind of miracle, but not what he required. His privacy was precious to him, but not his hours and days, not his sleepless nights. Such was the time of his life in which he dwelled. He woke up at midnight and made coffee for himself. He wouldn't sleep anyway. He tried to read and fell asleep. He awakened and waited for the dawn. He brushed and flossed. He fidgeted.

Why, during the night, did it abruptly thrust him out of sleep to think how cleverly Bethany had deserted him? His heart thumped and she was too clever by half. She had worked out a solution for him and she had let him down. She had said: "No more explanations, because it's obvious, isn't it?"

It was obvious and it wasn't enough.

The message his clutching of the sheets sent him was: *I can't handle it.* By the time he got out of bed the sheet was rolled into a wet club.

Okay, today was another session at HumanHouse. Okay, he decided to tell the truth to his good friends and enemies.

By the time he walked through campus, in full morning, his eyes still rasped by the sleep-lorn middle of the night—and the bicycles floated past with the lovely dreamy faces, and the students with backpacks, the stooped or athletic boychildren, girlchildren, perpetual children, the elderly faculty—and the dewy earnestness and innocence of everyone's striving to make a career, plus the goddamned sensual anxiety and comfort of campus—he was no longer a jittery insomniac. He was an alert fuzzy-headed insomniac.

He heard his own footsteps from afar as if he were very tall. Up the eroded stairs of HumanHouse, past the violets with their frayed yellow petals and their black wolf faces, past the everready, loose-lipped coffeemaker, he pushed into the room. Now he was ready to play the game. Pete Positano was there already. "Pete," he said, "you win."

"What do I win this time?"

"Something, Pete. You haven't had the story right, but now I'll just hand it over."

He told them about himself, about Bethany, about her, about them. He left out the true loves for whom he had advertised. They didn't need to know that. He left out Bethany's name. They didn't need to know that. He left in his need and lack and loss and grief. "I've been dying for the love of an inappropriate woman," he said. "What do you make of that?"

"Uh-huh, uh-huh, uh-huh," said Rod. "Is that the story?"

Even Pete didn't say: Is that all? What are you leaving out? Watkins was as grateful for his silence as if he had chosen to go easy. As he talked, he watched Pete's eyes glow with Watkins's discomfort; sympathy or satisfaction brought that wetness of light—it didn't matter what brought it. Watkins had fallen into disclosure. Pete was with him now. He was leaning forward and listening and nodding his head sharply; he was giving feeling back to his old friend. "I've had this woman in my head every minute of the day or night, I don't think she should be there but she is, I have these times when I can't stand myself or anyone and I want to die but I think maybe she'll change her mind so I run the routines, I don't die, no, I won't do that—"

Rod, concerned but a little sleepy; Fred, thinking about himself and checking Watkins's obsession against his own accommodations to his wife and to Pete; Chuck, sturdy and sad and measuring and not getting any love from his inappropriate woman, either.

A lot of words by Watkins. An avowal. A difficult partial confession slid through him.

A silence.

"Who is it, Wat?" Pete asked.

Watkins stared. No one repeated the question. Even Pete knew enough not to ask again.

Rod got up, left the room and came back with a foam-and-cloth cudgel, lumpish of form, made in Venice, California, and said delicately and mildly: "Depression is blocked anger. Here, it helps to pound. Hit, please." He yawned. "Pardon. Hit the floor. Hit the pillow. Hit me."

Watkins picked up the padded thuggish weapon and said pedantically, "This is called a slapstick. Too big to pick your teeth. It makes people feel funny on stage when someone—"

"Naming it! Words! Mindfucker!" Pete flailed the air from a half-lotus position. "Come on, man, *hit it!*"

Watkins waved the foam bludgeon in the air. He felt foolish. "Come on!" Pete screamed. Watkins let it topple. It looked limp. He felt disarmed. "Come on, come on!" He slapped it twice, softly, against the floor. He felt nothing. He felt nothing.

"I don't feel like it," he said.

"Goddamn, we're wasting our valuable time, Wat."

Softly Rod said, "Watkins must feel you're manipulative, Pete. He must feel you are pressuring."

"Shit no! I wouldn't lay a heavy trip on that mindfucker because I want to assist the snotty bastard."

"*I* feel," said Watkins, "I feel, Pete—"

"Hit it, goddamnit, why are we talking? I got better places to be! Why can't you acknowledge your feelings?"

"I'm angry. I'm depressed. I acknowledged. I don't feel like hitting a pillow with a piece of foam."

"Hey," said Chuck, "why don't we wrestle, Wat? You ever wrestle?"

"Not since I was a kid. Oh, with my kids some when they were babies—"

"Let's wrestle. You want to wrestle?"

"I don't—"

"Come *on.*" Chuck's hoarse voice startled everyone. "Come on, you bastard!"

Watkins lunged at him. They rolled on the floor. An immense heat suffused Watkins's chest and shoulders. A nail scratched his neck. He pulled his head down. He flipped around. He tried to press Chuck to the carpet. Chuck twisted. Watkins was embracing this thick, muscular, sweating, middle-aged engineer's body —this poor stub whom he had pitied so when he spoke of his nonangry wife. Chuck was grunting and whooshing great moans. Watkins started to laugh, but there was no time for it, no breath. He was fighting for his life. There was slime on his chest, shoulders, cheeks. He pinned Chuck twice, but maybe Chuck was letting him do it. Chuck was surely stronger, younger, more thick with clotted rage. Or perhaps Watkins was so angry he was stronger than he was supposed to be and Chuck was thinking about not hurting him—was that possible?

Watkins pinned him panting to the carpet. Chuck tapped his back. You can get up now.

"You feel better?" Chuck inquired.

Tears were coming from Watkins's eyes. He wanted to apologize and tell everyone not to feel bad for him, those were selfish tears, they were only for himself, he hadn't earned anyone's pity.

"You feel better?"

"Yeah, Pete. Okay. So you win a round. I feel better."

>———15

Bethany had never returned the key to his house. A normal man might worry that she would come in unannounced or when he wasn't home; Watkins worried that she might not. Another man might fear she would surprise him while he was with another woman, rattling her equipment and tromping around, indignant. Watkins knew she had no intention to do so. Nor would it happen accidentally. No indignant rattling or tromping; no eyes suddenly red, blinking, wet, conjunctival with jealousy. No crazed astonishments. Not unless it was what suited her.

She may have kept the key because of some sentimental memory or memories of him, using it as a paperweight. Clear eyed, she might mist for a moment or two, no worse than a dose of Murine.

Or she may have kept the key because she plain didn't notice. When she noticed—oh dear, what's this?—she might return it. Or more likely, she assumed he could afford to make duplicates if he needed them. And because there was a touch of delicacy in Bethany, practical delicacy, as demonstrated by her energy on his behalf, she would not return the key now because, at this time, tardy in the closing-down of their afternoons, it would seem symbolic of something—of the closing and the locking—and who needed such symbols?

She may not have kept the key at all. She may have left it behind a cushion or under the dish drainer.

She may not have given it a thought. Circumstantial evidence, based on the psychological profile, with testimony from personal experience, not hearsay, indicated the latter, according to counsel. Key didn't interest Mrs. Andrews.

Watkins was proud of his ability to avoid harassing Bethany. It was something to cling to. Self-respect never hurt a person. Although the town was small, and one's habits and routes in such a town were predictable, and he could easily have placed himself unobtrusively in her path now and then, at the Safeway or the tennis courts, for example, he did not. He shopped for himself at different hours. He drove down different streets from the ones she frequented. He avoided the tennis courts at the hours when she played, before her kiddies got home from school. Mostly he did that.

Sometimes he didn't, and his heart thumped with the possibility of seeing her and the shame of searching for her. He didn't catch a glimpse of her except when he did, and then he regretted this hungry hollow yearning. I guess, he thought, that's what insulin shock feels like. It's the opposite of the runner's high. Also the experience of the loss of self-respect lets a person know that his original idea, which was to behave with dignity, no weeping in public, no moping or begging, was the better one. If he happened to drive past the courts, stop, stroll, push through the bushes and catch her eye just as she was arching her back for a serve, well, he would merely tip his hat and wish her a good day.

Unfortunately, he didn't wear a hat.

Sometimes he had pleasant dreams about Bethany and sometimes he had less pleasant ones. Sometimes he was asleep when he had these dreams, and all too often he was awake. In her tennis whites the tennis saint appeared at HumanHouse, confronting Pete, His Radiance, and Rod, and sturdy Chuck, and unsturdy Fred: "Boys, I've heard so much about you. The truth is, boys, you're not as interesting as tennis."

Or at a stoplight on E Street, he was in despair when this lovely woman in a red sports car, it was the dentist's, drove alongside and they were both waiting for the light to change and it turned green but he shouted, "Stop! Wait!" and she asked, "What do you want?" and in his dream he said, "True love," and she glanced at her watch, she checked it against the clock in front of the Navajo jewelry shop, she said, "Oh, then get in," and he abandoned his fairly new Saab, he climbed in beside her, they drove off, leaving the other motorists honking at his automobile just abandoned like that on E Street . . .

All of which tended to mean that when Bethany really did telephone again ("Hi! It's Bethany! You remember Bethany Andrews?"), Watkins put an easy smile on his face to cover his surprise for the no one who was watching ("Hello, Bethany, how are you?"), as if it were the most ordinary trivial social touching of base and not simply what he had been praying for, asleep and awake, living for, dying for, while he moped around Davis and Dixon and Woodland, and ran off to Las Vegas or Los Angeles or San Francisco in search of the true love which Bethany had sort of tried to arrange for him. He was going to handle this telephone call like a solid baseline player.

"Time to ask how go things, Wat."

"Fine."

"I mean our project. Time to ask, if you haven't just been lazy, which one turned out to be great and which merely good."

"All good I guess, Bethany. Maybe none great?"

"Not even one?"

"Define *great*, Bethany."

"Oh. That's a question, I guess. Kudos for sharp thinking, Wat." She considered the problem of communication, private need and where a man like Watkins might locate his hopes in collaboration with a woman like, for example, Bethany Andrews. "It could be . . ." she began.

His heart. His face. His shame.

"It could be we should confer on this in person, Wat."

She hung up. She did not say when. She did not say wait. She just took it for granted that he had nothing better to do than to stay where he was until she got there. He might take the ragged layers of newspapers from the floor near his reading chair and remove them to the utility stairs, he might organize his bills and receipts, opening envelopes and stacking the bills to be paid, he might look to see if any apple cores were where apple cores didn't need to be, in the sink or in an ashtray, he might tuck the quilt tight around his bed, he might push the ashes into his fireplace with the little fireplace broom, he might turn on his answering machine so that he wouldn't be tempted to answer any calls, he might . . . It was presumptuous of her to imagine he had nothing better to do than these finicky household chores, and it was correct.

He might hide in a drawer the clippings about Justice Victor Lonkin.

He finished and he waited. He did not look out the window or listen for the sound of her motor. He washed his face and he scrubbed his ears with a cloth. Perhaps this was an hour of solitary confinement.

She came bustling in with lots on her mind and in her arms, much to accomplish, such as much avoiding of his eyes—"Hi, Wat!"—and a paper bag gaily printed with the tricolors. "It's lunchtime anyway," she said—anyway what?—"but I was in such a rush, I guess—"

He stood by to let the whirlwind pass.

"Aren't you going to relieve me of my burdens? You expect me to carry things to the kitchen just as if I remember where the kitchen is, Watkins, in your little hideaway condo?"

In a hurry, with one child to pick up at soccer practice and another child to deliver to a piano lesson, Bethany did not surprise him with one of her marvelous picnics. Besides children, she had Watkins to manage, and one of her marvelous picnics packed in the French wicker basket would be wrong management for this occasion—overkill for what she had in mind. Instead, she had stopped at the Gormet Boteek on E Street, which she always called Elm Street, for a couple of Cheese McCamembert sandwiches on McFrenchbread, cole slaw, potato salad, and it came with choice of Offbrand Kola, strawberry pop or V-8 juice or beer at a slight surcharge. She knew enough to get one beer for him, one juice for her.

"McHeineken's," he said.

"Now don't make fun of me," she said. "I didn't have to look for snacks at all. I could have made you scramble something."

"This is just like old times, Beth."

"These are new times, however."

Finally, with things arranged on the sideboard, she met his eyes. "I've not forgotten you, Wat. With all my chores, driving hither and yon, I've had lots of time to think of you. I still squeeze you in mentally."

Bethany can appreciate me, he was thinking, that's one of her charms for sure. But without necessarily caring for me. Every other woman spends so much energy on being winsome. She doesn't worry about it. The other women are suing for love and more love, or they're hurt and they give it up absolutely, or they're hurt and this is worse—twist around like snakes and bite everything in sight, including their own tails.

He corrected himself: Every other woman *I* know.

Every other woman *I* deserve. (Further correction.)

Linda King, for example, she might even be as smart as Bethany. She just didn't have everything she wanted. She lined things up in a jumble. She got herself in a life jam. Bethany was unusual about life's distresses. She thought eternal youth was in her grasp, and by God, she might have it. For Watkins, on the other hand, it was too late for the latter.

"Maybe I'll have eternal middle age instead."

"What? Are you mumbling again? Wat, rinsing off your silver, you do a rotten job on the silver, I can't hear you if you mumble."

"How come you didn't pick up McPlasticware?"

"This is festive. Life is a festival, Wat, shall we dine? Feed the beasts their lunch first, then converse or whatever."

Bethany played at tennis even when she wasn't playing tennis. It was her uniform, it was how she revealed and concealed herself. She wore country-club tennis whites to do the shopping and to car-pool the children and meet her lover, or she wore tennis colors, or sometimes she wore jean cutoffs, like a girl just hanging out at the high-school courts on a summer's day. When she wore jean cutoffs she often chewed gum. Watkins had not figured out which mood called for spearmint, which for juicyfruit. Rather than ask her, he hoped to apply pure reason—his secret weapon which he always kept in reserve, like the hydrogen bomb.

Best after sex with Watkins, she used to say, Bethany preferred tennis. When she gave up sex with Watkins, it wasn't because she liked him less than tennis. But perhaps she liked him less than before, since liking a person depended on so many other things in a life. In any case, she preferred tennis best of all because the complications—other than finding partners and opponents among the first-ranked women and the second-ranked men, plus working around the household duties and the obligations to be a hardworking and devoted wife—were entirely practical and manageable: training, focusing, concentrating, riding a winning streak. This relative simplicity, it turned out, had not been the case with her first-ranked lover.

No, Bethany wasn't trying for eternal youth. Perhaps Watkins merely thought she should fail, like other people; choose a failing game, like others. Bethany was just slipping through on her own terms. She was one of those rare ones who succeeded. She didn't even mind, for example, what the sun did to her skin. What a needful Watkins did to her heart—she was not out of touch with facts—was more drastic than the sun and required taking action.

Even during the years when they used to be together for their few hours a week, Watkins sometimes strolled in full urban legal pinstripe down to the public park in the center of Davis where Bethany met her fellow athletic housewives. They were all neat, slim, girlish women, but Bethany was the neatest, slimmest, most girlish, lacking the stringy and harassed look of some of them, clinging to their teens and their twenties while adolescents of their own sulked at home.

At the Pleasant Valley Country Club, where she also played, perhaps there were creamier women. Watkins didn't prowl around those courts. Although blinded by love, he read the little suncrinkles around her eyes and mouth as portents and blessings; fair women get that in their thirties, their mid-thirties, their late thirties; the sun wounding added something to Bethany. He wanted to watch the tracery grow. For Watkins, every tiny fact of history added something of value to Bethany, even fate unlinked with history. The sun and the bruising of the mild California seasons, the scratching of wind and effort, gave mystery to her soul. The body, for Watkins, reflected this as quality, not as diminishment; it received the weather, the stress of children, his love. Bethany's epidermis was the package Bethany came wrapped in. Oh, and when her slim arms and legs flew about him, and then tightened around him; oh, Bethany.

"Deuce again!" she might cry, laughing. She usually won at tennis unless she was competing against some teenage boy hotshot, playing hooky from school. After school she liked to be home to attend to her own children. She would jump into the shower, and then was dripping and fresh and laughing and her hair lank as she sat with them and their Grape Nuts and fruit and she was discreetly directing raisins and bananas in their direction but not pressing unwanted health upon them. They would be healthy. No sweat. They were hers, weren't they?

Yet, in her smiling easy way, she tried so hard!

Sometimes, of course, she hid out with Watkins a while into the late afternoon. The kids were old enough to fill their bowls with Grape Nuts without mom's encouragement, and so what if they didn't bother to slice the banana in and sprinkle raisins without a little psychic reward, such as mom pasting the Chiquita sticker in the middle of the good forehead? Tomorrow was another day for potassium and iron. And she would do their homework with them later anyway, curled up, relaxed as a laughing child on their beds. Once, she told Watkins, her eldest son sniffed her and said, "What's that?"

"Some new soap," she said; it was the smell of Watkins— potassium, iron, zinc and all the good juices that come out of a man and a lady likes to rub into her skin, taste on her tongue.

"Smells like punk to me," said the boy, Bruce.

After that incident of the homework session with Bruce, she had to allow time for a shower, no matter what. If her son could smell it, maybe her husband could, too. Though of course children have sharp senses and her husband had less sharp senses, maybe dulled by flying tooth enamel and gum and composition and the chemicals of his office. Or by habit, boredom and no tennis in the open air.

Her sniffing was quick and accurate, brisk, loving, tender and practical. Even when she blew on his wet chest, blew on his nipples to make them scrunch and squeak, blew on his crotch to make him wiggle and wriggle and arch his back, she sniffed and whistled and giggled and drew all the interesting fragrances into her interested nose, filtering and relishing along the way. "Nice. Nice."

When she wrote his advertisement for the Bay *Guardian* and collected the letters, she made her preliminary judgments with a nice nose for amusement. Bethany relished each of Watkins's future loved, lovelorn ladies. She decided against making photographs a requirement; inflamed members do better with inflamed imagination, she decided. Calcium also helps children, builds strong bones and teeth.

In Watkins's case both his imagination and his body were frequently inflamed. With Bethany's brisk, loving, tender and practical intelligence, it was all the same for her purposes, whichever. Before coming to see him she had decided to continue the compassionate process of separating herself by denying him her limbs on this farewell occasion. It was only fair. He would suffer and so would she. They would be even. How to compare the needs of two different persons? For all practical purposes, for all reasonable analysis—even. So easy just to have a farewell sexing, a lot of wet grabbing and squeezing, and so utterly selfish of her such would be!

In her mind she made the sacrifice lovingly. She used to like the sensations which tricked and tickled through her when his big meaty hands grabbed and squeezed her narrow tight athletic buttocks—his kisses lumbering there, too—but she was too intelligent and imaginative and compassionate to give herself this pleasure at his expense. She had her mind made up. Some sacrifice on her part was called for. A farewell fuck, she had decided with measure, would hurt him more than it would give her pleasure. She wanted no tears and poignant memories. McPoignancy, McTears . . .

"Eat the nice sandwich," she said.

"You look good. You don't look nervous. I'm nervous."

"Drink the nice beer."

She had made the sacrifice in her mind, so it was really not necessary to make it in the flesh. The flesh is as naught, it is null in the eyes of divinity, her parents' Christian Science had instructed her. Wasn't that something! All that giggling from all that tickling came from *nothing*! Isn't the human mind amazing, to conceive away the husk like that?

Watkins was not the sort who merely agreed with the person he adored. He merely adored her; to understand her was going too far.

"Not necessarily you don't!" she said, laughing.

Bethany, Lady of No Sorrows.

Bethany, unvirgin of my most marital unmarital days.

Tennis Saint, Bethany, bless me off the court. Bethany, from whom I seem to seek pain—for who but a painseeker would seek comfort from thee? Bethany.

Had he spoken of God? What question was she answering? "I don't know how God works, I don't even know how my serve works. But sometimes it works just right, that's all I know. And when it's wrong, I'm playing anyway."

"You're an optimist," he said.

She showed her small childish teeth in her sun-wrinkled smile. "I'm just living from day to day. Time runs on before it runs out. That's all I count on. Is that optimism?"

It was unnecessary to answer. In her own way she was very intelligent. She had made a decision about the limited utility of words. Yet she did improve his thought.

Since she had been able to make the wise decision not to lift her arms and legs around him one more time, since she had made it firmly in her mind, it was no longer necessary to keep to this resolution in her body. What does the body matter when the mind is resolute?

The day was dry and warm, the house was dry and warm, even California sport clothes were an impediment if a person was thinking and moving with a swift metabolism; the colors were light and cool, but the colors of bodies, the pinks and tans and browns and gleams, the ooze that caught the refraction of afternoon sun, the fair and the dark of bodies, were awfully much ahead of anything any designer could put on a healthy young avid housewife, a healthy middle-aged greedy lawyer. Since she had left him forever—except, of course, for wishing him well forever—she wanted to stay with him a while now. Since their love affair was ancient history, but here they were just visiting during a nice familiar hour or two, why not remember that history had much to teach? What did the body matter when the spirit was so strong? Why not do what she wanted to do, since her resolution not to do it was so clear, unambiguous and reconciled? Since nothing could shake Bethany's will, why not, herself, give it a little tremble? Just to prove how intelligent and reasonable and full of good will for Watkins she was, and yet full of lovely memories, failings in the thighs, openings, spreadings, liquefactions, oh, dreamings, too.

Since she was giving him up—losing him, she would almost say—why not keep him a while longer? Not forever, of course; this was the real world. Bethany recognized the limitations of the real world, where a person could not both have and have not simultaneously and forever. Such was the nature of marriage and love and responsibility and pleasure. But a while, anyway. A really clever person could recognize the nature of the real world, and deny its nature for a moment, and escape. As long as necessary. Could a person ask for more? Bethany couldn't.

Logic was one of Bethany's strong points. She could not only anticipate what her opponent would do at singles, and several strokes ahead, but she could also anticipate what both opponents would do, plus her partner, at doubles. With all the ifs here, the tangle of possibility and probability and alternative, why, it was highly mathematical in nature. Watkins used to say she played tennis like chess, and how this pleased her! How well he knew her!

Yet, of course, there were velocities and muscles and aerobics and calculations to tennis, backs to strain and second serves to bluff, which added something quite enjoyable to the mere logic of a sedentary game like chess, which only involved one other person at a time.

Bethany had a secret even from shrewd and loving Watkins. What she would never let him know, like a truly passionate player, but a player intelligent about her irrationality, was that she knew what everybody was doing, two, three, four strokes ahead, or what they might do, and how she might properly respond, lobbing and rushing. But she really didn't know what *Bethany* would decide to do when the ridiculous fuzzball came tempting toward her, growing larger by the millisecond.

That was a secret from Watkins and a mystery to Bethany. One thing she knew: It gave her the capacity to become a victim.

Nobody must suspect this about her.

But as long as opponents and partners kept her secret—they kept it only because they didn't have it to keep—she was in a reasonable situation. She was strong, not a victim, not a loser. They would just think her marvelous. Therefore, perhaps she was.

Nevertheless, it concerned her sometimes.

"Watkins," she asked suddenly, "are you dumb and pitiful? Or are you smart and pitiful?"

"Whatever," he said.

"Or are you just being silly?"

"I'm not prepared to answer that question in the affirmative. I require a little rescue, not destruction."

"That would be nice for you." She cocked her head, thinking of him. This was a relief. It was truly wearisome to think of herself. "You have a little smile on your face. It's sort of defiant. Do you feel like crying?"

"I don't think so."

"Go ahead if you want to. I won't think less of you."

"Don't you already?"

She smiled and touched his hand. "Always the same, Wat,

205

always the same. Positive you don't want to undress me good-bye one last time?"

He didn't move.

She smiled and her lips moved. *Well?* Although she had decided firmly against it, and also for it, often a person can rush the net against a lobbing game.

Still he didn't move, but he asked: "Am I anything you want, Beth?"

She winced. How did he perform this trick with her? Just when it was clearly tennis, not love, he had the filthy talent of being able to change it into what it was absolutely not supposed to be. That was the whole trouble with Watkins. If only he could perform as he was supposed to, and let her perform as she was supposed to, they could both be at their best—she at hers, anyway.

It would even be better for him, she sincerely believed. If he didn't stir up the beast and the soul, they could be so lovely together. They could be immortal. It could be a kind of immortality; not really, of course, but the immortality of a game well played.

Instead, he pulled this same old nasty stunt, and she was wincing, and there came age, not just the middle age she was beating back with her good bones and her good exercise and her good alertness, but her future old age. She could feel it fitted like a paper mask over her head. This isn't Halloween! she wanted to cry. This isn't some awful festival or dress-up!

This was just supposed to be another warm dry afternoon between Bethany and Watkins in Davis, California.

"Am I anything you want, Bethany?"

Her voice didn't belong to her. "A whole lot of things I want," she whispered. But she often came from behind to win. She was a good sport, but she was a winner. Her voice now belonged to her again: "You're nice. You're telling me the truth. You really have a permanent dream about me—" He still had an advantage, but not completely. She was getting her strength back, she was forward and moving, she was bent a little at the knees and waiting for whatever came her way, she could take the pressure.

206

"It feels that way, Wat. Your dream is nice. You, you, I don't want to say it, you love me."

"Yes."

"That's something a person could want. But my dear, isn't it silly?" She remained tranquil and smiling at him, a girl again; her invisible sun-dried and crinkled old age disappeared. She asked, "Now do you want to? good-bye?"

"No," he said.

"Would you like me to ask you specifically again?"

"No," he said.

"Would you? I mean would you for me?"

"No."

"I'm asking you now again. Will you, Watkins?"

"No."

And her eyes squinted shut and her mouth opened and the tiny little-girl teeth gleamed and glinted and the laughter which poured out of her mouth was a shower, a flood, an avalanche—how pleased she was! She was choking and rippling with it, for a moment almost uncomfortable, and then just rippling along with giggly girlish pleasure. How pleased to be denied! She took her time about it.

He waited.

She took her time. At last, when the stormlet had passed, she hiccuped a little and said, "Good. Stop. Then we can go on to the next point with no distraction."

"You mean doubt?"

"I mean distraction," she said. "There never is any real doubt with me, except of course I really do like you and remember you when I remember to think about you, which is not too often, so . . . This is far from the passionate longitude of New York, my dear, although the latitude is close. But the longitude; no. So better make the best of it. So on to the next point. What next for you? I'm here to go on to the next point, Wat."

That wasn't a lemony smell of Bethany's skin. It was more like lime. There was also a green oil or acid or both in Bethany's smell.

"Wat?" she was asking.

207

Maybe I have the best of Bethany, he thought—the Best of Bethany, when I want all, including the worst!—when I enjoy longing for her. The best of her might be this wanting her; wouldn't that be awful? Like a twelve-year-old's mooning over a glimpse of white underpants, pink knees, a child's snowy expanse of soul.

Worse than awful—silly. A legal person with an endowed chair and a silly heart.

What if he looked up her sister in San Diego? Maybe her sister, recently divorced, could be his Bethany, needing not a lover but a mingle.

Foolish, silly and unnecessary.

He decided there were two possibilities here. To be foolish, silly and unnecessary or to stop. Both solutions were difficult. He had drifted into a black hole of foolishness, some Bermuda Triangle in the ocean of middle age, and the edges of it heaved over him when he tried to climb out.

Not trying hard enough, not getting his elbows and knees into it. Why couldn't he learn from the law student he overheard in the Coop Coffee House, earnestly imploring a young woman: "I'm in love with you on a limited scale. I truly want you and need you and respect you up to a point." And the young woman was bobbing her head and taking it in and weighing the matter, giving it all due consideration.

When they made love (on a limited scale and up to a point), did the law student and his friend do the same things Bethany and Watkins used to do? Bethany's flushed cheekbones and that freckling on her breasts, wasn't it something that could happen to anyone with fair skin and the standard-issue maze of capillaries? Bethany freckled like that when she took a game in straight serves. Bethany freckled like that when Watkins happened to encounter her husband in the mall. ("Nice to see you Watkins. Glad to see you again Watkins. I've heard so much about you Watkins, may I call you that?")

So it had come time to say good-bye. The dentist may not have known he knew, but he knew. When Bethany's husband greeted Watkins in the mall, something took away the easy sportsman's

and dentist's and solar investor's ability to ventilate comfortably. He left out the breath of comma between his politeness and
Watkins's name. He knew. Bethany's good sense was superior
to Watkins's bad judgment. Her husband knew. Watkins loved
her, and her husband knew; and those kids, that law student and
his lady in the Coop, perhaps they still had leisure for the careful
exploration of options. Bethany did not.

"Are you still literally in love with me or is this how you pass
the time?" Bethany asked.

"Well, some kids I know answer that question: up to a point."

Bethany sighed. "If I could only believe that." She shook her
head. Rapid motion plus daily shampoo caused her hair to shim-
mer. "Trouble is, I suspect deep in your heart of hearts you're
mad for me. You're crazy for me. You crowd me, Watkins."

"I'm sorry. I'll try to be cheerful about it."

"I mean when you, uh, and you do it so nicely, you're biting
your tongue afterwards to keep from blurting out things. You're
willing to take it as I take it, Wat, but you just can't. Your flesh
is strong enough, but the spirit is weak. I'm sorry."

She gave him one of her accusatory looks—the clear space
above her nose growing a quick net of pale eyebrow. The look
just seemed to come from someplace. It was judgment, and there
was friendly California fierce in it. Probably her children received it when homework wasn't done by bedtime, or the
kitchen chores, or their beds made. God knew when her husband might receive it, shot straight out of the fair and blue.
Then, since she was a devoted grudge noncherisher, the nose
unwrinkled itself and she was nicely indifferent again. "Men
like to be in control, don't they?" she asked.

"I'm not, however."

"But you'd like it. You'd rather have control of things than a
nice life. Me, all I prefer is a nice life, so I get the control as a
bonus." She came as close to nostalgia as she would allow herself
just now. "You were a part of it once."

"I'm sorry."

"It's not your damn fault."

He smiled. She was upset, a little. At least. She wasn't perfect.

"You're washing around, Wat, in your own juice. Some of those women out there might be terrific."

"Some are. They all are. Just *I* am not."

"Now you're cooking, Wat. Knowing that, I think you could try a little harder. What about the one in Las Vegas?"

"Linda was terrific. It's a whole way of life being with her."

"Linda..." she said thoughtfully. She wasn't going to ask, but she cocked her head at him. How he said her name, Linda, must mean a whole story of intimacy and heart-rending drama. "Linda." Briskly she added, "Linda King, I remember. Did you keep the order? Maybe I put her fourth because I didn't want to put her first. Now what?"

"Okay."

"I want to know," she said.

He didn't ask what. She wanted to know if he was on the track of true love or false love. Wasn't it obvious?

"I want to know," she repeated, "if you miss me."

"That's not kind," he said.

"Did I ever say I was kind? Did you ever think me kind? Was that ever part of the deal?"

"I had my thoughts about you."

"That was your idea for me. It had nothing to do with Bethany, Mrs. Andrews. Another reason, although I don't need any reason, to decline the kind offer to be your dream loved one." She smiled. "Anchorwoman of the Universe, Wat!" She let the smile go to pale. She must have given him some consideration. She was in a rare explaining mood. "I needed your body and you needed my soul. Only I really needed *your* body and you had some other soul in mind. Isn't that odd? You gave me too much credit, Wat."

She sniffed and surveyed the little stone and plaster and redwood house. It didn't show his disarray. He remembered how once she told him all he needed was a drive-up teller window and it could be a fancy small-town bank. Free coffee for depositors. His cleaning woman put most things in place, towels folded, books lined up, even papers straightened with a quick darting shake. And she never lost anything. He knew where his cleaning woman put things. He had stripped down the machinery. He had an instinct for care and precision. He too had the possibility of logic; Bethany appreciated this in him. What a shame that a great love came to distress him.

Without meeting his eyes, she added, "I do think about you, also. I miss you." And since this was too airy she quickly added, "I missed you, goddamnit." And since this was too much: "A habit is hard to give up." And since this wasn't enough: "Wat my dear—"

"Why are you here?"

"I wanted to make sure. I know you've been away weekends. Never mind how I know. Has it been fun?"

He shrugged.

"Well, was one of them okay? All you need is one."

"All of them were," he said. "None of them."

"Oh dear. Let's be serious now." And she fumbled in her tennis bag for her glasses—that was how serious it was. The glasses darkened in the glare of the courts but here, inside, had only a pinkish cast. "Enough of this lovemaking, let's see where you stand—it's done with dreaming," Bethany said, "like the movies. Shadows and dark and you're dreaming all the time. I think that's how I do it to you, Watkins."

"I'm used to nightmares. This isn't it. You're an unlikely nightmare, Beth, with your seven little tennis dresses plus your funny tee shirts and shorts. Do you remember Pete Positano?"

"Oh, no! If you're buddying around with Pete, I've *got* to find you a woman."

"You don't have to, Bethany."

"That's my dream." She was upset. Probably she had been upset for a while. Watkins didn't necessarily know what was going on with Bethany. Being a lover gave no special privileges. She turned her eyes toward the light so that the treated lenses of her glasses darkened. She was impatient with herself, not just with Watkins. She would say it fast: "You were part of one dream, Wat. Where we loved each other and crept into each other's arms and hid there all day all night, or at least some afternoons but not Fridays when I carpool early—"

"I didn't know you cared."

"And now you're part of another dream where I do something truly kind to you—I find you someone. Oh dear. Now I rescue you from Pete Positano, besides."

"What do you have against Pete?"

She shrugged her shoulders, lacking words to express.

"I didn't know you cared," he repeated dumbly.

She put her thin and wiry brown hands on her hips. She grinned. "Because you listened so nicely," she said, "you want to do what I believe I just suggested—?" He was shaking his head. "—one more time? for friendship? this afternoon?"

She was suggesting an ordinary consolation and regret, sealed with a lot of kisses. There is no Hallmark card for the parting of married lovers. *To a Special Friend from a Special Married Woman.* She wanted one more sweet before she gave up snacks. She wanted to say good-bye in a way that suited her, especially since her household arrangements for the afternoon were timed out.

"That would not be kind," he said.

"Oh?" She looked sad and impressed despite herself by the brave brave boy. She intended to do only her best for him. For herself, after today, after this afternoon, she wanted nothing at all, except perhaps a touch of indifference. That gift was difficult for Watkins. It wasn't a service for him to offer.

She studied him in silence a moment. She seemed to be humming. He expected her to stamp her right foot, a gesture she performed after humming, while deciding whether to serve fast and hard to the backhand or fast and hard to the forehand. "Ummm, ummm, ummm," she said. And then she stamped her foot chipperly: "Okay! To work! With Old California courtesy we seek to end your mumbles and bumbles, Wat."

Mumbles and Bumbles was her name for suffering, sorrow, mourning and grief.

She riffled a little packet of letters now to be discovered on the table among the scraps of their picnic. A magician, she had just made them appear. She knew where everything was stored. She fondled them with her clever small magician's hands. "Our mistake, dear, was really mine. My mea culpa error is what I admit. We went with the most convincing *writers*. But you don't need articulation, dear, you need mute silent understanding. So using a different standard, I'm sure, with a little patience, we'll find someone in this group to whom we can offer your Power of True Love. Dear Watkins: Like you, perhaps only a little less than you, I so want you never to be lonely and always more happy."

"None of them worked out, Bethany."

"I think that's clear. But you only tried four."

"All four. You've got to stop this playing with me. I need you."

"Only the first four on the list."

"I need you."

"So you've deposed. The fault was all mine. Now try the second four on the list."

"Pardon?"

She had a report for him. "It's your good-news network, Wat. I've looked at the next in line—really not bad. I'm taking all the dither out of it. For you only, this special offer. I've ranked them five through eight, and in my opinion, golly, they're only marginally less promising than our first choices, darling."

He looked at her with his tongue clotted to his palate. He performed the act of silence. It had been Victor Lonkin's most recent political move. They had cooked abalone on the beach at Monterey, and each of them had made a first wife of the girls who helped them out of their wet suits, and for a few weeks Vic had been a justice of the California Supreme Court.

"First, to reward you for your efforts, all your cooperation, just one more time. Let's one more time, darling. This time doesn't count, but let's. Just because I'd like to, darling—don't you think?"

"I think I'm going to die," he said.

"Oh dear, changing the subject—that's such a wily-attorney thing to do. Wat dying first, leading the way for the rest of us."

"I'm not a pioneer," he said.

"I trust you're not making vain threats, Wat."

213

She made it difficult for him to grow mawkish in her presence. She set up a case which excluded pitiful remarks. If he mentioned Vic, she would be sure to point out how he was using his old friend for selfish purposes. And of course she would be right. One more thing about Bethany: her intelligence fitted her as neatly as any of her other habits.

"Well, to take up that subject, Wat, we'll all get there in due course. I'll be there too, dearest, is that what you want to hear? But Wat, if you're *not* going to rip and claw at my clothes in your mortal delirium, why don't you at least listen to me—try numbers five through, if you have to, ten?"

Her mouth was hilarious. Her eyes were cool and bright. The way was open. Filled with only the two of them, the house was empty. Certainly Linda King had at least been a possible; therefore it was only a matter of persistence, time and a favorable crossing of the immutable laws of average and need—

Bethany, not numbered, out of series, was tugging at his belt.

True Love Reply to My Soul.